THROUGH A
BRICK WALL,
DARKLY

BARBARA YATES ROTHWELL

Order this book online at www.trafford.com
or email orders@trafford.com

Most Trafford titles are also available at major online book retailers.

© Copyright 2015 Hebe Morgan.

Print information available on the last page.

ISBN: 978-1-4907-6788-8 (sc)
ISBN: 978-1-4907-6789-5 (hc)
ISBN: 978-1-4907-6799-4 (e)

Library of Congress Control Number: 2015920145

Because of the dynamic nature of the Internet, any web addresses or links contained in
this book may have changed since publication and may no longer be valid. The views
expressed in this work are solely those of the author and do not necessarily reflect the
views of the publisher, and the publisher hereby disclaims any responsibility for them.

Any people depicted in stock imagery provided by Thinkstock are models,
and such images are being used for illustrative purposes only.
Certain stock imagery © Thinkstock.

Trafford rev. 12/14/2015

www.trafford.com

North America & international
toll-free: 1 888 232 4444 (USA & Canada)
fax: 812 355 4082

*Thanks to Josh and Ambini
and their parents, who gave me the idea.*

'For now we see through a glass, darkly; but then face to face: now I know in part; but then shall I know even as also I am known.'

I Corinthians 13, v 12.

S HE knew now, for good or ill, who her birth mother was. And she wanted to know, quite desperately, who was the other, shadowy, misty, unimaginable person—the one who had, in a single moment, created *her*; because she was real, someone you could touch, speak to, see, smell, hear: someone who had importance far beyond that moment of—what? Passion—anger—despairing love—deep affection— lust? Her father.

She knew she was beginning to be obsessed with the search; that it was probably useless. Just a few weeks more and she might have known for sure; now it was too late, and she should forget about it, let the dream go, settle for what she had, what she had always had since babyhood: a loving home, caring friends. And her children, whose parenthood would never be in doubt.

But it had become a habit to scan the faces of elderly men as she passed them in the street, trying to see, trying to imagine if *he*... and knowing always that it was a waste of her time. Now she came out of the café where she had indulged in a chocolate cake of supreme sweetness, and found herself being winked at by a man of perhaps seventy. *I have to stop this*, she muttered to herself, turning her head away from him. *This is madness!*

~~~~~

FOUR episodes stood out in Andrea's memory. There were many more, of course, times of happiness, of the pointless miseries of childhood, of achievement. But the four brief moments had been like small windows opening on to a dark landscape, and they had stayed with her when other moments had been blown away by time.

'You adopted?' the eight-year-old who had no need of assertiveness training had demanded.

1

Andrea had flinched slightly. 'Yes.'

'Who's your mum, then?'

'You know my mum!'

'No—your real mum. Mrs Martin's not your *real* mum. The other one—the one who borned you.'

Andrea stared at the child. She couldn't think what to say. She had always known she was adopted; the Martins, her dear Mum and Dad, had never hidden the fact. That word—adoption—held neither fear nor mystery for her. It was simply a word that hung harmlessly in the back of her mind, and she had never wanted to search beyond it.

Now she saw the word hanging before her, blotting everything else out. Miss Jarrow, her teacher, lost patience with her blank eyes. Andrea, shamed, wet the bed for the first time since she was a baby. The Martins worried over her.

But she wouldn't tell them what was bothering her. In some obscure way she felt guilty—guilty because her mind was searching for answers without knowing what the questions were, guilty because she sensed, even at the tender age of seven, that she might upset Mummy if she told her what had happened.

In due course the pain and confusion grew a tough skin, and she was able to ignore them for most of the time. Adoption, though, never seemed quite the same again.

When she was twelve: 'Bet you'd like to know who your mother is'. This from her best friend, Audrey, as they changed after sports.

'No.' said Andrea, combing her hair. 'Why would I want to?'

'*I* would! I'd be really curious to know. I wonder where she is now.'

All the way home, Andrea struggled with the concept of a birth mother, a woman who really existed, who was more than a shadow in the corner of a young girl's mind. She dreamed that night, vague and threatening shapes forming and re-forming to fill her sleeping mind; and when she awoke they were still there, unseen, fading slowly as day brightened.

She was sixteen, a bridesmaid for the first time, when Aunt Susan, matron of honour, leaned over to her at the reception. 'Your turn next!' she teased.

Andrea blushed red. So far there hadn't even been a boyfriend. 'Not for ages, Aunt Susan,' she smiled.

'Well, you're looking very petty, my dear. How proud your mother would be if she could see you now.'

'She—she...' Turning her head, Andrea caught her mother's expression. 'I—I think she is.'

Aunt Susan put a hand on her arm. 'You know what I mean, dear.' There was a knowing gleam in her eye. '*Someone else* must wonder every so often what became of her little girl!' She squeezed Andrea's hand. 'I think she must have been a pretty girl, don't you? She had a very pretty daughter.'

What could she say? She smiled swiftly and slipped away, taking refuge with the younger set. Across the function room she could see Aunt Susan chatting to one person and then another, and she had a stupid and alarming sensation that she was spreading gossip. 'Yes, the bridesmaid, Andrea—adopted, you know, but *so* pretty!'

Andrea watched Lucy Martin talking animatedly to the elderly clergyman who had performed the marriage ceremony. Perhaps for the first time she saw her as a person detached from herself, an adult who was not simply a parent, but a woman in isolation, almost a stranger.

She saw the lively eyes, the quick-moving, expressive hands, the slim, energetic body. She recognised that she loved her, but now the love had subtly changed. Now, something intangible, something hardly understood, had slipped treacherously between them, and Andrea sensed, with a pang of loneliness, that Aunt Susan's casual (possibly even well-meant) words had had a greater effect than either of them could have expected.

Lucy Martin glanced across and their eyes met. She smiled affectionately and then turned back to the vicar. Andrea took a deep breath and moved away. That was her mother. *She was!* But somewhere—somewhere was another woman whose claim had never been considered.

When Andrea was twenty-two, after she had graduated and was in her first—temporary—job, she sat in a coffee shop with her friend Samantha.

Outside, the traffic moved slowly under the spreading branches of plane trees. In the early summer the girls strolling past shop windows wore bright dresses; the scene was peaceful and conducive to taking a long lunch.

'You know Nick,' Samantha began, with her eyes down.

'*Of course* I know Nick, Sam!'

'Well...'

Andrea regarded her friend with a small smile. 'You don't mean you've finally got him trapped?'

3

'Andrea! What a way...!' Sam pulled a face. 'But yes, I think so.'
'When?'
'Last night. We went to the theatre, and afterwards—he proposed!'
'Proper job? On one knee?'
'Hardly! In the theatre restaurant? But it was—oh, so romantic!'
'And you said yes, of course?'
'Before he'd finished!'
They laughed together. Andrea studied Samantha's face. They had been friends from schooldays on, and they knew each other as well as good pals can. But now Sam had moved ahead, taken a step into the mystery of being a grown woman; Andrea, considering the fact, felt a sudden and unwelcome sense of separation. It could never be quite the same for them again.
'When's the great day?'
'A couple of months. No reason to wait.'
'And then what?'
'Oh, you know!' Samantha shrugged, a little embarrassed. 'Kids, I suppose.'
'Will you like that?' Andrea regarded her curiously.
Sam hesitated for a moment. 'I'm not really a career girl, you know. Not really.' She smiled up at Andrea. 'I'll love it.'
'And Nick?'
'He says three!'
'Sam!' Andrea laughed, taken aback. She wondered briefly if she would ever want children. 'That's a big step.'
'I know.' Samantha's cheerful face—quite an ordinary face really, but full of character under a fringe that never submitted for long to comb or hairspray—became unusually solemn. 'There's so much to consider. Expense, of course. But things like—will they be healthy? Will I be a good mum?'
'Of course you will.'
'Will Nick be a good dad?' She grinned shyly. 'I think so.' Then, after a tiny pause: 'I've wondered sometimes about you, Andrea...'
'What about me?'
'Not *you*, exactly.' She looked straight into Andrea's eyes. 'I've wondered—how could a mother give up her child?'
Andrea sat very still. *Am I very immature? Or have I been hiding this from myself?* Because she had never tried to imagine how it had been, that separation soon after birth, for the mother who had borne her, carried her for nine tormented months (they had

been tormented, surely, with adoption the outcome?), and finally allowed her to be taken by a stranger into a life that should never have been hers.

Samantha looked stricken. 'I've upset you. I'm sorry.'

'No.' Andrea pulled herself together. 'It's just—I've never really thought about that side.'

'You must have.'

'No.' She shook her head. 'Never'. Why? 'I think it's because—because I've had such a good life with Mum and Dad. I've never needed to regret anything.' But now, she knew, she would have to think about it. And for a moment she felt the pain of loss. That comfortable existence must now be underwritten with the previously unimagined distress of an unknown woman who, for whatever reason, had been able to give away the child she had—what? Loved? Hated? Not wanted? Long desired? Had she, that baby, been an *inconvenience?*

The 'why' of her situation crowded in on her. She gave Samantha a swift smile. 'I must go. I've got to buy something for tea. And I have to be back at work in twenty minutes.' She ignored the anxiety in Sam's eyes. 'Tell Nick I'm delighted he's finally seen sense.' A quick hug and she was gone.

'If I ever have children,' Andrea told herself as she gazed absently at the deli counter, 'I shall know.'

2

Life was determined to be serene for Andrea. Where other friends failed to find temporary work, Andrea succeeded without difficulty. And although the job she really wanted took its time coming, it was only a short-time wait for the future she had trained for. Her degree was a music BA, her chief instrument the violin.

When she had shown musical promise, Lucy and Harry Martin had fostered it. At five she was learning the piano, at seven she took to the violin as if she had been playing it for months instead of minutes.

In due course she led the school orchestra. It was understood that she would go on to study music at tertiary level; she gained prizes and certificates, and stared hopefully into the future—a future which, at seventeen, she hoped would include a solo career.

But when she arrived at the Conservatorium, eyes wide with the excitement of it, she found that her skills were fairly standard among gifted children, and by the time she completed the degree course she knew that solo performance wasn't an option in a world where, if you hadn't made your mark by eighteen, you might as well forget it. It was a tougher world than she had anticipated.

And so she sensibly devoted herself to the next-best option, and applied for an audition with the state's premier orchestra. Perhaps she would one day be concert-master (would it then be 'concert-mistress' or was there a unisex title that covered the role?) and that would be glory enough.

The back desk of the second violins was perhaps less than she had hoped for. The conductor seemed a long way away. The sound she was hearing during concerts took a bit of getting used to in those early weeks, but she persevered. Her life was a blend of beautiful music, rushing to rehearsals, gaining experience while trying to ignore the crustiness of certain visiting conductors and the too-easy familiarity of others. She lived at home, which gave her hectic life a basis of permanence (unlike many of her friends, who combined the day-to-day bustle with having to cope with small, expensive and inconvenient flats). But she felt, all the same, that something was missing from her life; that music by itself was not everything.

And when she met Joseph Coombes—who, surprisingly, was not a musician, but a teacher of mathematics in a senior high school—she discovered what the missing ingredient had been.

She fell—'hook, line and sinker', as her father unimaginatively remarked—and music and individual freedom (of which she had been a great supporter) fell, too, into the pattern of living which she knew at once was right for her.

'What do you want out of life?' Joseph had said, quite early in their relationship. They were lying on the grass overlooking the water that was the centre point of the city, she pleasantly tired after a long rehearsal, he wearied after a battle with a difficult class. They had a flask of coffee between them, half empty, and some sandwiches that had spent the day being crushed in Andrea's capacious bag.

'That's a big question.'

'Life is big,' he said around the remains of a chunk of hastily carved ham.

'I don't want to waste my training,' she said, half wondering if this was a moment to be taken seriously. Up to this point their friendship—their blossoming love—had been fun, a way to relax with someone she liked and trusted. If Joseph was going to begin with meaningful questions she would have to do some equally serious thinking about answers.

'Training should never be wasted,' he agreed. 'But how are you going to use it?'

'I am—already,' she protested. She turned to look at him. 'What about you?'

Joseph sat up slowly. He gazed down the hill towards the river. For a moment she wondered if he had heard her; he seemed distant, unreachable.

'Maybe I won't want to teach maths all my life,' he said finally. 'I believe in education...'

'Doesn't everyone?'

'Perhaps. But I believe in it as a life experience. Not just a way to keep kids quiet in school. Not as a way of earning a good living. I see it...' He hesitated. 'I see it as a quest...'

She sat up, her arms around her knees. 'A quest for what?'

'For...it's difficult to explain. I suppose I mean that, for me, educating children is a way of changing the world.' He glanced at her, daring her to laugh at him. But she was smiling, and in the smile he saw something he wanted, a sympathy, an understanding that, unexpectedly, made his head spin. 'Am I a fool?'

Andrea shook her head. 'I think I know what you mean. It sounds wonderful.'

'Really?'

'Really!' Shyly, sensing that their friendship had shifted in some way she could not quite work out, she put out a hand. 'Good luck with your quest!'

Joseph took her hand in his and held it, staring down at it, asking himself if he dared take the next step. 'Andrea—do you think...?'

She waited before saying 'Yes?'

She smiled again. All at once she felt older, more mature than Joseph, and what was happening made good sense. 'Yes, I think I could,' she said, and he turned on her a wide grin of such delight that she caught her breath.

'What I mean,' he said quickly, dropping the remains of the sandwich and taking both her hands in his, 'is something permanent.'

She laughed. 'I know!'

He frowned. 'You're not taking this seriously. What I'm trying to say...'

'Joseph, I know what you're trying to say.'

'You do?' He took a deep breath. 'Then I'd better say it. Andrea—shall we get married?'

'I think that's a marvellous idea,' she said, and was oblivious of a passing couple as Joseph leaned forward and kissed her.

Those were special years, years of fun and hard work. Andrea found a part-time job teaching music to children who really cared. She loved it. But performance was still her main delight, and the morning rehearsals, the evening concerts, the camaraderie and the heady pleasures of playing some of the greatest music in the world under the batons of some of the finest conductors—these never failed her. She would return home to the small town house she shared with Joseph exhausted but happy. It seemed as if this was how it always would be.

Then she became pregnant.

'Are you sure?' Joseph asked the question men so often find necessary.

'I've seen the doctor.'

'We should have gone together.'

'Why?'

He shrugged. 'My baby too.'

She crossed the room to him (they were making supper together on one of her free evenings) and put her arms around him. 'I'm sorry. I was just afraid...'

'What of?'

'Well—of being wrong, I suppose. Of getting our hopes up and then...' She stood back and looked up into his face. 'You are pleased, aren't you?'

Joseph put his arms around her and held her gently. 'Pleased? I'm—I'm choked!' He gave a small, satisfied chuckle. 'I don't know how we'll manage, but we will. Somehow.'

'Manage what? Do you mean money?'

'We two,' he said, hugging her, 'are about to become three. Of course it'll take a bit of managing.'

Andrea smiled. 'Other people seem to manage it. People you'd think couldn't possibly cope.'

'And so will we!' He led her by the hand to the couch and sat her down. 'Let me get you a cuppa. We should celebrate.'

Joseph managed it very well. He used his mathematical skills to start a bank account for the baby, took out insurance against everything he could think of, saw to it that Andrea got enough rest. And she managed well, too, until the day she felt somehow under the weather and stayed in bed. When Joseph came home she was pale and in pain, and he got her to hospital just in time. The baby, apparently managing its own pregnancy less well than its parents had, arrived in a flow of blood and Andrea's helpless tears. Joseph held his own tears back until he went home that night to an empty house.

But they were young and healthy, and a year later Andrea embarked on motherhood once more (with anxiety she hoped she had kept from her husband, who was himself hiding his own fears); and this time all went swimmingly well, so that she was able to play in the orchestra right up to the week before little Bethany arrived, round and pink and, of course, totally irresistible. On this unarguable fact parents and grandparents agreed completely.

A couple of years later Daniel was born. 'Our pigeon pair,' Joseph said proudly, gazing down at his son, and holding his squirming daughter against his shoulder.

'I've never known what that means,' Andrea said, still sleepy, and Joseph shrugged.

'Lost in the mists of time.' He put Bethany down on the bed. 'Does this complete our family?'

Andrea gave a faint smile. 'I don't need to do it again. I shall be able to remember what it's like.'

'So?'

'Two's probably enough.' She yawned widely, and Bethany shoved a small fist into her mother's mouth. 'No, darling— Mummy's tired.'

Joseph scooped the child up and bent to kiss his wife. 'I am so proud of you,' he whispered. But she was nearly enough asleep, and summoned up only the bare ghost of a smile for him to take away with him.

So life became more complex. Two busy parents, two increasingly active children; a recipe for many of the troubles of the world. Lucy and Harry took over when it got too difficult; Joseph's parents were too far away to be called on for help. The days slid by, and then the months and years—classes, concerts, rehearsals, hours of practice for Andrea; seemingly endless marking of books and preparation of study notes for Joseph. All tiring, all demanding—all challengingly exhilarating. They felt they had the world at their feet, that they had found the secret of good parenting, good timing, a good and mutually satisfying approach to marriage.

They saw all around them that not everyone was so serenely balanced, and wondered. Her friend Samantha's marriage dwindled and died. But Andrea and Joseph were still in love, still preferred each other's company; and if they had had time to think about it they would have agreed that they were enjoying the slow, happy development of their life together.

'I wonder how many grandchildren we'll have,' Joseph said quite idly one day, when Bethany was a beautiful fourteen.

'Please!' Andrea said, not quite laughing. 'She's still a child.'

'Have you seen how people look at her in the street?'

Andrea turned and stared at him. 'People?'

'Well, all right—men!'

'No,' Andrea said firmly, trying not to show panic. 'I haven't.' But she knew he was right. Bethany was a beauty; she had a way of lifting her head that was captivating, a smile that invited friendship and perhaps more, in the most innocent way imaginable. 'Do you think she's a flirt?'

'No. I think she hasn't a clue what she's got.' He grinned at his wife. 'Easy enough to see where she got it from, though.'

'Oh, Joseph!' Andrea sank down beside him. 'You get them through all the childish things, and it seems as if one day it'll all be easier. But it's never easy, is it?' She put her head on his shoulder. 'I love them both so much. I don't want either of them ever to get hurt.'

'That's not possible.' He moved to make her more comfortable. 'They have to bear their own hurt just as we had to.'

But Bethany and Dan, surrounded by comfort and love, showed no signs of becoming the kind of children who get into the newspapers for the wrong reasons. Andrea was as blessed in her son and daughter as she had been in her parents. It almost seemed as if life was trying to make up for those first days when, as she sometimes thought with a shudder, anything could have happened.

'We're so lucky!' she said to Joseph on Christmas Eve. 'So blessed!' and he agreed, looking around him at the red and gold and green of the Christmas decorations catching firelight; at the tree, groaning under its burden of tinsel and gifts; and finally at Andrea, who seemed to him then and always to be exactly as she had been when they first met.

'You two!' Bethany laughed, catching them kissing under the mistletoe as she brought in logs for the stove. They held out their hands to her and she entered the circle of their arms. Daniel would be in later, after his dinner with his footy team.

'God bless us every one!' Joseph said, and laughed a little to offset the emotion of the moment.

When they called her to the hospital, Andrea felt a momentary panic, then pulled herself together. Chest pains, they had said. Indigestion probably, she thought, changing out of jeans and sweater. Joseph was healthy; he exercised, he ate sensibly, he was hardly ever ill.

At the hospital they said they would have to do more tests. Joseph was lying in a network of tubes and wires; things beeped and hummed. It all felt most unlike the Joseph she knew. But there was the usual twinkle in his eye for her. She searched his face.

'What have you been up to?' She bent and kissed his cheek. 'Trying to frighten me?'

He took her hand. 'Nothing to worry about, my love. They're just being super careful.'

But it was more than that. Andrea felt a fragility in the hand she held that had never been there before. Suddenly she felt frightened for him—and for herself. Life without Joseph was something she had never contemplated. When they wheeled him away for tests she watched him go with foreboding.

Daniel arrived while she was waiting. 'But he'll be all right, won't he?' he said, just a little anxious in a situation new to him. None of them had ever seen Joseph really sick.

'I'm sure he will be,' she assured him; and as she said it she felt a shiver run through her at the thought that—*no*, she told herself, *don't even think it. He has to be well—for all of us.*

When Bethany came down the corridor half an hour later—and Joseph was still not back—she saw the drawn look on her mother's face and stopped suddenly. It was the hardest thing to do, to go on and say, with as much cheerfulness as she could muster, 'What's he been up to, Mum?'

She bent down and kissed Andrea; she punched Daniel lightly on the shoulder in greeting. But the waiting had told on Andrea. A smile was a strain. 'He'll be OK, dear. Just having tests. They're being very careful.'

Then the waiting again. Magazines, a paper cup of coke, coffee that tasted like nothing for Andrea, a chocolate bar for Bethany.

Conversation, then silence. Nurses came and went on swift feet, smiling quickly, impersonally, as they passed. Other relatives waited to hear about other patients. It was strange to think that in this silent place so many dramas were being played out.

'How long?' Daniel demanded irritably. 'Why doesn't someone come?'

'They're being very careful,' Andrea said automatically, then realised she had said it twice already. She smiled at Bethany, but the smile was one-sided and revealed too much. Bethany took her hand and patted it gently, as if she were a small child in need of comfort.

'*And that's what I am at the moment,*' Andrea told herself. '*Oh, Joseph, my dear, for God's sake be all right!*'

A doctor came. She thought it was the one who had been fiddling with the tubes and wires before Joseph was taken to wherever he now was. There was a nurse behind him, and it was on her face that Andrea saw the truth. She stood up, her hand held out as if to ward off something unbearable. And if the nurse's expression of compassion was accurate, what she was about to hear could not be borne.

'Mrs Coombes...' The doctor gave an involuntary sigh. Andrea thought, *It's late—he's tired. He shouldn't have to tell me. They should have sent someone else.*

'Mrs Coombes, I'm so sorry. Your husband had a massive heart attack as we were conducting the tests. We operated straight away, but there was nothing we could do.'

Andrea frowned slightly. What was he trying to tell her? A heart attack didn't have to be fatal these days. Perhaps he meant...

'Your husband died, Mrs Coombes. I'm very sorry.' He stood there for a moment, almost like a naughty boy who had been caught out in his naughtiness. 'If there's anything we can do...'

The nurse emerged from behind the doctor. 'Let me get you a cup of tea,' she said, and the expression on her face was so tragic that Andrea nodded slightly, as if a cup of tea was just what she wanted at this moment when everything seemed to have ground to a halt. She was trying to think of something to say, but nothing would come.

It was Daniel who spoke. 'You should have told us earlier.' His young voice cracked with emotion. 'Mum could have seen him.'

The doctor shook his head. 'It was very quick. And it would have been very distressing to watch while we were trying to revive him.' He put out a hand to Andrea, thinking she might be going to faint, but she shook her head.

'I'm all right, Daniel—Bethany.' She took their hands. 'Do you want to come with me to see your father?'

For a moment she thought they would refuse; but then they fell in beside her, taking her arms protectively, and they followed the doctor along the corridor to where Joseph was waiting for them.

3

'It was just so sudden,' Andrea said later to Lucy. 'No time for anything. No chance for saying goodbye. No—no anything.'

'How have the children taken it?'

'Bethany is looking after me like a mother. Daniel is very angry about the whole thing. He'd like to sue someone, I think.' She managed a small, dry smile. 'But it seems there was nothing to be done about it. Joseph, my nice, healthy Joseph, had a heart condition no one had ever suspected, and suddenly—pouf!—it couldn't take any more.'

'And what now?'' Lucy asked with compassion, noting the hollows under the eyes, the faintly trembling fingers.

'I don't know. I can't seem to think. I thought it might be better once the funeral was over, but it isn't. I keep expecting to see him there, in his chair, at the table. Weeding the garden— all those things. I get into bed and it seems huge and empty without him there. I just never, ever, thought that he would go like this. I always expected that we would grow old together, two dear old dodderers driving our children mad and spoiling the grandchildren.'

'I feel so helpless,' Lucy said, wishing she could properly share this grief. 'What can I do?'

'Just be there,' Andrea said flatly, standing up and moving around the room as if sitting had become intolerable. 'I keep thinking—when there are so many awful marriages in the world, or so we're told, why did my good, lovely marriage have to end like this?'

'Who knows? Who knows anything when it comes down to it?' She felt tears very close and wondered if weeping together would help this child, this grown woman who was her child, this child she had nurtured as her own and loved so dearly.

Somehow they did the things that needed to be done. They went to bed at sensible times, rose in the morning and showered and put on make-up and tried to make it easier for each other and for the children—Bethany the mothering one, and Daniel the angry young man struggling with the knowledge that there was now no father-figure, no masculine influence to help him through the coming years. And, subconsciously, Andrea waited for Joseph to come home from wherever he had gone; and was devastated again and again when, waking in the early hours, she felt the bed beside her empty and cold.

One day she went out into the garden that Joseph had tended so well. She sat under the silver birch he had been proud of and saw that there were flowers around her, colour, a gentle breeze stirring the leaves above her head. The rose bushes had been pruned—who had done that? Daniel? Bethany? Perhaps her father? There were magpies somewhere pouring out their liquid song. A willy-wagtail flew down almost to her feet and gazed up at her, unconcerned by her size and hoping for food.

It came to her that in the weeks since Joseph's death she had seen everything in greys; life had become a black and white film, all colour leached out of it by his passing. And it came even more strongly that he wouldn't have wanted that to happen. That he loved her, and Bethany and Daniel, far too much to want them to suffer for ever.

There, under the silver birch, she felt him very close to her for the first time. She had never thought of herself as psychic, but in that moment she knew that he was there, somehow, in some form, and that he was telling her the time had come to put the past behind her and start forward again.

How would he have put it in life? 'Come on, old thing! Enough's enough. Get your hat on and let's go!'

There were tears then. She didn't want to let go of the grief. Without it she felt she would have lost him for ever. She allowed the tears to fall, flooding her, exhausting her, and then, standing, putting her hand on the rough bark of his tree, she said goodbye.

'Darling...'she murmured. 'My darling!' And it was over.

Lucy saw the change in her, but made no comment at first. Bethany was away for the weekend and Daniel was with his mates somewhere. The two women had time together. After a couple of hours, Lucy said, 'What happened?'

Andrea smiled, still a trifle wan, but an improvement. 'Joseph told me to get my act together.'

'How did he manage that?' Lucy was intrigued. There was colour in her daughter's face.

'I was—well, I don't really know. I don't believe in messages from beyond the grave. But I was under the silver birch, and...' She took a deep breath and told her mother how she had felt his nearness. 'Joseph wouldn't want endless mourning for him, would he? He wasn't a *mourning* sort of person. I just had this huge feeling that it was time. Time to start again, to celebrate him instead of making myself sick with longing.' She stared across the room, trying to rediscover the sensation she had had. 'He's gone, that's the point. He really has gone, and no amount of grief will bring him back again. And while I get older,' she held down a sudden desire to sob, 'he will always be young. I'm right, aren't I?'

Lucy held out her hands. 'Of course you are. And so is he. It would be no memorial to him to spend your life as a black-garbed widow. You are young enough to have a whole new life. You have us and you have your children. You're not alone, darling.'

'Then that's that!' Andrea leaned back in her chair. 'There'll be bad times, but good times too.' She gave the small smile again. 'He was rather special, wasn't he, Mum?'

'Very special.'

'I think I'm going to cry...'

Lucy stood. 'You go ahead and cry. I'll make a cuppa. Tea or coffee?'

Andrea, from behind one of Joseph's handkerchiefs (they were big enough to soak up the tears she had recently shed), laughed instead. 'Coffee! With extra caffeine and two sugars.'

Lucy, in the kitchen, offered up a prayer of thanks for the return of her child. Suddenly she felt like singing, but spared Andrea that experience until she was stronger. She had so wanted her to get on with her life, to know that there was still so much to do and so many places to go that a normal lifespan would hardly contain all that could be done.

She wondered if she should offer suggestions for the future, and decided against it. Perhaps Joseph would oblige! He seemed to have done a good job already.

'Coffee!' she announced. 'Hot, strong and sweet!' and saw that a corner had indeed been turned. Andrea was sitting curled up at the end of the sofa, glancing through a magazine. Everything would be all right.

All the same, the months ahead were not easy. Andrea began teaching violin again, and found a small part-time job in a local school, running a choir. Bethany and Daniel, once they saw their mother coping, relaxed and picked up their interrupted lives. And Lucy went home to Harry and kept an eye on things from a distance.

The empty space in Andrea's life remained empty. She thought it was perhaps like losing a limb—wasn't there something about a 'phantom limb' that ached and hurt even though there was nothing there? She had a phantom Joseph, who seemed to be about to come into the house at the times he would normally have returned, who was in the bathroom when she went to bed, but never came out, who failed to prune the shrubs in the garden or take out the refuse, in the odd moments when she almost forgot that he would never be there again.

These moments always shook her. But gradually they grew less, and one day she found that she had spent the entire day without yearning for him once. Briefly she felt guilt; then her good sense told her that she had nothing to feel guilty about, and she relaxed and let her body and mind lead her into a state of comfort. She bought a dress without his compliments to guide her, and wished that he could have seen it. But those days were drawing to a close, and she was able to admit that she was glad of it.

Joseph, somewhere, nodded with satisfaction. 'Well done, old girl! Knew you could do it.'

'Oh, you!' she said aloud. 'Oh, *you*, Joseph, my darling!'

And she began to wonder what she should do to fill the empty space.

Later, she was unable to say what had led her to thinking of her birth mother, that shadowy figure who had never seriously impinged on her life.

Lucy was all the mother she had ever wanted. But somewhere, in an outer darkness of her mind, another woman stood, faceless, nameless, a stranger; and it all at once became necessary to know more about her.

Why? She asked herself this several times a day. Why rock a boat that, until Joseph's death, had sailed merrily on its way without hazard? Why open a can of worms? Yet why should it be a can of worms? she demanded silently. Why could it not be an enriching experience to find the woman who had given one life?

Because it often was not enriching, she replied firmly. Because she didn't need to know. Because—because it might hurt Dad and Mum! That was why. They had given her everything, personal,

17

spiritual, emotional, and—no less welcome—financial support and security. How could she now do something that might rock *their* boat?

But the niggling questions stayed. And one day she decided that, for good or ill, she must have an answer. She picked up the phone and called Lucy, her hand shaking a little at what she was doing. After this moment, after this question, things could never be quite the same again.

'Mum? Hi! How are you? And Dad? Yes, I'm feeling good. No, Bethany's still away. Daniel wrote—yes, wrote!—to say he'd be back in a couple of weeks.' She listened to Lucy's news, grunted, nodded, laughed. Then, 'Well, yes, there was something.' It was so hard to say. 'Look, Mum—if this upsets you we'll say no more about it, OK?'

Lucy stood very still. She felt she knew, even before the words were spoken, what this call was about. Now it had come, after all these years—and how did she feel? 'Go on, dear.' She could sort out her feelings later.

'I've been thinking. I'd like to find out something about my...' *My what? Not my mother; I'm talking to my mother!* 'My birth mother.' It was said. It felt very odd. For the first time she had really given a name, however inadequate, to the figure in the background.

Lucy took a deep breath. 'That sounds a good idea. What made you...?' She was pleased that her voice remained quite normal.

'It's been coming on for weeks. Are you upset?'

'Of course not.'

'After Joseph—I suddenly felt I needed to know. I don't really know why. And I've no idea how to go about it. But I think I have to do it. Will Dad mind?'

Lucy laughed. 'He's got more sense. This has been at the back of our minds ever since we first had you. I thought it would come up when you were a teenager, but it didn't. If you feel like that about it you should certainly do something.' She hesitated. 'Have you thought that it might not be a happy situation—that you might find someone you couldn't—love?'

'Yes, I've thought.' Andrea stared through the window beside the phone. It was done, or at least started. 'Mum, when *you* look back in time you see your parents and their parents and all those going back for ever. You can recognise features in other members of the family, just as I can with my kids. But I can't recognise anything further back than myself. Do you understand? When I look back there's a brick wall, or a curtain or something—it's blocking out where I came from, why I was abandoned by the people who should have wanted to love me...' Her voice trailed off. 'I understand, darling.' The warmth came down the line as an expression of deep affection.

'Somewhere, perhaps, there's still a grandmother who wonders where I am. Brothers and sisters, perhaps.' These were new thoughts. She had never tried to look beyond the fact that there was this woman... 'I've got to think,' she said suddenly. 'It's all getting too big.'

Lucy held the receiver tight. There was so much she wanted to say but mustn't. Andrea had to make these decisions for herself. 'Let us know,' she said. 'Keep in touch. If you need money or anything...'

Andrea felt tears forming. In a moment her voice would begin to wobble. 'I'll get back to you. And Mum—I love you. I love you both! It won't change that.'

4

It was a matter of writing letters and ringing people up, of finding out where the adoption authorities were who could help, of asking the right questions in the right quarters.

She had been born in Western Australia, she knew that. Lucy and Harry were both westerners; they had brought her over east when she was barely a year old.

'Why?' she asked.

'Work,' her father said. 'My company relocated to Sydney and I went with it.'

'So my—my birth mother...?'

'Let's give her a name,' he suggested. '*My birth mother* is too much of a mouthful.'

In spite of herself, Andrea laughed. 'What would be appropriate?'

'Belinda, Lucinda, Deborah, Delilah...?'

'Hang on! What about Mary, Jane, Betty? The others sound like something out of grand opera.'

'What then?' he said.

She pondered. 'Ma', she said. 'Short, to the point, *and* appropriate. And not a name I've ever used with Mum.'

'Ma it is.' He nodded. 'Now, what was the question?'

'She—*Ma*...' she giggled slightly, 'gave birth to me in WA. So that's the place to begin, isn't it?'

'As good as any other.'

She regarded him fondly. The slim man had given way over the years to a measure of rotundity, but it suited him. He was looking at her with equal fondness; she knew how much he cared. 'You'll tell me if it ever becomes painful to you, won't you?'

'I certainly will! But I don't expect to have much pain myself. My concern would be that you might find yourself in a situation you can't handle.'

'I'll be careful.' She stared past him, through the window into the garden where sun and shade made a pretty picture. 'The worst we know about her now is that she let me go for adoption. There could be any number of reasons for that, from good to bad.' She turned to look directly at him. 'Do you know anything bad? From back then?'

He shook his head. 'We weren't told anything about her. Just that you had been fostered for the six months after you were born.'

'Six months? I'd forgotten.' It suddenly seemed that she had always visualised herself handed over in the first weeks of life, a tiny babe wrapped in a white shawl (that was right: she still had it, Bethany and Daniel had slept in it), passed from an anonymous figure in hospital white to the young couple whose own problem of childlessness had led them to this dramatic moment. 'So I could look around—and see...'

'Oh, yes! You were wide-eyed all right. Didn't miss a thing.' He smiled slowly, reminiscently. 'You were a beauty.'

She was thinking, *So I must have seen her, recognised her, perhaps, cried when she let me go—no, of course not! I was fostered. So who looked after me then, for those months? Who...?* She said, 'Did I cry? When you took me?'

He shook his head. 'Not a drop! Tried to grab my glasses while I was driving. Wet your mother's dress—we weren't very good with nappies at first. A happy child—always.' He glanced at her. 'Still?'

'In spite of everything—yes, I think so. I find it bubbles up even when I wish it wouldn't.'

'Yes—a happy child!' He patted her hand. 'Still!'

Harry glanced across to where Lucy was sitting, gazing out of the window. She had been doing that for the past ten minutes or so, a long time for a lively body like his wife.

'A penny?' he suggested, and she blinked and turned to him. 'What?'

'You were deep in thought. I offered you the going rate.'

She gave a quick smile. 'Just thinking.'

'About Andrea?'

She let out a breath she had been holding for too long. 'You can always tell, can't you? Yes, I was wondering about Andrea.'

'Has she upset you?'

She didn't answer at once. The distant, thoughtful look came back, and then she turned to him and met his eyes squarely. 'Not upset. I don't think it's that. Maybe disturbed, but for her, not for me. I don't want her to find this—this woman and then discover that it would all have been better left alone.'

'She's going to call her Ma.'

'Ma?'

'*My birth mother* was a mouthful. She suggested "Ma"—and it made her laugh. I thought laughter was better than the intensity she was feeling.'

'I hope she's doing the right thing.'

'We shan't know until she does it.'

Lucy regarded him silently. Then, 'Are *you* upset?'

He hesitated. 'Well—not upset, no. Slightly troubled, as you are. I would have been happier if the problem hadn't come up.'

'For the same reasons?'

'I think so.'

Neither spoke for a while. Then Lucy said in a quiet voice that did not hide her concern: 'I don't want to lose her. I've loved her so much, right from that first moment. I don't want to lose that. I feel as if—as if this woman might somehow take some of the love she has for us...'

'That's foolishness,' he said gently. 'Love grows to whatever size is needed. If this—if Ma turns out to be the sort of woman we would like her to be, then it can only be good—for all of us. If not... well, that's something Andrea would have to cope with. We can help, but we can't do her suffering for her.'

'You're quite wise sometimes, aren't you?' Lucy grinned at him and got up. 'I need a cup of tea. What about you?'

He followed her into the kitchen. 'And whatever happens,' he said, holding her shoulders for a moment, 'we've had Andrea for over forty years. This Ma—well, she didn't know what she was missing. Perhaps it's our time to be generous.'

Lucy filled the kettle and plugged it in. 'Do you remember,' she said, 'all those years ago, how awful we felt when I couldn't get pregnant? Do you?'

'Vaguely. It's a lifetime ago. We were different people.'

'I felt so let down. Marriage, then babies, that's what I thought.' She laughed briefly. 'Such pain I felt. Such pain. And then, after all the arrangements and disappointments and people telling us what to do and what not to do—Andrea!' She pulled a face. 'Your mother told me it would never be the same as having my own child, and for a while I believed her. Then—well, we were a family and I was as happy as if I had given birth to her. And that's how it's always been. It couldn't have worked out better.'

She turned to him urgently. 'That's what I don't want to lose. Don't want to spoil. She's *ours*, Harry. Whoever gave her birth, she's ours, now and always. I don't want to lose that special feeling.'

'And you won't! You won't, my dear.' He kissed her. 'Harry, Lucy and Andrea. Now and for ever. Make the tea! We've brooded long enough.'

5

'**I**'m thinking of trying to find my birth mother, Bethany.'

Andrea watched her daughter carefully. Bethany was curled up on the sofa with an after-dinner coffee. The girl looked up quickly.

'Really? Gosh! How exciting!'

Andrea's eyebrows went up. 'Is that how you feel?'

'Why not? There's always been that sort of blankness about the past, hasn't there? I think it would be really cool to know.'

'What would Daniel think about it?'

'How does anyone know what Daniel would think? Try him.'

'I might. Next time he rings.'

They sat in silence. Andrea was conscious of a relaxing of tension within her. Had she then been so scared of raising the subject? Bethany was staring into her coffee cup, thoughtfully.

'What about Gran and Grandpa? Would they mind?'

'I asked. They seemed quite OK about it.'

'It might change things.'

'Yes. It might.'

'For better or worse?'

'I wouldn't know until the time came.'

'What if she turned out to be a real stinker?'

'I have to take that chance.'

Bethany said, 'What if she wanted to be your real mother after all this time? Take you over, know what I mean?'

'She couldn't. Gran and Grandpa are my "real" parents. You can't wipe out forty-five years.'

'She might be—well, grasping. Wanting money or something like that.'

Andrea put her head back on the chair and stared at the ceiling. It was all true. She was taking a big risk. But she didn't see, now, how she could avoid some action.

'Perhaps I won't be able to find her. She might be dead. Or she might not want to see me.' *Am I doing the right thing?* 'I have to do it, Beth, now I've started it. Otherwise I'll never be able to put it out of my mind.'

Bethany regarded her across the room. 'Then go ahead. I'd like to know, anyway. Maybe she's terribly rich and...'

'Bethany!' Andrea stood up and pointed a finger at her daughter. 'No flights of fancy, especially about money.' She laughed. 'Let's keep our feet on the ground.'

Bethany stared up mischievously. Then, as something struck her, she said, 'I wonder who your birth *father* was.'

And Andrea, who had not yet asked herself that question, sat down again and felt a moment of panic. What, indeed, was she doing? Would it be a can of worms? Was there still, somewhere out there, the man who had fathered her? Someone must have! Did he know about her; had he ever cared about the baby he had never cherished? Where had he been when she was fostered out?

She stood up, feeling slightly storm-tossed. 'That's a question for the future. Enough to look for her.'

Bethany watched her leave the room, sensing the turmoil she had raised. 'I'd want to know,' she murmured to herself. 'If I found *her* I'd need to find *him*.'

And so Andrea embarked on her journey of exploration. Buoyed with warmest good wishes from family and the few friends she had let into the secret, she set off on the cross-country Indian-Pacific railway for the seclusion she would find there, the limbo into which she could prepare herself for a future wreathed in clouds of uncertainty.

As the last of the waving hands—and Lucy's anxious eyes—disappeared into what now, symbolically, felt like a closure on her secure past, Andrea stood by the door for a moment, hit all at once by a sensation of panic such as she had never in her life known. In that searing moment she wished she had never thought of this crazy scheme, had been content to carry with her to the grave the cloudy patch that concealed—what? While she made her way to a small cabin (another womb from which she might well emerge to become someone completely different) she began to see that patch rather as a place on her body that had grown numb through surgery. A nerve destroyed under the surgeon's knife. The thought satisfied her. Emotional surgery was surely as valid as a more physical cutting. Having your parents cut out of your life as debilitating as losing, for instance, a leg or an eye.

Momentarily she sensed Joseph—in reality or in memory? Did it matter?—and he was saying, as of course he would, 'Come on, old girl! You've not done so badly, have you?' So she sank down in the comfortable chair by the window she would not have to share with anyone, and the panic left her, a little shaken, but at least with her sense of humour intact.

'Go away, Joseph!' she said out loud. 'You're far too sensible. If I want to wallow, I will.'

(Was there, somewhere unreachable, a gentle laugh?)

Andrea settled herself, and watched the scenery sweeping past beyond the window. A new sensation filled the space left by the panic, a bubbling, small but unmistakable, which, allowed to grow, would become hope and excitement and, perhaps, fruition for a search she had at one time never expected to make.

The journal she had decided to keep lay unopened as the train made its way up through the daunting, craggy hills that had beaten back so many of the early explorers. She would see all this again one day. No need to record it.

For three nights and the intervening days the train carried her on. It was inexorable, unescapable. Not a train one could decide to leave on an impulse. The stations, once past Port Pirie, out of reach of the kind of civilisation she knew, seemed more like wayside halts. The desert, the scrub, the unimaginable flatness of the Nullarbor Plain—that vast area once below the sea, where, she had heard somewhere, one could now and then find sea-shells that had lain there for millennia—all these were disturbing, a warning, perhaps, that nothing else she had known in her settled existence was the full reality. The Australia that she loved was a compendium of experiences, far beyond what one could learn by being a typical city girl.

Andrea took the lesson to heart. If she had flown to Perth, she realised, she would have been able to deny the savage reality of the country she lived in, just as she had been able to deny the realities of her own existence. City to city, she would have missed all this.

She stared out of the window on the final full day as they drew towards the mining town of Kalgoorlie. The red earth was pocked with old mine workings, the abortive efforts, she imagined, of hopeful men years ago who had tried and failed. Success, supposedly, would have developed into a real mine.

So she prepared herself for whatever would come in the days ahead—success or failure in her quest, and if success, then what?

Joy, rejection, confusion, anger, a real home-coming? Well, she would take what came. Seeing her native country at ground level had been a revelation, and perhaps a blessing.

She began to gather her belongings together. Early the next morning she would be in Perth, the place where she had been born. 'Day one,' she said aloud, 'of my new life!'

6

Andrea liked Perth the moment she saw it. It was so small after Sydney, so clean, so free of huge, towering buildings, its proportions just right to her approving gaze as the taxi took her towards her city hotel.

The lovely Swan River (even denuded of its original black swans) gave a sparkling focal point to this intriguing city. 'I shall enjoy it here,' she said, and the driver glanced up and met her eyes in the mirror.

'First visit?'

'Yes.'

'On business?'

For a brief moment she hesitated. 'No—family.' She had said it. Her heart gave a sudden bump. Somewhere here, among these buildings, the shadowy figure of Ma, her birth mother, might still live.

Now she was ready to move on, to discover what was discoverable. And to reject nothing. That was what the bleak Nullarbor Plain had taught her. *Australia is what it is—and I am what I am,* she said silently. *And nothing can change the truth.*

She paid off the taxi and entered the hotel. A shower, something to eat, then—action stations!

The voice on the phone was the one she had heard in Sydney during her first, nervous approaches to the adoption society.

'Mrs Coombes! Welcome to Perth. I hope you are comfortable.'

'Yes. Thank you. It's very nice.' She paused, clearing her throat. 'May I come and see you?'

'Of course. When?'

'Today?'

'Certainly. If you come at three you'll just be in time for a cuppa.'

A cuppa is a cuppa anywhere. Andrea smiled. 'I'll like that.'

The office was in an older style house. Its need of external painting and a less than manicured front lawn indicated that the organisation's funds were not going into glossy upkeep. Andrea found that fairly comforting. She had been a little nervous of glass-walled offices and exotic pot plants, with staff to match. She felt the sudden turmoil in her stomach as she opened a gate that squeaked and walked up a red-painted concrete path that led to a half-open front door. Pushing it, she stepped inside.

'Mrs Coombes?' The voice came from a room on the left of a long passage. Andrea peeped around the door. A middle-aged woman, perhaps early sixties, with shoulder-length hair, and dressed in a blue two-piece with a flowery scarf, was coming round a desk covered with files, hand out-held in welcome. 'How are you? How was your trip? Do come in and sit down. I'm sure you can do with that cuppa.'

She swept out of the room, presumably to a kitchen somewhere in the back of the house. Andrea sank down on to a couch and let her breath out in a long sigh. She felt as if she had hardly taken breath since leaving the hotel. This place, homely, unprepossessing, was a repository for so many different kinds of distress. That filing cabinet—to how many disrupted lives did it bear evidence? She closed her eyes for a moment, her head swimming. Then she heard the rattle of tea cups and pulled herself together.

'I should have introduced myself. Cathy Farwell. Do call me Cathy.'

Andrea accepted to cup. 'Andrea.'

'Now,' Cathy said, settling herself comfortably in an easy chair, 'we can talk. I have nothing else for over an hour.' She smiled at Andrea. 'You've come a long way. What do you want to know?'

Andrea sipped tea, gaining time. She wondered what the answer should be. At last, 'I suppose what most people in my position want to know. Where did I come from?' She stopped. 'Who am I? Am I still who I thought I was until...' She sipped again, confused.

'Of course you are. Nothing's going to change that.'

There was something very comforting about Cathy. 'Then—how do I find out? I've been trying to imagine it, the process.'

'This organisation—Response WA—can undertake a search for you.'

Andrea stared. 'Can you?'

'Oh, yes. We're used to it. If that's what you want.'

'I thought I'd have to do it all myself.' Such a load off her mind.
'You charge for it?'

'Oh, yes. We have to. It means going through all kinds of documentation and so on. A bit of a minefield for many people.'

'How long?'

'Depends. On the complications. Some are easy, some are not. Have a biscuit.'

Andrea leaned forward and took one without looking, her mind far away. 'So—what do I do now?'

'Look, we're jumping the gun.' Cathy sat up and put down her cup. 'Tell me about yourself.'

Andrea stared out of the window at the suburban traffic flowing past beyond a scruffy, ill-kept hedge. Where to begin? At the beginning, as far as she knew it.

'I was adopted at six months old, after I'd been fostered...'

Cathy was a good listener. The story came, hesitantly at first, then fluently as she spoke of a happy childhood, faltering only when she came to the unbearable pain of losing Joseph. Cathy's eyes warmed in sympathy.

'Then, somehow, I found I needed to discover my background. I don't know why. It had never happened before. Perhaps because of the turmoil after Joseph...'

They sat together quietly. It seemed unnecessary to say anything. At last Cathy stirred.

'I'm sorry for your loss. It must have been very hard.' Then, more briskly, 'But you're a sensible woman. You've come through.'

'I've never, ever, told the whole story to anyone.' Andrea smiled pensively. 'You'd think I'd be content to let well alone. I'm sure that there are many—adoptees who have worse tales to tell. You must meet them in your job.'

Cathy gave her a very level look. 'I *am* one of them. In my case a double whammy. Adoptee *and* relinquishing mother. I'll tell you one day.'

Andrea stared. 'That's terrible. Terrible! How have you coped?'

'Sometimes not well. Now...'

'Do you know—I mean, who your mother—have you found your—your...?'

'Daughter. Yes, I found my mother. She didn't want to know. And I know where my daughter is, but I haven't tried to contact her.' She gave Andrea a tight smile. 'But this is your problem, not mine. This is what we can do...'

30

At dinner that evening, in a corner of the hotel dining room, Andrea let her mind slip back over the momentous afternoon. Cathy had taken copies of the documents, including Andrea's birth certificate, and made notes of the details Lucy had provided of those first days, lost in time for Andrea—the foster home, the adoption papers, pieces of a complex crossword which, hopefully, would eventually make complete sense.

For a moment she felt like calling it all back, all that evidence of another, unknown life. But the slope she had set herself on, a toboggan slope of the emotions, would not let her off until she reached its end. Whether that end would bring tears or laughter she wouldn't know until the toboggan tipped her off. She smiled at the metaphor. It reminded her of holidays in the Victorian snowfields with her parents.

And *that* reminded her that she must ring Lucy and report developments.

'Yes, Mum, it was a good trip. I'm glad I took the train.'
'And what have you done today?'
'I met Cathy Farwell. She's going to do the search for me.'
'That'll be a help. How long will it take?'
'How long is a piece of string!'
'Silly of me! Your father's here. Would you like to speak to him?'
'Of course. But Mum—it's all right. You're not to worry.'
'I won't, darling. Really I won't. Only...'
'Put Dad on, Mum. Please?'
'Take care, Andrea. Won't you?'
'I'll take care. I miss you both already.'
'Oh, me too, dear! Oh, dear, I'm being silly again. Here's Dad.'

'The umbilical cord is a lifeline,' Andrea said into the silence of her bedroom as she put the receiver down, cutting off the clearly emotional voices of Lucy and Harry. 'And so is the phone cord! I think I shall sleep tonight.'

The waiting was a torment. Sometimes she wished she had undertaken the search herself, the time hung so heavily. And yet she found plenty to occupy her, in or out of the city. She gloried in amazing beaches, ate in pasta restaurants, Vietnamese cafés, found Indian and Italian cuisine, took free buses around the city and trains that ran up the centre of the freeway. The public library offered comfortable reading on wet and windy days—autumn was well advanced—and the art galleries, public and private, drew her in when Cathy had once again said it was early days, and not to worry.

Then came the phone call she was waiting for. Somehow she could tell, as soon as she heard the voice, that Cathy had real news for her. She sat down on the bed and held the receiver in both hands—both shaking hands.

'Can you come over? I don't want to say this on the phone.'

Andrea said. 'Just—is it good or bad?'

'That will be for you to judge, my dear. But it looks good on the surface.'

'I'll be there,' she glanced at her watch, 'in twenty minutes.'

'I'll put the kettle on.'

The gate creaked, the front door was ajar, and as Andrea pushed it open the kettle began to whistle in the distance. She stood in the office doorway as Cathy looked up.

'Well?'

Cathy smiled widely. 'Looking good! Take a seat. I'll only be a moment.'

By the time she returned with the tea-tray Andrea felt more in control of herself. She waited patiently while Cathy put a cup before her, accepted a biscuit, leaned back and crossed her legs. 'Shoot!'

Cathy lifted a file from her desk and removed a piece of paper. 'Your mother,' she said, savouring the moment, 'is seventy-three, and still lives in a Perth suburb.' She glanced up at Andrea, whose face had paled. 'You OK?' Andrea nodded, holding the arms of her chair with white-knuckled fingers. 'She has not been told that you are looking for her. That's your decision.'

Andrea picked up the cup and put it down again. Her heart had given a mighty thump, and she thought for a second that she might actually faint. She could see Cathy's concerned face, but it seemed a mile away.

Somewhere, in a corner of her mind she had hardly visited until recently, a dark door had opened. A gleam of light shone through, and she was all at once terrified of what that light might be about to reveal. This plain, undistinguished room was to be her birthing chamber, and she felt desperately unready to be re-born. In a flurry she stood, clutching her handbag to her, filled with the panic she had first felt as she left Sydney behind her.

'I can't...' she began. 'Not now. I have to go! Sorry! Sorry, Cathy—you've been—I have to go.'

Cathy put out a hand. 'Let me get you a taxi, Andrea. Please?'

'No. I want to walk. I need to.' She pulled herself together a little. 'Don't worry. I'll be careful. I just can't...'

Somehow she left the house; somehow found her way into the city. How far she walked she had no idea. Cathy, watching her leave, had murmured, 'But you'll be back, my dear. You haven't come this far to give up.'

Sleep came late that night. By morning Andrea felt wrung out; but she also knew that it would be impossible not to go on, whatever that mystical opening door might disclose. She rang Cathy.

Soon after lunch they sat together in the office. Andrea attempted an apology, but Cathy dismissed it with one sweep of her hand.

'It's an amazing moment. The wonder is that we don't all go mad.'

'It was the door opening,' Andrea said obscurely.

Cathy nodded. 'Too many closed doors in our lives.' She regarded her visitor thoughtfully. 'You're looking better—but I guess you didn't sleep well.'

'Whoever invented the phrase "tossing and turning" had me in mind.' She managed a smile. 'I'm ready now.'

'Right! You were fostered at three months. I haven't yet been able to find a reason for that. You were with a foster family for the next three months, then the Martins adopted you. But you know that.'

Andrea frowned. 'I always imagined I was illegitimate. Was I?'

'No. Your birth mother was married.'

'Then why...?'

'Could be any number of reasons. Her ill-health, perhaps. Or you might not have been her husband's child. Or she might have been a widow, or divorced.'

'Or I might have been an inconvenience,' Andrea suggested acidly.

'Some of us probably were. But *it wasn't our fault!* Remember that. We had no choice over our own conception.'

Andrea sat silent, thinking deeply. 'What now?' she said at last.

'We can approach this lady and ask if she wants to make contact.'

'I've come this far,' Andrea said, almost to herself. 'I can't stop now.'

'Then we'll call her and see if she wants to take that step.'

Andrea nodded slowly. 'I'll wait till I hear from you. I—I can't altogether take it in.'

'Of course not. We'll give you a call.'

When that call came, Andrea held her phone and let it ring several times.

'We've located her,' Cathy said. 'This is the bad news, I'm afraid, Andrea. She's in hospital. Terminal cancer. Didn't sound overjoyed. But she says you can visit her if you want to.'

'Then she must be at least a little curious about me. Mustn't she?'

'It would be odd if she weren't.'

Andrea's legs gave way and she sat down on the bed. 'Oh, Cathy! All this was for that? How long has she got, did they say?'

'Not good. You know hospitals—no info, but sounded a bit gloomy about her chances.' She paused, waiting for Andrea to speak, but Andrea was silent. This news, on top of everything else, had taken her breath away. 'So do you want to know where she is, Andrea?'

'Yes.' It was a whisper down the line.

She scribbled the name of the hospital and the ward number. *An address to what?* she was asking herself. A happy reunion? Frustration? *Oh, God!* she thought wildly, *why did I ever start this?* 'And—her name?'

'Mrs Claudia Shepherd.'

A real person. Someone with a real name. The mists of ignorance began to disperse. You had to take seriously a person with a real name. Mrs Claudia Shepherd!

'Thanks, Cathy.' Funny, her voice sounded quite normal. 'What do I do now?'

'You can go and see her. Perhaps you should warn her. Let the hospital know you're coming. Something.'

'Will you come with me?'

'No way, my dear. You're on your own in this. You have to be.' She made her voice warm and confident. 'See her for a short while as she's sick. Tell her you'll come back again. And—Andrea—good luck! We'll be thinking of you.'

Andrea paused by the ward door. The importance of the next few minutes suddenly overwhelmed her. There was (was she over-reacting?) an almost mystical aspect to the meeting she had so longed for. But how could you over-react to seeing, for the first conscious time, the mother who had conceived you, borne you for nine long months, delivered you into a world that would, all too soon, separate the two of you, set you on a course that, long after, would bring you full circle to meet...what? Whom? A stranger whose only link was that once you had lain, protected, in her womb.

Was that a link sufficient to bridge the gap?

She entered the room. Two beds, one unoccupied. For a panicky second Andrea hoped that the empty bed was her mother's. That she was out for an X-ray, or a bath, or anything that would put off the inevitable for another moment.

But the name over the other bed was the one she was looking for. *MRS CLAUDIA SHEPHERD.*

Andrea stood very still. The woman appeared to be asleep. Then she saw that the eyes were open, just a little, and that they were regarding her with what hardly seemed an appropriate lack of interest. It occurred to Andrea that perhaps the stomach-churning excitement was hers alone. Somehow she had expected— hoped?— that this thin, pale woman lying in a hospital bed would be showing emotion commensurate with the occasion: a reunion that would be a turning point in the private histories of each of them.

Mrs Claudia Shepherd showed no such emotion.

'You've found me, then,' the woman said. And Andrea, confused, replied, 'Yes, I found you.'

Such little sentences. She wanted something bigger to happen, something that would match the magnitude of the moment.

'You'd better sit down, then.'

If the past days had seemed bizarre, this meeting capped them in its sheer extraordinariness.

Andrea took a chair from against the wall and put it beside the bed. Not too close to that enigmatic figure. She needed space. And suspected that this woman, this Claudia Shepherd, trapped in her bed, needed space even more pressingly.

What do you say? She tried to smile, but her facial muscles seemed to have gone into some kind of spasm. 'How do you do?' was altogether too trite. '*Mother!*' was unthinkable. She made several attempts, while the woman in the bed lay silent and inscrutable, and finally managed, 'I hope you didn't mind me coming?'

Mrs Shepherd shrugged slightly, hardly moving the bedclothes pulled up to her chin. 'It was bound to happen, I suppose. One day. You're only just in time.' Before Andrea could reply, she said, 'I suppose you want to know why I let you go?'

Andrea cleared her throat. 'There's so much I would like to know. But only if you want to tell me. I haven't come to upset you.'

'Haven't you?' Thin eyebrows rose, and an odd expression flickered in the eyes. 'I would, if it was me.' Andrea, watching every movement of this unknown face, fancied there was a malicious glint there. But surely this was no occasion for malice?

'I'd like to know whatever you want to tell me,' Andrea assured her. 'And perhaps if—when—we get to know each other better...'

'Not much chance of that,' the woman said in that thin, unwelcoming voice. 'You're lucky to find me alive. I'm on borrowed time—so they think.'

'Perhaps,' Andrea said bravely, 'you were waiting for me to find you?'

This stranger who was her mother gave a short, dry laugh. 'A bit of a mystic, are you? No, you can forget that. I haven't been waiting for you or anyone else.'

Andrea, not knowing what to say, bent to her handbag and took out an envelope. 'I brought you this.' She opened it and removed a photograph, herself at two years old. 'I thought you might like to have it.'

Mrs Shepherd glanced at the snap, but left her hands under the covers. 'I knew you'd be pretty. But you shouldn't have bothered. It's too late for that.'

Andrea swallowed down her desire to say, 'It's not too late! It's never too late while there's still life.' She looked around her; said instead, 'Are you comfortable? Is there anything I can bring in for you?'

Claudia Shepherd shook her head briefly. 'There's nothing I need.' Her expression was forbidding, and Andrea felt a wave of depression rising within her. So long, so far—and for what? She had imagined embarrassment, tears, even anger and withdrawal; but this woman was fully in control of herself, and seemed to have no interest in the strange encounter. 'Just to be left alone.'

Andrea hesitated. She reminded herself that she was a grown woman, a widow with two almost adult children; that if this (how to describe her? *Ma* no longer seemed appropriate), this *stranger* were to prove to be a brick wall, *she* was entitled to pick at the bricks and try to make a hole. Beyond the wall was a wealth of knowledge relating to her, Andrea; and—suddenly feeling both annoyed and assertive—by golly, she was going to get at it!

'What should I call you?' she asked firmly.

The sunken eyes recognised a change in the wind, and a flicker of amusement crossed the emaciated features.

'The name's Claudia. Or would you prefer "Mummy"?'

Andrea met her eyes. 'No, I have a Mummy already.' She gathered together the thoughts that had been racing panic-stricken through her head. 'Claudia—you say we haven't much time. I'm sorry to find you so sick. I had hoped we might be friends, discover each other, perhaps. Not like this, in a hurry. Not after so long.'

'Bad timing. If you'd come next week I'd be gone.'

'And you think that would be good? Not to have met.'

'What's the point?' Claudia coughed, a dry, uncomfortable sound. 'We've managed without each other up to now. Why dig anything up at this late date?'

'Because...' Andrea began, swallowing hard against a sob of frustration that wouldn't go away, 'because I need to know. I need to know where I came from, what my background is—*who I am.*'

'How will it change you? For good? Can you be sure?'

Andrea thought of that brick wall. Dig through? Scale it and see the view from the top? Locate a way around it? 'Can't you see,' she said urgently, 'that to know *something,* whatever it might be, would be better than knowing nothing?' She stopped to draw breath and control a voice becoming strident with disappointment.

Claudia seemed quite unmoved by her passion. 'Once you know, you have to carry it for the rest of your life.' She coughed again. 'You've had a good life. Don't be greedy.'

'Greedy? Is that how it seems to you? I have a right to know—haven't I?'

Claudia's eyes closed wearily. It was a clear message. Andrea sat for a moment, letting tense muscles relax. She felt a deep sense of rejection, and wondered why she had not anticipated this particular reaction.

'How do you know I've had a good life?' she persisted.

For a moment the tired eyes opened. 'Look at yourself. It's all there.'

Andrea stood and replaced the chair against the wall. 'You're tired. I'll come tomorrow.'

'Please yourself. Send the nurse in.'

Andrea regarded the enigmatic figure that had nothing and everything to do with her. She left and went to the nursing station.

'Mrs Shepherd would like to see the nurse.'

'Certainly.' A quick, professional smile.

'She's very sick.'

'I'm afraid so.'

Andrea was suddenly seized with a need to say something to someone. Anything! Anyone! 'Mrs Shepherd is my mother.'

The nurse raised her eyebrows. 'She told us she had no family.'

'Well, she had me.' She was already regretting the impulse. 'She's my birth mother. This is the first time...' (*I will not cry!* she told herself fiercely).

'How very interesting,' the nurse said. 'Are you all right, my dear?'

'Yes. I shouldn't have said. And please don't say anything to her. Or anyone. Please.'

'Of course not.' Sympathy, automatic and swift. A tissue for the two tears that had escaped. That smile again. 'All right now?'

Andrea nodded. 'Thanks.' She turned away, glanced towards the door behind which Claudia was—what? Asleep, or savouring their recent reunion? Asleep, probably. She sighed. So much for high hopes.

7

'**N**o good?' Cathy said, pouring the healing tea.

Andrea sank back in her chair. 'Weird! Not at all what I expected. I thought I was prepared. But she...' Words failed her. She moved her hands helplessly. 'I don't even know how to describe it—or her.'

'She's very sick?'

'Yes. Yes, very. Actually, she looks terrible. I don't think she could possibly last much longer.' She gazed into her tea cup as if an answer could be found there. 'It was almost,' she said in a low voice, 'as if she was mocking me. I didn't expect that.'

'Her own defence mechanism?'

'I don't think so. I didn't sense anything defensive. It was more as if—as if she had closed a door and wasn't going to open it. Yes.' She looked up. 'She's a closed door, Cathy. So I have to find a key.'

They sat, companionably silent. Andrea was reliving that enigmatic meeting that had for so many weeks past filled her mind almost to the exclusion of all else, and had now proved to be so—so... She shook her head, deeply confused.

Cathy hesitated. 'It might explain—you were taken into care, Andrea. *Taken.* She didn't make the decision.'

Andrea stared at her. 'I didn't realise.' She considered for a moment. 'So there must have been something—something...' She frowned at Cathy. 'Why?'

'I haven't been able to discover.'

'They wouldn't take a baby unless there was a very good reason, would they? But what?'

'I don't know. Unfit mother? Alcohol? Abuse of some kind? I'll try to find out.'

'This might be the key I'm looking for.' Andrea sat up. 'I'm going to see her tomorrow. I may try this on her.' She grinned, suddenly hopeful once more. 'She's not going to beat me, not after all this time.'

'That's the girl!' Cathy refilled the cups.
'Yes, Mum, I've seen her'
'And?'
'I wouldn't know how to describe—it was bizarre, Mum, just bizarre. She's dying of cancer. I think I'm only just in time. But she's—she's an enigma.'
'I'm so sorry, darling. Not a good meeting?'
'She's like a closed door. So I have to find a way in. I'm afraid—Mum, I really didn't take to her. And she didn't seem to want to know anything about me.'
'How disappointing for you. So what will you do?'
'I'll see her tomorrow. Mum, I was taken from her. She didn't give me up. That's a whole different can of worms, isn't it?'
'I didn't know. My dear, I didn't know!'
'There's something in there, Mum. Something I have to discover. I don't know how, but I'll do it. Somehow...'

Andrea carried a small pot of African violets into the room. Claudia was awake, staring at the ceiling; when she saw Andrea her eyes registered the fact, then slid away. Andrea put the pot on the window sill.

'You came back, then.'

'Yes. Did you think you'd put me off?' She pulled the chair towards the bed and sat down. 'How are you, Claudia?'

'Nothing changes.' She cast a sardonic eye over her daughter. 'Haven't you anything better to do?'

Andrea regarded her with a greater sense of control over herself and the situation than she had managed the first time. 'No, not at present. I've come from Sydney to find you. Why would I give up now?' She took an envelope from her bag. 'This is the photo I showed you. I'm leaving it with you. And this...' She took out another snap taken of Bethany and Daniel at the beach the previous year. 'These are your two lovely grandchildren.'

She propped them against the water jug. Claudia said nothing, but her eyes flickered towards the pictures.

Andrea hesitated briefly, then produced another likeness—Harry and Lucy, taken at last year's Christmas party.

'Mum and Dad,' she said quietly.

This time Claudia turned her head slightly, almost unwillingly; then returned painfully to her original position. 'I said you'd had a good life.'

'They're good people. Don't you want to hear about them? About my children, Bethany and Daniel? Doesn't any of it interest you?'

Claudia's eyes moved slowly to fasten on Andrea's face. There was little expression in them, only a shadow of that silent mockery Andrea had sensed. 'It's got nothing to do with me. Why should it have? More than forty years. Too much water under the bridge.' She nodded briefly towards the photographs. 'They're strangers. You're a stranger. Whatever happened all those years ago...' She began to cough, and Andrea held a feeding cup of water to the dry lips, her hand under the back of the dying woman's head.

The first time I've touched my mother since they took me away, she was thinking as she laid the head back on the pillows.

'Get over it,' Claudia said as soon as she could speak. 'What is it you want?' Was the closed door opening a crack?

'I know you didn't just give me up,' Andrea said carefully. 'I know I was put into care.'

The tired eyes opened. 'Who says?'

'The official records.'

'Then what *do* you want?'

'To know why. To know who my father was. You were married. So what went wrong?'

The long silence could be denial. It could be an effort of memories being unearthed. It lasted long enough so that Andrea began to think that the door was closing again before she had had time to peep through.

'Tell me,' she pleaded.

Claudia shifted in the bed as if it had suddenly become uncomfortable. 'My business, all those.' She closed her eyes. 'I had you. That's all. They had their reasons for taking you.'

Andrea took a deep, frustrated breath. 'My father?'

'You wouldn't want to know.'

'Claudia! You're not being fair. This is information I have a right to. A moral right! What harm can it do to you now?'

The wasted figure in the bed gave a faint snort that might have been laughter. 'Moral! There wasn't much morality involved.'

Andrea leaned forward. She wanted to threaten, twist an arm, *pinch* information out of this stubborn stranger. But she mustn't.

'Claudia—was my father your husband?'

'Were you legal, do you mean?'

'Well—yes.'

'What if you were?' She suddenly lost patience. 'Oh, go home to your kids and your *Mum and Dad!*' (It was nearly a sneer). 'I'm not the person you hoped for. Take what you've got and go.'

Andrea sat very still for a moment to let the turmoil within her die down. Slowly she stood and replaced the chair. She picked up her handbag and stood looking down on the dying woman, those cold eyes closed once more. Briefly they flickered open.

'Take your pictures.'

'They're for you.'

As Andrea started for the door, Claudia suddenly said, 'What do you do?'

Startled, Andrea swung round to look at her. 'What do you mean?'

'Career girl? Or stay-at-home?'

'I'm a musician.'

The eyes followed her as she returned to the bed. 'Do you play?'

'Violin.'

'Are you any good?'

'Pretty good. But I haven't played for a while.'

'Why not?'

'My husband died.' She said it flatly. This wasn't a time for emotion.

'How?'

'Heart attack.'

Claudia seemed to be taking the information in, digesting it. It was the most hopeful moment in their brief contact.

'What's your name?'

Puzzled: 'Andrea Coombes.'

'Is that your full name?'

'No. Andrea Frazier Coombes.' She frowned. 'Did you name me?'

'Oh yes, I named you.'

'Was Frazier your maiden name?'

'No.'

'Whose, then?'

'I liked it. That's all.'

'But...'

'*I liked it*'. The eyes burned briefly. 'Now go. I'm tired.'

Andrea sighed. 'I'll see you tomorrow, Claudia.'

'I don't suppose I'll be going anywhere.'

The same nurse was on duty. 'If Mrs Shepherd's condition should change,' Andrea said, 'can you contact me?'

'Give me a phone number.'

As she took it down a thought struck. 'Does she have an official next-of-kin?'

'No. Sad, isn't it? To be alone at a time like this.'

'She seems to like being alone.' She smiled at the nurse. 'I'll see her tomorrow.'

8

'**O**dd,' Andrea said to Cathy. 'She suddenly wanted to know what I did for a living. Seemed almost interested—well, no, that's an exaggeration. But I left some family photos with her—and I'd love to be a fly on the wall. Will she look at them or not? Will she pick them up?' She grinned. 'She's a real toughie, Cathy. But she's made me really determined to see this thing through. I'm *not* going to let her beat me!'

'Attagirl!' Cathy said, and lifted the teapot once again.

'Oh, it's you.' Claudia turned her head away. Andrea noticed that the photos were still on view. She put down a bunch of Singapore orchids.

'I'll get a vase.'

'Let them do it. Earn their money.' The voice was no more than a breath of air.

I bet they do that, Andrea thought. She stood at the foot of the bed. She was feeling quite buoyed up today. *Like it or not, Claudia, you're going to tell me something.*

She went across the corridor to where she had seen a sink and a collection of vases. She chose a tall one and filled it with water, then quickly arranged the flowers and carried them back.

'There! I'll put them on this other table.' She stood back to admire them.

'You don't give up easily.' The paper-thin voice was still antagonistic, but Andrea, turning, sensed a subtle change.

'No, I don't.' She smiled cheerfully. 'Do I get that from you?'

'I doubt it. You only got one thing from me.'

'Life?' Andrea drew the chair towards the bed. 'Well, for that I thank you, Claudia. As you said, it's been a good life.' She regarded the face, pale as a peeled almond, small enough in its wasted condition to belong to a child. For the first time she felt real sensations of pity. What had brought this woman to such a depth of bitterness that she could show no warmth to someone who might be her only living relative?

'Am I the only one?' she said.

Claudia turned her head on the pillow and stared. 'The only what?'

'Your only relative?'

'Why?'

'Well, someone will have to look after things when you—when it's...' She foundered, fearing to offend with those so final words: death, when it's over, when you're no longer here to handle your own affairs.

'When I'm dead. Go on, you can say it.'

'OK. When you're dead, Claudia, someone will have to clear up your things.'

'Nothing to clear. I've paid for my funeral. Given everything away to one of those do-good places.'

'Salvos? Red Cross?'

Claudia shrugged.

'Do you have a home?'

'Rented. Paid up. Moved out.'

Andrea regarded the woman with a frown. 'There must be something.'

The cold eyes registered brief amusement. 'Thought you were going to be an heiress, did you? Bad luck!'

'Certainly not. I was thinking of you.'

'I do my own thinking, thanks. Always have, always will.'

Silence lay between them. In Andrea's case it was laced with frustration. Welcome interruption came in the rotund shape of a woman with a trolley. Andrea accepted a cup of coffee. Claudia shook her head irritably.

'They never let you alone. Always some busybody, checking out that you're still alive. Fiddling with this.' She indicated the stand with a plastic bag of fluid and a tube that disappeared into the bedclothes in the direction of her left arm. 'Don't know why they don't just let me go.'

Andrea was tempted to make a sarcastic remark, but held it in. 'They want you to be comfortable as long as possible.' She put the coffee cup down. 'Claudia—can you tell me a bit about your family? Your parents? Help me to understand what happened to me.'

The silence threatened. She thought, *I'll never get anything out of her. Never!*

Suddenly, Claudia said, 'My mother died when I was seven. I was the only one. My father was killed in the war. North Africa. I never knew my grandparents. I had no aunts and uncles, no cousins. Children's home. I married when I was twenty-four. Ben Shepherd.' She stopped and gave a short, throaty laugh. 'His bad luck!'

'Why?' Andrea, fascinated, demanded.

The sunken eyes turned towards her, seeming to look at her properly for the first time. 'Why? *Because*, that's why. He was a fool and I was a bigger one.' She stopped for a moment, staring past Andrea. 'Well, we both paid for it.'

Here was the chink in the wall, the rift in the mists of silence. Andrea hesitated to speak in case the tiny promise of revelation were to disappear for ever.

'How?' she asked at last, cautiously. 'How did you pay?'

Claudia let out a long breath and shifted wearily in the bed. 'Keep searching,' she said, and the dry coughing began. When she could speak again it was in a voice in which Andrea detected an emotional change. The words themselves offered no comfort, but there was the smallest indication that, somewhere behind the expressionless face and the bitter speech, something had warmed. 'Keep searching and you'll find out. I shan't be here to see it.'

Andrea regarded her thoughtfully. 'A clue?' she suggested at last.

'Not on yours!' Claudia gave the shadow of a humphing snort. 'You've had all you're getting. If you're daft enough to dig it all up, you can do it on your own.'

'Right!' It was a challenge. She accepted it. 'I'll be in tomorrow.'

'Suit yourself.'

She stood at the end of the bed, and found herself smiling. 'Are you as tough as you seem, Claudia?'

Those sunken eyes gleamed for a moment. 'You'd better believe it.' It was the nearest they had come to finding a rapport.

'I'll see you tomorrow.' Andrea collected her bag and stopped by the bedside. 'I *will* come tomorrow!'

'Your choice. Can't stop you.'

They exchanged a glance, puzzlement on Andrea's side, a defensive lack of expression from her mother. Unsatisfying, but a tiny step forward. Andrea nodded, smiled. 'Take care, Claudia.'

She was at the door when Claudia said, in the voice that bore the spice of malice that had so defeated Andrea: 'What happened to the other one?'

Andrea stood very still. She could make no sense of the words. Slowly she turned. 'Which other one? Claudia! What do you mean?'

But she was playing her game again, eyes shut, body almost hidden under the thin hospital blanket. 'Claudia! Please!'

No response from the fragile figure. Andrea, not sure what she had heard, wanted to shake her, force her to explain. But she was beginning to know this strange, eccentric parent of hers. *Tomorrow will do*, she told herself. *I'll ask her tomorrow.*

'It was so extraordinary,' she said to Cathy. 'I still don't know what she meant. *The other one!* The only thing I can think is...'

'Yes?' Cathy was watching her carefully as she struggled with a new concept.

'Do you suppose—do you think I might have a—a sister or a brother? A twin, maybe?' She put her hands to her face. 'It's all becoming more bizarre by the minute. What do you think, Cathy?'

'It was an odd thing to say. Nothing else?'

'No. The wretched woman pretended to be asleep.' Andrea gave a nervous laugh. 'I'm so muddled...' She stood and went to the window, looking out blindly, then swung round, her mind made up. 'She's got to tell me what she meant. I'll see her tomorrow and *make* her.'

'How?'

''Ve haf vays of making you talk!'

'I think the hospital might object to pulling out fingernails.'

'I'll be subtle. I'll offer her money.' She laughed, feeling slightly less traumatised now that she had made her decision.

'On her deathbed?' Cathy smiled. 'From what you say she's virtually divested herself of worldly things.'

'I might break down. Cry and scream.'

'I'd better come with you. You may need someone to vouch for you.'

'Don't worry.' Reaction set in, a small wave of dejection overcoming her. She sat down and sighed. 'Oh, Cathy, I wonder if I'd have bothered if I'd known all this.'

'Once the need to know hits you, you don't have much choice, my dear.'

'You're right. Well...' She gathered herself together. 'I'm off! See you tomorrow.' She stopped at the door. 'I don't know what I'd have done without you, Cathy.'

'My pleasure.'

'You always make me feel as if my problems are the only ones you have to deal with. And yet...' she gestured towards a pile of papers on the desk, 'you must be dealing with so many other damaged lives.'

'Each one unique. Every one of us an individual. All the stories the same and yet quite different.'

'You're a wise woman.'

'Wise? I wonder. Experienced.'

Andrea twiddled her fingers in farewell and left. Cathy sat for a moment. '*Very* experienced,' she murmured, and went back to her desk.

Andrea sat in her hotel room and regarded the phone. She ought to ring Lucy. Or Bethany. But at the prospect of trying to describe Claudia's behaviour over the phone her courage failed her.

'Tomorrow,' she promised. 'After I've seen her again.'

She let herself out and locked the door and went in search of her dinner.

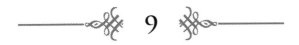

9

The bank balance was beginning to moan under the weight of her hotel bills. She would have to find cheaper accommodation—somehow. Surely, Cathy would know of somewhere bearable? She did.

'You can have my spare bedroom,' she said, apparently without stopping for thought.

'Oh—but...' Andrea looked at her quickly to gauge her reactions.

'No "but"! The room is there. No one is using it, and you're welcome.' Cathy paused for a moment, then said, 'It would be a kindness to me, really. And we do seem to hit it off—don't we?'

It was morning, just after nine, and Andrea aimed to get to the hospital about ten. The load of worry over accommodation now lifted, she felt a rush of excitement, and with it came determination. Claudia must open up. She must! She couldn't keep throwing out these challenges at her new-found daughter and then recede—like the tiny crabs that dug themselves in at the water's edge and left nothing but the traces of their sharp little claws. This woman's claws were all too evident.

But Andrea was going to see to it that the tide came in too swiftly this time for Claudia to take cover. This could well be the last opportunity for persuading (*forcing?* she wondered) some sense out of the stubborn creature.

'Because she's simply got to give,' she said to Cathy. 'Time's running out.'

She bought a single orchid blossom at the hospital's flower shop and made her way with determined step towards the ward. In her mind she was going over her opening words to Claudia. It would go something like, 'Claudia, we don't have the time to play games...' or perhaps, 'Claudia, I haven't come this far to be...' She would be firm.

The nurse met her as she entered the ward. 'Oh, Mrs Coombes—I'm so glad I saw you coming.'

Andrea stood very still. 'Yes?'

'I've been trying to ring you. I'm so sorry, my dear. Mrs Shepherd...'

'She's gone.'

'I'm afraid so. She went into a coma very early this morning, and died about half an hour ago. Here!' She saw Andrea's face whiten. 'Sit down. I'll get you some water.'

How silly, Andrea was thinking, *to feel faint because of this woman I didn't even like.* And there was some relief in admitting that she had indeed found Claudia unlikeable, though perhaps this was not the time to say so. The nurse brought water, and Andrea sipped. What now? Without Claudia to answer questions, even if the answers had to be torn out of her, where could she go on this great quest?

For a moment she felt a sense of the load lightening, but it lasted only briefly. However difficult this latest blow made it, she would have to press on. There were too many unanswered questions, and she knew that if they remained unanswered they would hang around her for the rest of her life.

She was never sure what she said to the nurse as she was taken to a side ward where Claudia was lying, cold and thin and pale, flown from a life that, from what Andrea had gleaned, had been far from satisfactory—into what? She stood and looked down at the remains of her mother, and found no feeling within her except the frustration of not knowing.

'I'm sorry, Claudia,' she murmured when the nurse had gone, 'I can't mourn for you. You made that impossible. But I am sorry that we found so little pleasure in each other. It could have been different.'

The thin face, now beginning to look like a marble copy of itself, had lost that mocking expression that had been so annoying. Andrea touched the cool brow gently and turned away.

'She left this for you,' the nurse said as Andrea returned to the nursing station, and handed her an envelope. It was unsealed.

'Did she say anything?'

'Not really. She was too far gone to speak. Just handed it over and whispered "my visitor". You were the only person who ever came to see her, so...' The nurse shrugged. 'Such a strange lady.'

'Yes, she was.' Andrea opened the envelope and slipped her fingers in. What she hoped to find she had no idea, but certainly not the photographs she had left, torn across in a final defiant gesture. She held them for a moment before looking into the envelope, just in case there might have been a message, something to indicate that Claudia had cared even microscopically about this family she had never known. There was a slip of paper. In shaky letters it said, 'Look at the papers'.

Andrea stared at it. It seemed to make no sense. She was confused, a little angry, feeling that same mockery now coming from beyond whatever the line was between life and death. She turned to the nurse. 'Thank you for what you have all done for her. I don't suppose she ever managed to say thanks. She was an unhappy woman.'

'You get all sorts in nursing. I'm sorry you didn't have better luck with her.' She hesitated. 'I think everything has been taken care of. Mrs Shepherd made all the arrangements for—for afterwards before she came in.' She smiled at Andrea with understanding. 'You won't have to take on any unwanted burdens.'

'Thank God for that!' Andrea said with feeling. She glanced back at the door behind which Claudia now lay, and had a momentary spasm of conscience. 'Perhaps I ought...'

'I don't think so. It's not my business, of course, but...'

'No, you're right. If I hadn't come here until after she had died, I would never have known...'

'We make our own lives,' said the nurse gently. 'A woman like Mrs Shepherd has the same opportunities as the rest of us to make it a good life. But for some it seems they always choose the hard road.'

'Of course you're right.' Andrea held out her hand. 'Anyway, thanks.'

She wandered out into the streets of Perth and took the first free bus she saw, alighting some minutes later within easy distance of King's Park. It was one of Perth's loveliest days, sunny with a light breeze that ruffled leaves and kept the air sweet. As she walked up the hill to the park she let her mind float over the few, the very few meetings she had had with the strange woman who, so oddly, was her mother. Now that it was over she felt a sense of disbelief that there could ever have been that contact between them.

Had Claudia ever held her with that overwhelming love that Andrea recalled from those long-ago days when her own children had been tiny? Had she kissed dimpled knees, smelt that perfume of newly-bathed and powdered baby, lain on the bed to watch the tiny child beside her, asleep, and pondered on the wonder of it all?

Somehow, recent events considered, it seemed unlikely.

She treated herself to a coffee and a superbly wicked piece of chocolate cake. Beyond the café window she could see the wide stretch of water that made Perth so special, and beyond that the hills that separated this city from the rest of Australia. *Isolation,* she thought. *Like me. Alone in a world that seems increasingly weird.* She recalled a nursery counting song sung in early school days. The tune was there, but the words eluded her for a long moment, then suddenly sprang into her mind. She hummed the verse to herself under her breath.

'...one is one and all alone, and evermore shall be so!'

But that was ridiculous. She was in no way alone; Lucy and Harry, Bethany and Dan, and now her new friend Cathy—she was surrounded by friends and family, people who loved her. So why did she feel like weeping? Why should she weep anyway because of a mocking, ill-wishing woman who was now dead, even if she had left so many questions unanswered?

Because she was my mother, Andrea whispered into her coffee cup. *In spite of everything, she was my mother. And one should wish to weep for the death of one's mother.*

She took the envelope out of her bag and stared at it. Strange bequest! Torn photographs and an enigmatic message. Not much to inherit from one's only surviving parent. At least... A thought struck her. *Was* Claudia her only surviving parent? She wondered what had happened to her father—if indeed Ben Shepherd had been her father. What a mess! Why...? Why...? So many questions. And at this moment she had no idea how she would find answers.

She looked again at the torn slip of paper. *Look at the papers.* What did it mean? The newspapers? Some papers that only Claudia knew about? Newspapers sounded more likely. She finished her coffee and the delectable cake and paid at the desk. Suddenly she was filled with determination. She was *damned* if she'd be beaten by that—that... 'My mother!' she said out loud, and laughed briefly, pretending she had not been noticed by two women sitting at an outside table.

'Claudia,' she murmured as she made her way to the bus stop, 'you will not beat me. If there is anything to be found, I will find it!'

'She died. I don't know if she would have told me anything else. She seemed to take pleasure in being annoying. Tantalising, perhaps.'

'So what's next? Are you coming home?'

'No, I'm not beaten yet. There's something—something. I don't know what, but I'm not giving up just when it's getting interesting.'

'Take care, dear.'

'I will. Love to Dad. See you one day...'

The obvious thing to do was to go to the city library and have a look at the newspapers for the period during which the mystery began. Those months of her own earliest childhood, the time she knew nothing about; that was where to start.

The librarian found the records of the State newspaper for the month that marked her fostering. With the strangest sensation—not fear, not even curiosity, but an odd mixture of emotions—Andrea started her quest. On the screen came a page of news, seeming now so old-fashioned and quite unimportant that she flicked to the next one. It was daunting, she thought as she watched the page slide into place, that what was of such importance to one generation should be so inconsequential to another.

She had hoped, perhaps foolishly, that something would jump out of the page and seize her attention. Without even knowing what it was she was looking for, she ran her eyes up and down the screen until she had to stop, to blink and look around her, to reassure herself that she really was still in the present year, and not thrown back in time.

What *was* it she was hoping to see? A name, perhaps—Claudia was unusual enough to catch the eye. 'Shepherd', 'Benjamin', even perhaps 'Andrea'. But not that, of course. They didn't publish children's names in that sort of case. *What sort of case?* That was the trouble—she didn't even know why she had been fostered, *taken in care*, and she didn't know what Claudia had had in mind in that final cryptic message.

Perhaps it was all a posthumous set-up, anyway—a final snarl from an unhappy woman.

She went through the papers for that first month, then decided she had had enough for one day. Outside the sun was shining, and on an impulse she took the train down to Fremantle—Freo, as the locals call it—and walked along the harbour-side. The fish and chips tempted her, and she sat, eating slowly and with relish, while her mind spun through the events of the day and she tried to make sense of them.

The water sparkled invitingly. Elegant yachts moved with slow grace like swans to their moorings. Gulls flew and screamed and swooped on anything that looked half edible. The town, lying behind the water-front, had its own elegance, a relic, well-preserved, of Edwardian charm. No skyscrapers thrust their way arrogantly to change the skyline; this was a place, she told herself, where she could be happy if she ever wished to move from the east coast. *How Joseph would have loved it!* That pain was slowly dying, leaving a warm glow like embers; the memories were comfortable. Briefly she wondered where life would take her next.

Back at the hotel she rang Cathy and brought her up to date. Tomorrow, she said, she would try again. Though she might be hunting in quite the wrong direction. She only knew that she had to keep on until she found something.

And the following morning, after an hour spent staring at a screen that gave her nothing of importance, she did indeed find something.

The headline said, *WIFE ACCUSED OF HUSBAND KILLING.* There was a grainy picture of a woman being hustled into a car by a policeman; Andrea stared at it until her eyes watered, trying to see some resemblance. But she hardly needed that proof. The caption said it all. *'Mrs Claudia Shepherd (27) being taken into custody after the suspicious death of her husband'.*

Andrea sat back. Her heart was racing. Whatever she had expected, it had not been this. She stared again at the picture, but the woman of forty-six years ago could hardly be expected to look like the old lady dying of cancer, whom Andrea had so recently seen.

That explained so much: being taken into care; Claudia's refusal to talk; even the torn photos. How much 'time' had she done? How badly had it affected her? How would one cope with life after prison? For a brief, compassionate moment, Andrea felt a deep sense of pity for her mother. Whatever she had done...

'Well,' Andrea said aloud, with no one near to hear, 'what she did was kill my father!'

Said like that, it sounded ridiculous. What could lead a woman like Claudia, who had seemed, in spite of her taciturnity, to be an educated person, someone who had known refinement, to kill someone?

She made a note of the date and the page. It was enough for now—necessary to get away and think it out. It cleared up a couple of things, anyway: both her parents were now dead, no need to search hopefully for a father. She wished—how she wished—that she had known these new facts before Claudia had slipped away from her. She could imagine going into that aseptic room, closing the door, advancing on the bed (yes, all right, *menacingly*—she felt she was owed that), and demanding to know the truth. Instead of which...

'Do I have the energy?' she asked the empty room. 'Is it even worth going on, now that I know—*that?*'

And she knew at once that there was no way back now. If she was to have any peace of mind from here on she must uncover the rest of the story. But how? What was the next step?

In the Art Gallery café nearby (*how much coffee will I drink before this is all cleared up?*) she leaned back in her chair and watched the passers-by. The confusion in her mind was slowly dying down; in its place a kind of blankness that was probably another aspect of shock. It was not every day that one discovered that one was the child of a —*murderess?*

Andrea sipped the coffee thoughtfully, and then took from her bag a notebook that she had been using for jotting down the details of this strange journey; on which she had embarked, she now thought, without really being prepared for what might emerge. She flipped through the pages, scrappy reminders of Claudia's few caustic comments, her own memory-joggers of phone numbers, addresses and so on. It all looked pretty silly now. If she had known it would lead to this—this revelation, would she have started it? Well, yes, she could hardly have left it there. She gazed without seeing into her cup. *If I don't go on, if I don't find out finally what all this was about, I shall never get it out of my mind.*

She finished her coffee with resolution and moved out into the sunshine with a new spring in her step. The first thing would be to get copies of all the records of the murder trial, any references to children involved, the whole caboodle! Whatever might be hidden there in those old reports, it was all a part of her own life. Whatever had been done by these particular adults before she was old enough to understand had shaped her life, and she was entitled to know.

It's war, Claudia! You can run, but you can't hide. Andrea laughed drily at her own dramatics. At the library she made her request to the librarian, and went back to her search. Now she knew what she was after. Would there be a reference to the child in the case? The child! Some pictures, maybe. She would recognise herself, even in grainy black and white. Lucy and Harry had so many photos of that time when she had mysteriously become their daughter. That time that was so closely linked to *this* time that she was even now staring at on the screen. This time that told her why Claudia had mentioned 'the other one'.

The headline said HUSBAND KILLER'S CHILDREN. The picture was of two babies, in the arms of two women who were presumably some kind of welfare workers. Neither tiny face was visible, and the children's names were not given. No clues. Except—Andrea pushed her chair back, her heart racing. Except the fact that there *had* been another one, the small boy being taken into a car, a child she had not really believed in. Her brother.

She read down the page. The twin children of Claudia Shepherd, now awaiting trial for the murder of her husband, were taken into care following a court order. The three-month old babies, a boy and a girl, had been cared for by a neighbour, Miss Bella Carding, who told our reporter, 'I could have looked after them. I've known them since they were born. But the magistrate thought otherwise'. It appears that there are no relatives.

Andrea took a deep breath. She felt giddy. What would it have been like, all these years, if she had had a brother? She couldn't even imagine it.

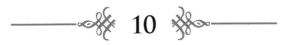

10

'So what do you think?' Andrea was standing by the window in Cathy's office, too strung up to sit. 'I mean, isn't it all too—too...?' Her voice tailed off.

'We weren't expecting that, were we?' The use of 'we' was somehow encouraging. Cathy's face was expressing sympathy for Andrea's dilemma; but at the same time there was a gleam in her eye that said she found the situation intriguing. 'What do you want to do?'

Andrea shrugged. 'I've no idea. It's a mess. I keep wishing...'

'That you'd never started it?'

She grinned fleetingly. 'That I'd hit Claudia over the head and demanded the truth!' She moved to a chair and sat slowly. 'Can the other baby be found? Only...'

'Only?'

'I don't think I want to know.'

'You're really doubtful?'

'I am—very. There was something basic about wanting to find Claudia. It's somehow not the same with—with the other one.' She turned to regard her friend. 'What should I do, Cathy?'

For a long moment Cathy was silent, thinking deeply. She was acutely nervous of advising anyone in this kind of situation. But she and Andrea had become so much more than professional and client. So much more! She took a deep breath. 'If you don't follow this up—just as you did with Claudia—you're going to be bugged by it for ever. It's the same thing, really, all over again. So—are you glad, or not, that you went on with your hunt for your mother? If you are, deep down, then you may find the same happens with the search for this other baby. And even though it is going to impact on someone else's life, he will have the right to reject your advances.' She patted Andrea's hand. 'If we find him, whoever he is and wherever he is, he remains a free agent. If he says he doesn't want to meet you, then I shan't tell you where he is.' She sat back in her office chair and swung it gently from side to side. 'Who knows, he may thank you for looking for him.' A thought hit her. 'He may have been looking for his own family roots for years.' She grinned. 'You may be the answer to his prayers.'

'Some answer!' Andrea's eyes were looking into a place where Cathy could not follow. After a brief moment she sighed and glanced quickly through the window. 'So—out there I may have a brother. Do I want a brother? I don't know.'

'It's not really a question of wanting, is it? He is a fact! It's a question of how much of a disturbance you want to make in his life—and in your own.'

Andrea's face all at once registered a kind of dismayed humour. 'He might take after Claudia!' She shook her head slowly. 'I truly don't know, Cathy.'

Two cups of tea gave them something to do while Andrea pondered. Her emotions were running in two different directions, almost simultaneously, she felt. It made confusion. It made making a decision really difficult. After a while Cathy turned to look at her. 'So it's no?'

Andrea stood up, suddenly feeling positive. 'Oh, what the hell! Let's do it!' She closed her eye briefly and bit her lip. 'You're right as usual. If I don't find out where all this is going I shall never rest.' She held her hand out and Cathy clasped it. 'Let's see if there are any more bogeymen in my family history.'

There was a hiatus, a strange gap in which nothing seemed to be happening. Andrea did aimless things: shopping for clothes she didn't need or particularly want; sitting through films she didn't enjoy because her mind was elsewhere. As she sauntered through the city shops, or sat under an umbrella outside a café for one of the endless cups of coffee, she found herself staring at men walking towards her or crossing the street, wondering, 'Is that him? My brother?'

'*I'd better stop this*,' she told herself firmly, when one of them gave her a broad wink and a grin. '*I'll be getting run in*.' She smiled swiftly at a policeman who seemed to be eyeing her thoughtfully. 'Lovely day,' she said brightly, and he nodded. (*It's true—they really do look far too young!*)

Then, just as she had decided to tell Cathy she had changed her mind, cancel everything, her phone rang. She opened it, her heart suddenly doing its double thump. If this was Cathy, and if...

Cathy was saying, 'Yes, I've found him!'

How did she feel, now that it had happened? How would one relate to someone who had once, if briefly, been so close, so intimately a part of one's life; even if that had come to an end so long ago, before either of them could have been conscious of what the future might hold?

She wondered if, when they were separated, they grieved for each other, missed the close companionship of the womb, and then perhaps the playing together, grabbing for each other's fingers or toes. For an imaginative moment she tried to search her memory for any trace of that sudden, quite brutal separation; but there was nothing there.

So this man, this mid-forties man who knew nothing of her or of Claudia, was out there, waiting, wondering perhaps, maybe resenting the detective work Cathy had put into finding him. 'What did he sound like?'

'Surprised, of course. Wondered why. Natural enough. Not *anti*, I think.'

'What now?'

'He says you can ring him.' She gave the number. 'Tomorrow.'

'It all sounds a bit alarming,' Andrea said, beginning an emotional back-down. 'Perhaps I won't bother.'

'As you like.' Cathy's serene acceptance, no pressure, no 'you ought to' do this or that, which left everything open, was at once comforting and slightly frustrating. 'Oh, his name is Gerard Scobell. A self-employed accountant.' She hesitated. 'He sounds nice.'

'That may not be enough.' Andrea sighed. 'Look at Claudia. Look what she's got me into. What if he does take after her?' She thought for a moment. 'OK, I'll ring him. That can't hurt. Thanks, Cathy—you're a pal.'

The voice that answered was pleasantly masculine, though with an understandably cautious edge to it. 'Scobell,' he said; and Andrea, heart thumping, took a deep breath.

'I'm Andrea Frazier-Coombes. Cathy at the adoption place gave me your number.'

'Yes, I was expecting your call. But I don't really understand...'

'We were both adopted as babies.'

'Yes.'

'I searched for my birth mother recently, and found her just before she died of cancer. I thought I was the only child, but she indicated that there was another one, presumably my twin...'

'You are saying that this woman was also my mother, and that you and I are—twins?' There was disbelief in his voice.

Andrea swallowed down a throb of nervousness. 'It seems so. Look—we can't talk about this on the phone. Can we meet somewhere?'

There was an uncomfortable silence. 'I'm not sure about that. I'll have to think about it.' He paused again. 'I'll let the adoption woman know. Soon. Probably tomorrow. I have to think it through.'

Tomorrow and tomorrow and tomorrow! 'Yes,' she said. 'Yes, of course.'

'You perhaps don't appreciate the upheaval this could cause, Mrs...'

'Frazier-Coombes. Andrea.'

'I mean—I know nothing about you.'

'We start level, then. I know nothing about you.'

'Yes—I suppose so. Well,' he clearly wanted the conversation to end, 'the adoption person will get back to you. Thanks for ringing.' The line went dead.

He thinks I have an ulterior motive. She wondered if he was married, if finding a twin sister might be the last straw in a rocky relationship—so many hazards in these human contacts. She felt a slightly shaky reaction to what (she now assured herself) had been quite a courageous act on her part. But at least he hadn't told her to get lost.

The call from Cathy suggested a meeting place and a time. Andrea suddenly felt a wave of excitement, an adrenalin rush like the heady sensation before a teenage 'date'. Even while telling herself that the whole thing could fall disastrously flat, she knew she wanted to meet this man, to look for signs—physical, emotional perhaps—that would seem to validate their sharing of genes. Sleep eluded her almost until dawn. She had a shower, paid attention to her make-up and hair, chose from her limited collection of clothes the ones she felt met the situation.

Then she sat down and laughed at herself. This was her brother she was meeting. Brothers and sisters, she imagined—not having had first-hand experience of the relationship—were not deeply concerned about each other's dress sense. 'All the same,' she said into the mirror, checking her lipstick, 'I need to make a good impression.' With a sudden giggle, she wondered if this Gerard Scobell was taking particular care not to cut himself shaving.

The rendezvous was a café with a wide forecourt where tables were well spaced. 'Thus making it possible,' Andrea murmured as she stood at the entrance and searched with her eyes, 'to talk without being overheard. Good thinking.' Only three men were sitting by themselves. Which one was Gerard Scobell? Which one would she *like* to be Gerard Scobell? She felt light-headed, as if she might find herself tongue-tied, or worse, caught with another fit of giggles or (horror!) hiccups.

One man was obviously too old. One was the right age, casually dressed, reading a newspaper. The third was looking around him, seemingly waiting for someone. He was a smart dresser, with a small moustache that immediately put Andrea off and paradoxically made her at once decide that he was the one. She moved forward hesitantly towards him, and he stood suddenly, pushing back his chair impatiently, and raised a hand. She was just saved from making a fool of herself when a woman came swiftly from behind her and made a beeline for the moustache, which she kissed with every evidence of pleasure. Not him then! So perhaps he hadn't yet arrived.

Then the man with the newspaper laid it down and looked across at her. He stood slowly, and Andrea, after a moment, went towards him. With the table between them he said, 'Mrs Frazier-Coombes? Have I got that right?'

Andrea let out a long breath. 'Yes. You are Mr Scobell.'

'That's right. Will you sit down?' He came round and pulled a chair out. Andrea, feeling unnecessarily relieved (for what had she expected?) sat. 'Coffee?'

'Thank you. Cappuccino.'

He walked over to the counter and she watched him as he ordered. Tall, but with a very slight stoop (too long spent over the computer?) thick hair with a tinge of auburn, a relaxed air which meant that either he had no problems in regard to this strange meeting, or was very well controlled. She wondered which.

He put the coffee cup down in front of her. 'Did you want something to eat?'

'Oh no, thanks.'

He sat, and now he looked across the table and regarded her thoughtfully. 'We're not much alike.'

The comment broke the ice. Andrea relaxed, stirring sugar into the froth. 'We wouldn't have been identical. Not a boy and a girl.' Then she nodded. 'But you're right. We're not.'

Scobell leaned back a little, long legs stretched under the table. 'So what's all this about?'

'What has Cathy told you? At the adoption place,' she added when he seemed not to recognise the name.

'That you have been searching for your birth mother. That when you found her you discovered that you probably had a twin brother. And that *that* was probably me.' He ran his hand over his hair. 'I must say it all seems fairly bizarre.'

'It is.' Andrea marshalled her thoughts. She wanted to get as much information as she could into the briefest possible explanation. 'I found Claudia, my mother. She was dying of cancer, and just before I left her for what proved to be the last time she suddenly said, "What happened to the other one?" It was a shock.'

'It must have been.' There was sympathy, but he was keeping a space between them, a kind of detachment. 'Didn't she give you a clue?'

'Yes. She left a note. "*Look at the papers*". I decided that meant the newspapers, so I went to the library and searched back to the year I was born—*we* were born!' she said, smiling a little.

'And...?'

Andrea paused. The reality of what she was about to disclose was suddenly a burden to her, and she wondered if she had the right to make it a burden for the stranger sitting opposite to her. 'It's not a very nice story. We were taken in by the welfare and later adopted out because—because our mother, Claudia, went to prison.' She stopped and glanced at him. His face revealed nothing, not even really interest. 'It was a bad situation.'

'So Mummy was a gaol-bird!' Sarcasm! 'I think I could have lived out my life without knowing that, Mrs Frazier-Coombes.' He finished his coffee. 'I'm not sure what you want of me.'

He was getting ready to leave. It was important that she should know the truth, she was telling herself. In her bag she had copies of the newspaper accounts and her own copied notes on the whole drama as it had unfolded. She bent down and took the envelope out and put it on the table. Scobell stared at it with, she thought, some trepidation.

'This will tell you all about it. You can keep those—they're copies. After you've looked at them, if you want to, you can ring me. If I don't hear from you,' and she found herself hoping that she would, 'I'll leave it alone. It's your choice.' She pushed the envelope towards him and he took it, warily, as if he feared it might attack him.

'Right. Thank you. I'm sorry,' he said impulsively, 'that I can't show more enthusiasm for this. It's rather taken me...' He stopped.

'I know. That's how I felt.'

'But you went looking. I...' He looked at her more closely. 'You've been through it already, haven't you?'

'And come out the other side. The truth may hurt, but perhaps one can't ignore the truth, even if it is painful.'

'No. You're probably right. Well...' He stood up. 'Thanks. It's been interesting meeting you.' He held out his hand and Andrea took it briefly. 'If...'

'Your choice. I'll wait to hear from you.'

She watched him go. He was a slow mover; she was quite drawn to his leisurely air. And it *had* been interesting. It had also been fruitless. She wouldn't hold her breath.

As he went out of sight she found herself hoping that she would see him again. It would be a pity to lose a perfectly good brother.

'Yes, I've met him.'

'Oh good! What's he like?'

'A bit taken aback, as you can imagine.'

'It would be a bit of a shock.'

'He seems quite nice, Mum. But definitely holding back. He wasn't exactly enthralled to find out he's the son of a gaol-bird—his words, not mine.'

'No. It's not what one would hope for, is it? Does he—is there any resemblance? Between you and him? Or Claudia?'

'Not the slightest. He's tallish, brown hair, not exactly good-looking, but—oh, just an average sort of guy.'

'So what happens now?'

'I'm waiting to hear from him. It's up to him. If he doesn't want to know, that's OK. I can't put pressure on him.'

'It might be difficult for him now, Andrea, to turn away. Natural curiosity. Who can resist it?'

'Yes—oh well! I've done all I can. How's Dad?'

'Pretty good, dear.'

'How's Bethany's cold?'

'Just a sniffle now.'

'Good. Talk to you later, Mum. I'm going out for some lunch. All this emotional stuff makes me hungry. Take care!'

'And you, dear.'

Andrea sat back and regarded the phone absently. Perhaps she should pack it in, all of it. Let Cathy know. Ring Gerard Scobell and say she had decided it wasn't worth the effort. Go home!

The phone bell rang. 'Mrs Frazier-Coombes? Gerard Scobell here. I've been thinking—can we meet somewhere? There are one or two things I'd like to ask you.'

11

'I t's a mess, isn't it?' They were sitting in Cathy's office—Cathy was out. Gerard Scobell was on a chair, Andrea on the settee. He was leaning back, hands in pockets, body language saying that he was still not sure he wanted to be a part of this strange situation.

'Yes.' Andrea was feeling much more relaxed than at their first meeting. His suggestion that they should meet again took the load of responsibility from her. It made them, in some way, partners. 'Yes, it isn't a pretty story, I'm afraid. But it happened, so we can't ignore it.'

'I've had a good try,' he said, wryly. 'But in the end one has to know, I suppose.' He touched the envelope she had given him as it lay on the table before him. 'It's a *weird* story. Difficult to believe. Why did she do it, do you suppose?'

'She said it was self-defence. She would, naturally. If it had been premeditated she'd have got a longer sentence, presumably. I imagine the marriage was not a happy one.'

'She sounds a bit of a tartar.'

'She was all of that.' Andrea smiled slightly. 'Ours wasn't the joyful reunion one might have hoped for. She seemed to be consumed with malice.'

'So who were these other people the paper mentioned? Sir Kenneth something and a woman—Carding, I think.'

'Well, Sir Kenneth Frazier-Greenwood is a well-known orchestral conductor. I've actually played for him.'

'Played?'

'I play the violin. He conducted us in Sydney some time ago. He's a very eminent man.'

'And she worked for him as secretary.'

'Yes.'

'So he was only there as a character reference, I suppose?'

'I think so.'

'And thingy—Bella Carding?'

'She's barely mentioned. Just as a friend of the—the—of Claudia.'

'Claudia,' he said, as if he was trying out the name. 'Do I feel as if I ever had a mother called Claudia?' He thought for a moment, then shook his head. 'No, it doesn't feel right. I suppose your adoption friend...'

'Cathy.'

'All right then—Cathy! I suppose she's got the right person?'

'Meaning you?'

'Meaning me!'

'She seems sure enough. It all fits—dates, adoptive families, everything.'

Scobell was silent for a moment. Then he sighed. 'OK. What's the next move?'

'Well...if we accept that we are twins...'

'One thing! You said this musician chap was Sir Kenneth *Frazier*-Greenwood. And you are Andrea *Frazier*-Coombes. How come?'

She hesitated. 'I don't know. I don't understand. It seems odd to me...' she almost stopped, wary of revealing innermost thoughts, 'really odd that I should have his name *and* be a musician. It's been worrying me.'

Scobell was regarding her with some intensity. 'You think...? You think—what?'

'I wondered if they—he and Claudia—had been more than employer and employee. It's probably stupid. But I can't see why I should have his name.'

'Your adoptive parents didn't change it?'

'No. I was Andrea Frazier-Shepherd when they took me, then Frazier-Martin, and I kept it when I married.'

'Hmm. Odd! Is he still around—this music man?'

'Yes, he's here in Perth. He lives here, but of course he travels around a good deal.'

'He must be some age. We're not exactly spring chickens.'

Andrea laughed for the first time. 'Speak for yourself! But you're right. If he was thirtyish then, he's well into his seventies by now.'

Scobell was regarding her very thoughtfully. 'Do you seriously think...? I mean, if he was your—your father...'

Andrea shook her head rapidly. 'I don't really. At least, I don't think I do. It's just—well, *odd*. Isn't it?'

'Yes. But if he *is*, then he's mine, too.'

They sat in silence for a full minute. Then Andrea sighed deeply and stood up. 'I rather hope he isn't. It could be very—embarrassing.'

'For him as well.' All at once a new expression crossed his face, changing him from the somewhat dour person she had thought him to be. It was a flicker of amusement, even of devilry; and she could imagine him as he might once have been, a boy with a sense of humour that had perhaps not been nurtured by his adoptive parents. 'It could be very *interesting*—and worth watching!'

Andrea felt for the first time that she could ask him about his early days.

'Was it a good childhood?' she said.

He glanced up, surprised. 'Well...' He weighed his answer, and she kept her eyes on his face. At last he said, 'It certainly wasn't bad. I wanted for nothing important. Though they weren't all that well off, my—parents.' Now that this particular wasps' nest had been stirred up he found the parenting concept a hard one to evaluate calmly. He remembered the man and woman he had always called 'Dad' and 'Mother', and they seemed in some way distant, unreal, as if he had imagined them or seen them on film.

'Did you love them?' She asked it gently, knowing she had no right to pry.

He stared past her. 'Love? I respected them. I was grateful to them. And I think, in a way, I was sorry for them.'

'Why?'

'I think their childlessness was always a pain to them.'

'In spite of you?'

'Yes. I was a substitute. Sometimes—sometimes it made me feel I didn't actually exist as a person.' He shot a glance at her. 'What about you?'

'Not that. It was almost as if not having children of their own made it possible for them to have me. A blessing, really.' They sat quietly, sipping coffee, isolated in their thoughts, but with the sensation that a step forward had been taken.

'I never *looked* as if I belonged,' Gerard said suddenly, and again there was a glimmer of amusement in his eyes. 'Dad was about five foot eight and Mother was nearer to five foot two. So when we went out together either they or I looked like freaks. Dad would introduce me—"this is my son, Gerard"—and people would stare from him to me, and you could see them thinking *"adopted"*! As clear as if they had been white and I black.' He grinned quickly. 'It was OK until I got to thirteen, then I shot up. Up and out of range! I think I was a puzzle to them from then on. The cuckoo in the nest.'

'It's strange, isn't it?' she said thoughtfully. 'Genetics. The whole thing. I think that's one of the things that really started to bug me once I'd begun to wonder. I looked at my children, and they had a look of me and Joseph—very subtle, but it was there. But when I looked at my mother, at Lucy, there was no resemblance. Except, perhaps, mannerisms I had picked up from her. That was when I began to see it as a brick wall, something hiding the past from me. And it was why I quite suddenly needed to find someone who was—well, someone of my own. Do you know what I mean?'

He nodded. 'I think so. You've thought about it a lot more than I have, obviously. But yes, there's a wall there.'

'And so I needed to get over it, or round it, or through it. Somehow.'

'And are you glad you did—even though you ended up with Claudia?'

Andrea gazed past him, evaluating the journey she had made. It had certainly not been an altogether happy experience, but generally speaking... 'Yes, I'm glad. It's an amazing gift, to find a mother—even if it is Claudia...' She gave a dry laugh. 'And, of course, a brother! So very unexpected!'

'What next?' It seemed as if she never stopped asking Cathy this question. But she was finding it impossible to decide what her next move should be. Gerard Scobell had been acquiescent—by no means enthusiastic, but willing to see what else she could uncover. And Cathy was the source of comfort, of information—of warm friendship; and how she needed that at the moment!

'Will you be seeing him again?'

'Oh, I think so. I imagine he's now in the same position I was when you first found Claudia. Wanting to hold back, but needing to know. The trouble is, I don't really know what the next step should be.'

'Well, let's see what we've got. You know who your mother was, you've found the man who seems to be your brother, you have two possible contacts from that time...'

'But how can I go barging in and ask questions about something that happened over four decades ago?'

'Exactly! I suppose it depends on how much you want to know *all* the details of your birth.' She frowned at her desk, thinking. 'Because of what we've already discovered, you could really go on from here—if he's willing to—and leave everything else obscure. After all, Claudia was married to Ben Shepherd, so presumably there's a very good chance that he was your father. If he wasn't, then we're looking at a very different Claudia.' She gave Andrea a very straight look. 'What's bugging you?'

Andrea took a moment to reply. 'Only my name,' she said at last. 'I just find it so odd that my name should include *Frazier*. Why? What was he to her? Come to that, what was she to him? Why on earth did she give me that name, if there was no—well, you know what I mean. If they weren't *an item*, as we say now. There seems to be no point in it. Does there?' She looked up at Cathy. 'And I suppose that's why I feel that this thing isn't finished. As if there's perhaps one more corner to peep round.' She hesitated. 'I was saying to him—to Gerard—that for me the lack of knowledge of where I came from was like a brick wall behind me, blocking out my past. Most of that wall has come down now. But there's still a bit, and I feel that until it too collapses I shall be left with a—an impediment.' She smiled faintly. 'I'm greedy, Cathy. I want everything.'

'In that case,' said sensible Cathy, 'go for it! Go and see this Sir Kenneth. Try to find the woman who had looked after you—what was her name?'

'Bella Carding.'

'And then, if you get what you're looking for, go home to your parents and your children, and send me a card at Christmas! Or...' she said, drawing the word out mischievously, 'get to know your brother better. And if you don't get satisfaction, well, then, you'll have to put up with it. As we all have to. But one thing's sure—if you don't take it a step further you'll never know.'

'You're telling me to go ahead and mess up some more people's lives.' Andrea grinned. 'And as usual you're right.' She stood up quickly, as if she had suddenly had an injection of energy. 'I wonder how difficult it is to see Sir Kenneth. He has rather an austere look. And I know from playing under him that he can be quite authoritarian.' She stopped, a swift expression crossing her face. 'Actually, I think it would be quite awful to discover that he is indeed my father. He's not the kind of man one would want to call *Daddy!*'

Cathy laughed. 'Poor man! Let me know how you go.'

Andrea all at once felt very daunted. What she was about to do seemed foolhardy, and worse than that—extremely invasive. How could she go and virtually accuse the man of having had an affair with a woman who had eventually spent years in gaol for the worst of crimes?

So—she would have to meet Sir Kenneth Frazier-Greenwood, meet him face-to-face. Not as she had, well, not exactly *met* him—except for passing him in one of the back-stage corridors at the Opera House and receiving a gracious, impersonal nod from the elegant grey head. You could hardly call being conducted by him *meeting* him...*I'm babbling!* Andrea remarked silently. *If I talk to him like this he'll turn me out pronto.*

A letter? Brief note? Phone call? How would one contact him to the best advantage? How many minions stood between him and the general public? Should she ask Gerard what he thought? And should she introduce herself as a fellow musician, or as Claudia's daughter?

Too many questions. Anyhow, luck was on her side: he was resident in Perth for the rest of the year, with just a few brief visits to Asian cities to conduct their orchestras. She had checked his itineraries, and he should be here for at least the next month. So...! How to do it?

The orchestra's administrative office, repressively, would not give her his phone number, but would pass on a message to Sir Kenneth, and if he wished to speak to her... Oh, well, it would have to do. She gave Cathy's number and rang off.

It was two long days before he left a message on Cathy's phone, sounding slightly puzzled in a cool sort of way. He gave a number she could call, specifying a time in the manner of one who knows that his time is quite certainly more important than hers.

'Not "if that will be convenient",' she said to Cathy, pulling a face. 'Well, he's a great conductor, but I'm not sure if I like him.'

'One probably doesn't always get to be a great conductor by being liked,' Cathy remarked shrewdly. And with a sly glance at Andrea, 'Nor a father! What will you say to him?'

'Are you my daddy?' Andrea said with a laugh. 'Heaven knows, Cathy. It'll probably be a spur-of-the-moment thing.' She frowned. 'I saw him, you know, the other day at a concert. Before all this really got going. If I'd known...' Cathy grinned. 'There has to be a reason why Claudia called me Frazier, surely? Why else if he's not my—my father? And there's the music.' She flopped inelegantly on to a chair. 'I'm exhausted with all this mystery. Funny, I thought it'd be quite different. Much simpler. Either I wouldn't find my parents, in which case I'd go home and put it all behind me, or I'd find them and we'd click and become friends—or not. Either way, the end product would have been fairly straightforward. But this!' She waved a hand. 'All this confusion, malice, brothers turning up, Claudia dying when I'd hardly met her...' She fell silent. 'It doesn't feel like the sort of thing that happens to me.'

'Yes—Mrs Coombes?' The austere voice was reserved when she finally reached him.

Andrea fought to keep her voice steady and unemotional. 'I wonder if I might come and see you.'

'For what reason, Mrs Coombes?'

She paused for a moment. Then: 'I have recently discovered that I am the daughter of Claudia Shepherd, who died a short while ago. I know she was once employed by you. I would be pleased if you could fill in some gaps for me.'

There was a startled silence at the other end of the line. 'I should hardly think...' he began. 'How did you find out...?'

'Newspaper reports. You are mentioned as her employer. You gave a character reference.'

'But not at that time,' he said firmly. 'She was no longer in my employ when the—the scandal...'

'But you knew her,' Andrea pressed. 'And I met her so briefly. She died before we could get to know each other.' *I won't tell him that I doubt we would ever have got to know each other, even if she had lived.*

'Well...' Sir Kenneth seemed to be searching for a way out. 'Of course, I could possibly tell you about... But, good heavens, Mrs Coombes, it was over forty years ago! How can it matter what I know?'

Put the knife in, Andrea told herself. 'There's a bit of a puzzle about all this,' she said, trying not to sound too pushy. 'If I tell you that my name is Andrea *Frazier*-Coombes...' She left it hanging.

After what seemed minutes but could only have been seconds, he cleared his throat. 'That is strange. *Very* strange! I didn't know that.'

'She never told you?'

'I never saw her after she stopped working for me. We completely lost touch.'

Andrea asked, 'May I come to see you?'

'Oh, I don't think so.'

'It means a great deal to me.'

She heard him sigh. 'Well...I suppose if... You'd better—let's see...' She heard diary pages being turned 'I'm free tomorrow morning at nine forty-five. For about fifteen minutes. At the orchestra's rehearsal room. You know where it is?'

'Yes.'

'Please be prompt. I have a rehearsal at ten. Very well. I'll see you then.' The phone went dead.

'Well—that's given him something to think about.' Andrea found her hand was shaking as she replaced the receiver. 'Fifteen minutes. Cheeky devil!' Now she must plan properly what to say, what she needed to know. Surely the name they shared couldn't be a coincidence? Why, for goodness' sake, had Claudia called her *Frazier*? Why, if Sir Kenneth had had nothing to do with—with...? 'Ridiculous!' she said aloud 'Of *course* he can't be my father.' But— oh, there were far too many *buts* in this mess. Perhaps tomorrow would solve some of the mystery.

'Thank you for seeing me.'

Sir Kenneth regarded Andrea for a moment without speaking. Andrea, determined not to be over-awed, smiled quickly and settled into the chair he had indicated. Upright, she noted. Very formal. Not a chair to offer comfort.

'Please be quick, Mrs—er...As I mentioned...'

'Yes, I can be quick, Sir Kenneth.' She drew her thoughts together. 'I said on the phone that my name is *Frazier*-Coombes. I have discovered that I am the daughter of Claudia Shepherd, and that she was your secretary for a while before I was born.' She hesitated. 'You can understand that I am puzzled by the fact that she gave me your name.' She let the unspoken thought hang in the air.

'Could it not have been a family name of hers?' He was staring at her. 'I've seen you before, haven't I? I don't know where.'

'I'm in the Sydney orchestra, and you conducted us last year. But you'd hardly remember...'

'I remember faces. Not names. But faces.' He nodded. 'First violin. Behind the concertmaster.' The expression became

72

suddenly austere. 'What exactly are you hinting at, Mrs Frazier-Coombes?'

'What can you tell me about Claudia—about my mother? How well did you know her?' She leaned forward impulsively. 'I need to know about her.'

'It was a very long time...' He stood and moved to the window. 'I didn't know her well. She was an employee. I knew she was married. That was about all. She wasn't a chatty woman.'

'Did you like her?' Andrea hesitated. 'I ask, because the woman I found was not very likeable. I wonder if she had changed a lot because of her—her prison sentence.'

Sir Kenneth was silent for a long moment. 'No,' he said finally, turning and frowning at her. 'No, she wasn't particularly likeable. Not a sympathetic personality. Efficient and ambitious, I should think describes her. But she *was* efficient, and I wasn't looking for sympathy.' He glanced at his watch. 'I don't see how I can help you.'

'It was a long shot. The name puzzles me. Why did she...?'

'Who knows?' he said abruptly. 'At this distance, who can say? And does it matter? It's a good name.'

'It struck me when you came to conduct us,' Andrea said, determined to wring something out of this impasse. 'Then, when I saw in those old newspapers that you had been called as a witness—that you had known Claudia before I was born...' At the look on his face she came to a stop.

'You would be very unwise to go down that road,' he said. 'I hope you are not going to suggest...'

'I don't think I'm trying to do anything but find out about my mother. About where I fit in. Knowing about one forebears is important. And—there was the music!' She regarded him steadfastly, her heart doing a sudden double-thump in her chest. 'I just wondered.'

Sir Kenneth straightened a pen on his desk. The atmosphere had subtly changed; Andrea was conscious of it. He was having to take it seriously. She took a deep breath.

'Can you remember when you last saw Claudia?'

'She left my employment,' he said slowly, 'just before I went to London. That was the first of my overseas contracts.'

'I know. Eight months before I was born.'

The silence was oppressive.

'What you are suggesting,' Sir Kenneth said grimly, 'is impossible. Quite impossible. Why should you not be the child of Claudia's husband?'

'Perhaps I am. But I keep falling over the name. Why? If she had ceased employment with you at that time and you never saw her again, why call me Frazier?'

'I can understand your confusion.' He picked up his baton, a signal that the interview was over. 'But you must understand that making any connection between Claudia and myself in the matter would be most unwise. As you are well aware, someone who is in the public eye...'

'I am not here to blackmail you, Sir Kenneth!' She spoke sharply. 'Even if there was any connection beyond employing her... Damn!' A man's head had appeared round the door.

'Orchestra's ready, sir.'

'Ask Max if he will kindly start them for me, Stan. Five minutes. The Mendelssohn, I think.'

As the door closed he turned to Andrea. 'Your visit has been a waste of time, I'm afraid.'

'Not altogether. You have told me there was no connection. I must accept that.' She stood, picking up her bag, preparing to leave.

'I don't know you, you see.' He sounded almost fretful. 'If I knew anything about you...'

'Would that change anything? I'm Claudia's daughter.'

'If I may say so, that is little commendation. Claudia had a spiteful streak.'

'I know. It's bothered me too. But I'm not like Claudia. My parents are lovely people. It neutralises the other.' She watched him cautiously. There seemed to be a change in the wind.

'Perhaps.' He consulted the tip of baton again, pressing it into his finger as if he meant to hurt himself. 'I am an honest man, Mrs Frazier-Coombes.' The words appeared to burst out of him. 'And vulnerable. Especially today, when the media is merciless.' He glanced at her and she remained silent. 'But I will be honest with you. There was one occasion—just one...'

Andrea sat down again. Sir Kenneth turned away from her and she watched his back as he moved around the desk and sat in the chair. It seemed he was finding it difficult to face her, and she sat very still, her heart beating a little faster.

'Just before I left for London. Late one night after a concert. It meant little then, and nothing afterwards. I think today it would be vulgarly summed up as a "one-night stand".' He lifted his eyes briefly, warningly. 'Little could be gained by your making this public. Above all, I would not want to have my wife upset. And you can be sure of one thing—Claudia was far too sophisticated to allow anything to come of it. I don't understand why she gave you my name. But I am quite sure that you are not my child. If this helps you to understand your mother better, then...' He shrugged, and went to open the door for Andrea. 'I would not hesitate, of course, to call my solicitor if...'

'You have no need to worry,' Andrea said firmly, more firmly than she felt. 'It's not my intention to cause trouble.' At the door she turned. She wanted to say *'your secret is safe with me!'* but that would sound impertinent. 'I thank you for being frank with me. It was kind of you.'

As she walked slowly along the street towards a coffee shop she weighed what she had heard, pros and cons, the possibility of Sir Kenneth having put too much trust in Claudia's 'sophistication', the greater possibility that she was indeed not his, but Ben Shepherd's child. Without the musical gene—which she felt must have come from somewhere—and the extraordinary fact that she bore the great man's name, there would be no quandary. Why, oh why, she asked again, had Claudia burdened her with that name? Was it another of the woman's malicious moments, preparing the ground to stir up trouble later? It wasn't impossible. She would probably have enjoyed doing it.

And why, she wondered, had Sir Kenneth suddenly confessed to his moment of 'hanky-panky'? As she drank coffee and ate an excellent pastry she pondered on this. He said he was an honest man—was honesty his best policy? Perhaps he was afraid she would probe more deeply and discover he had lied. Yet he could have kept his mouth shut and she would never have known.

Anyway, where had it got her? If that regrettable moment had resulted in her birth, what did it matter? Except that now she had her teeth into the thing she didn't want to let it go. If Sir Kenneth were proved to be her father, it gave her a lineage reaching back into the mists of time. A background she could explore and legitimately (illegitimately, she corrected herself) claim as her own.

Of course, she conceded, the same could be said of the background provided by Ben and Claudia, but she feared those waters might be murkier and less promising than Sir Kenneth's.

'I'm a snob,' she murmured to herself.

12

'He's a proud man,' she said to Cathy. 'Of course he is. And while I was talking to him I suddenly saw what a huge upheaval it would be in his life if we are indeed related. I feel quite sorry for him, actually.' She smiled. 'I wonder if he got through his rehearsal OK.'

'So you don't think you'll get anywhere with him?'

'I don't know. I really wish I could talk to him again—just to find out more about Claudia, about what her life was like then. About Ben, only I don't suppose he knew him. Oh, just about anything to do with that time. But I can't see how...'

'Did you tell him about Gerard?'

Andrea laughed shortly. 'No, I was merciful. He was obviously struggling with what I'd already asked. I'll save Gerard in case I do manage to see him again.'

Cathy was silent for a moment. 'He rang me.'

'Who? Sir Kenneth?' Andrea regarded her in astonishment. Cathy nodded.

'He wanted to know about you. What sort of person you are, that sort of thing.'

'Good heavens!' Andrea sat back in her chair. 'And what sort of person am I?'

Cathy laughed. 'Honest! Not a stirrer. The sort of things he wanted to know.'

'Well, well! He's surprised me.' Neither spoke for several seconds. But Andrea felt that, in some strange way, this news made it more possible to make contact again. 'I wonder if I should write to him. Not make it quite so "in your face".' She thought for a moment. 'Yes—I think I will. What do you think, Cathy?'

'You could simply thank him for seeing you—that would show you are not only honest, but courteous.' She grinned. 'It's worth trying. Do it!'

Andrea spent the evening creating a letter which, she hoped, would both calm his fears and keep the door between them open for a little more time. By the time she went to bed she had, she felt, done the best she was capable of. She re-read it. It sounded genuine, it didn't threaten, it kept his pride and hers intact—she was determined not to sound peevish or demanding. It was, she decided, a friendly letter that demanded nothing in return.

In the morning she took it to the nearest post box and dropped it in, standing for a moment as she wondered what his reaction would be when he opened it. Oh, to be the fly on the wall!

'DNA,' she said to Gerard. They were walking by the river, close to the university campus. Families were picnicking; young men and maidens in the briefest of swim-wear were in the water, or wind-surfing with that sort of physical skill that seems to come easily to the young. They watched a couple come to grief, the sails collapsing into the water, laughter and shrieks of frustration floating to them on a gentle breeze.

'Oh, to be young again!' Gerard said.

'Did you ever do that?'

'Wind-surfing? No. It wasn't all the rage when I was a kid. I surfed. Swam. Climbed...'

'Climbed what?'

'Rocks.' He turned his head and looked at her. 'I was quite a good rock-climber.'

'I bet you were! I don't have a head for heights, so I wouldn't have been any good at that. I can't even watch it on TV. Those people who go up vertical cliffs like a fly on a wall.' She thought suddenly of Sir Kenneth. He should have the letter by now.

'So...' he said, 'you bearded the lion in his den. What happened?'

She brought him up to date. 'I'm hoping that my letter will make it possible to see him again, but I'm not holding my breath.' She hesitated. 'I didn't tell him about you.'

'Why not?'

'I thought he'd taken all he could.' She smiled at him. 'I'm saving you, just in case.'

They strolled companionably, not talking for a while.

'You said DNA,' he said suddenly.

'Yes.'

'Can it be done?'

'Yes. It might cost a bit. But there's a place...'

'And you think he'll do it?'

'I have no idea. But at least it would show, once and for all, whether he is or he isn't. Related to us, I mean.' She frowned. 'He may find it as important to know as we do.'

Gerard didn't immediately comment. 'I'm not altogether sure,' he said at last, 'that I want to do it, either.'

She regarded him with surprise. 'Don't you want to know?'

'In a way. But I can appreciate his feelings—not wanting to turn his life upside down.'

In a small voice, she said, 'Is that how it feels to you?'

He nodded. 'It's not like it is for you. You're really determined to get to the bottom of it. It was your choice. It wasn't mine. In my own probably stupid way I was reasonably content with how things were. My life wasn't perfect, but whose is? I was comfortable with my work, I didn't mind being on my own, I wasn't grieving for my parents, either the adoptive ones or the others. It hasn't been unalloyed joy to find out that Claudia was probably my mother. And I really don't care if I'm the illegitimate offspring of a famous musician. That matters to you because music is your thing. Not mine.' He glanced at her. 'I've probably made you cross. Sorry. But that's how I feel about it.'

'Not cross,' she said, feeling an acute sense of disappointment. She had hoped that he shared her enthusiasm for this quest. 'I'm sorry. I've assumed too much.' There was a bench nearby and she went to it and sat down. He followed her. They sat in silence, staring out over the panorama of river and trees and the white sails of yachts in the distance. 'I am sorry, Gerard.'

'Don't be. You've done what you had to do. And I think we probably can't avoid going on until we get all the answers. It makes a difference that I don't have children. I can see that you would want to know for their sakes as much as your own.'

She knew that he had been married, but he had been very reticent and she hadn't asked for details. Now, she did. 'Why no children?'

He didn't immediately answer. Then he said, 'There wasn't time. We were both twenty-five, thought everything was fine, looked forward to having a child one day, but not at once because we both had jobs and nothing else behind us financially. So we said we would wait a couple of years.' He fell silent. 'And then she caught one of these flu bugs and it hit her badly. It developed into pneumonia, and that revealed a heart condition nobody knew about. And she died. We'd been married just under three years, and the next thing on the agenda was a family. My parents died younger than they should have done—and I was on my own. No other rellies to take up the slack!'

'I had no idea,' she said.

'Why would you? I don't talk about it. It's over. I think we would probably have been happy together—we were until she was taken ill. It was quite a placid relationship—but it was good. We did things together, but we had our own space too. She wasn't interested in accountancy except as a means of making money to live on. And I wasn't really all that interested in her arts and crafts, though I knew she was good, and I hope I was encouraging.' He fell silent, and Andrea watched him as he gazed into the water flowing past them. 'I hope I was,' he said at last. 'And sometimes I wish I had shown more interest. But we did go rock climbing together occasionally, and we had some really good holidays. I think, on balance...' He glanced at her and grinned briefly, slightly shame-faced, 'On balance, I think it was a good marriage. I was devastated when she died.'

'I am so sorry.' Andrea put her hand out and touched his arm. 'We've both had to come to terms with loss. It's never easy.'

They sat in silence for several minutes. Suddenly Gerard shifted and stood up, impatient. He began to walk along the river bank, and Andrea stood quickly and followed him.

'If I do see him again,' Andrea said hesitantly, 'I ought to mention you. Even if he says he won't have the DNA done.' She glanced at Gerard. 'That would be all right?'

'Yes, I suppose so. You don't want me to meet him, do you? Because I'm certainly not keen on that.'

It was feeling more difficult by the minute. Andrea stifled a sigh. 'Of course not. You don't have to do anything that doesn't feel right.' She fell back a pace or two. 'But I have to—I have to go on, now that I've got this far.'

He nodded. 'Do what you need to do.' He stopped, looking out over the vista of water and sun and a clear sky without a cloud. 'Just look at it! What a place to live. I've never wanted to live anywhere else—is that very odd?'

'No. This is a country full of people on the move, but it needs some to stay where they are.' She laughed. 'I'm a bit torn now, since I came west. Over east, not many seem to know how lovely it is here. Some of them think it's all sandstorms, sharks and snakes.'

'Plenty of those,' he said, smiling at her. 'But worth it for days like this.'

They strolled on slowly, and when they came to a café they stopped and ordered coffee and cakes. 'At the very least,' Andrea said after they had sat companionably silent, enjoying the scene, 'it's been a very interesting holiday.'

The letter brought forth a brusque response. Sir Kenneth wrote in a strong hand, and it conveyed such confidence, such an appearance of authority, that Andrea was momentarily daunted.

But the message was less daunting. Yes, he would see her. At his home overlooking the river. On the following afternoon. Short, sharp sentences that gave nothing away.

The approach to the house was neatly kept. The front garden was immaculate, a tribute, probably, to the steady efforts of a full-time gardener. The house itself had a vaguely Georgian look about it, a well-proportioned façade with sash windows and a covered porch that might have been in one of the better areas of London, if it were not for the brilliant sunlight.

A housekeeper opened the door to Andrea, and showed her into a drawing room (it would have been quite wrong to describe it simply as a lounge room), tastefully furnished with the kind of chairs, couches and small tables that simply shouted 'antiques'! Music had done well by the knight.

To one side a door opened, and Sir Kenneth appeared, austere and unwelcoming despite excellent good manners. 'Do come through, Mrs Coombes.' He let her pass him and waved vaguely at a chair.

This was clearly his study. A wide mahogany desk was clear of papers; this was not the messy working place of the traditional artistic type. Books lined the walls. A broad music stand matched the desk and carried what she recognised as an orchestral score. A grand piano, its gleaming surface free of photos, its golden sheen reflecting the light from long windows, projected its rounded end into the room. Andrea was duly and sincerely impressed. The room—the house—bore all the marks of money and style, and it would not be difficult to imagine that it was a fertile ground for his musical activities. How could one not be inspired, she was thinking, with so much evidence of the goodies that success had already brought? But she cancelled the thought immediately as being tinged with malice. And malice was one thing they could all do without at this moment.

Sir Kenneth Frazier-Greenwood! She bore his name, but why? Unless he was indeed... But that was for science to decide. Her task today was to persuade him, almost certainly against his better judgement, to submit to a test that, whether it turned out to be in her interests or not, could only be a humiliation for him.

She regarded him from across the room before she moved forward to take the chair he had indicated. He was still handsome, even at this late stage of his life. He was just short of eighty (she had looked him up); in his successful thirties when she was born. He had always been successful, from the moment he had his first chance to wield a baton.

And that was another reason why he would want to refuse the test she would ask him to undergo; successful people don't look for failure. So she must handle him as carefully as she had ever handled anyone. But he must never see the kid gloves! She sat down and leaned back a little, taking a deep breath.

'What a beautiful room.'

He inclined his head. 'Thank you.'

Slowly he sat down behind the polished desk. He picked up a pen, twiddled it idly, then obviously decided that he was demonstrating nerves and set it down again, carefully, in the middle of a leather-bound blotter. 'Now—ah—Mrs Coombes...'

'Mrs *Frazier*-Coombes,' she said quietly.

He stared at her for a moment, frowning a little. 'Mrs Frazier-Coombes,' he agreed. 'What can I do for you?'

She reminded herself of their previous meeting, how at last she had departed feeling certain that she would never get any closer to the truth if it were to be left to him.

But today was different. There was a simple way of determining what the story had been all those years ago; simple and private and final.

'When we spoke a little while ago,' (she avoided any shakiness in her voice) 'you assured me that there was no way that we could be—related. Since then I have gone through the evidence of my mother's life once more, newspaper stories and so on, and it seems to me that there is a reasonable chance that the brief—relationship you had with Claudia may well have produced a child. The dates are right. If I am correct, I am that child. The fact that you knew nothing about it proves nothing. Claudia was a tough character. It would be in keeping with her personality that she would not have told you.'

She paused. He was staring at her broodingly, eyebrows low over dynamic eyes, and there was almost tangible antagonism in the air between them. 'Go on,' he said in a voice as grim as his features.

'What I have also discovered is that my friend Gerard Scobell may also be involved in this. It seems likely that he is my twin brother.' She watched as the eyebrows shot up in surprise, then dropped again in a mixture of puzzlement and distaste.

'Go on.' His voice was like ice.

'It would be very simple today,' she said, trying to infuse a little warmth into her voice, 'to prove this one way or the other. DNA testing will tell us if we are related. And I have been finding out about it. It takes so little time, it's so easy to do, and then we would know. I realise,' she said quickly, seeing him open his mouth to speak, 'that this would be unpleasant for you. I really do. But for me—well, I have to know. I can't explain that except to say that there is a part of me that is rootless, that doesn't know where it came from or, in a sense, where it's going to.' (*Oh Lord, don't let me cry! Don't let my voice wobble!*) 'If you can imagine it, when I look back into the past I see a brick wall with no way round it. And for some reason this matters to me. Very much.' She leaned forward slightly, eagerly. 'I will guarantee that the information, whatever it may prove to be, will never be released. I'll sign anything you want to prevent that.'

'If...' said Sir Kenneth, taking a deep breath, '*if* I did as you want me to, there *is* no guarantee, is there?'

'What do you mean?'

'I believe you have children. You will of course want them to know what their heritage is, and in due course their children will want the same information. And you want me to believe that you, and your children, and your children's children, will make no use of that knowledge? How unrealistic, Mrs...madam! Of course the news will get out. Of course the press will get hold of it. Of course my private life will be dragged through the streets for anyone to see and comment on. Haven't you seen how the newspapers, the media, delight in pulling down public figures?'

He stood up and looked away from her. 'I'm sorry. This is something I cannot do for you. I am not unsympathetic, but...'

Andrea lifted her head proudly. 'Perhaps it is time to give something back.'

He turned sharply. 'What do you mean?'

'Supposing the tests prove that we are not related. I shall go away and you will never hear from me again. That will be the end of it. But if I am in fact your daughter,' (she managed not to stumble over the word) 'then for forty-five years you have got away with something, you have managed not to face up to your responsibilities. What happened to me as a result of those traumas when I was a baby, traumas which, if you are indeed my father, you should have had a part in, all that passed you by.' She paused for breath. 'How can men cause babies to be conceived and then simply go away? My husband wasn't like that. My adoptive father isn't like that. Didn't you ever ask yourself if I was the result of your—your liaison with my mother? Didn't you?' She could feel passion rising in her, and suddenly she didn't care. She *was* passionate about this. It was her life, her very being that was involved. 'And if me, then perhaps that other child, too.'

He was staring at her as he sat down again. She felt she could almost see into his mind, see the wheels turning, the facts fitting or not fitting. All at once she was adamant that she would not leave this serenely beautiful room without some conclusion that she could live with.

'See it from my point of view,' she said, trying not to plead, controlling herself with an effort. 'I am asking you to take a simple test. It is private, completely confidential. You can do it here, in your own home. It would be over in a few minutes, and the results are quickly known. I promise you I shall make no claims upon you, now or ever. Can you imagine what it has been like for me, in these past weeks, to discover the truth about my mother? That was bad enough, but not knowing who is my other parent makes it seem somehow worse. If you can't understand that, I can't make you. But my need to know is very great, and I am appealing to you as a person who, because of your profession, your love of beautiful things,' (she waved an arm to include the room and all it contained) 'must surely have compassion and some—some *pity* for my present state.'

Into the silence that followed came the noises from outside the house—cars on the main road, a sudden gust of wind through the trees in the garden, a bird calling. Andrea moved back to her chair and sat down. She took a handkerchief from her bag and blew her nose. It didn't matter now if she showed emotion; it only mattered that he should know her for the sort of woman she was, that he should believe her when she said she would make no claims.

'Claudia,' he said into the hiatus between them, 'was a woman with many gifts.' Andrea looked up at him. 'A strangely convoluted woman.' His voice was flat, as if he had come to the end of some exhausting experience. 'She could have been successful at many things, but there was always something that held her back. As I told you before, our relationship, to use today's word for it, was very brief, the result of an evening spent together at a time when I was in low spirits. That is no excuse. But she was a very willing partner. I suspected, but never asked, that her marriage was not a success. She would not have been an easy woman to be married to. And I had no intention—afterwards—of carrying the relationship on. I was about to be married myself, and—I'll be honest with you—I didn't really like Claudia. She was an excellent secretary, but not a woman I would have wanted beside me on life's journey.' He cast a quick glance at Andrea, who was barely breathing in case she stopped the flow.

'There was no love involved.' He stood slowly and went back to the window, from where he could see into the garden below. 'No, no love. And I had assumed that she was taking precautions against—against the possible result of our—our...' The distaste he felt was clear on his face. 'That was foolish of me, no doubt. But she seemed a very sophisticated person who would have taken such precautions. And I was...' He stopped, as if to mention himself would be a betrayal; then swallowed and went on: 'I was, in spite of my age, quite naïf where women were concerned.'

'She was younger than you,' Andrea said quietly.

'In years,' he said. 'Only in years.'

'If you had known, what would you have done? If you had been told that your *relationship* had produced twins, what would you have done about it?'

'How can we tell,' he replied whimsically, 'what we would have done *if* this or that had happened over forty years ago?' She sensed a softening in his attitude. 'I like to think that I was—am—a man of integrity. I hope I would have done the right thing. But Claudia never came near me. Never tried to contact me. She stopped working for me about three months later, and as far as I was concerned she simply disappeared into the region of forgotten experiences. I heard eventually, from someone, that she had children, but there was nothing to connect me with them. I was busy by that time, travelling the world musically, getting married, establishing myself. I was shocked that she should have apparently committed such a dreadful crime, but if I had any feeling about it I expect that it was one of thankfulness that she was no longer in my employ. I gave such evidence—character and so on—as they seemed to want, and that was that.'

'And you never wondered?'

'I never wondered.'

'Not even when you knew that she had given me your name?'

Sir Kenneth hesitated briefly. 'I didn't know that until I met you the other day. The newspapers didn't give the children's names, of course, and it was a shock to me to hear you call yourself Frazier-Coombes.' He shook his head. 'No, I didn't know that.'

Silence fell between them. After a long moment, Andrea said, 'Which brings us back to the issue of testing.' She tried to smile at him, but knew that he would see desperation rather than friendliness in her expression. 'It matters so much to me, Sir Kenneth. To me, and to Gerard Scobell.'

'That's another thing,' he said. 'I don't know Mr Scobell. You are asking me to put myself, my reputation, everything, into the hands of two people I have only just heard of, and about whom I know nothing. Forgive me, but how do I know you are not simply on the make, taking some silly old fool with a bit of a past for a ride?'

Andrea bit her lip. 'I don't know how I can convince you.' She could feel tears beginning to rise up in throat and eyes. *It's hopeless,* she was thinking. *How can I ever persuade him?* 'I can only say that I have spent months looking for my birth mother, and finally found her. I have found a man who seems to be my brother. I have discovered things about my family background that I would give much to forget, but can't. I want only one thing more—to find out who my father is.'

'And then?'

'Then I can go back to my adoptive parents, whom I love, and to my children, whom I adore. My children, who may,' she said, with a sudden bright thought, 'be your grandchildren!'

His head came up at that. 'That is unfair!' he said sharply. 'You know full well that I have no children—my wife and I never were able—it's unfair to tempt me with grandchildren!'

The deadening silence crept once more into the room. Andrea gave a deep sigh and collected her handbag and file of papers together ready to stand and admit defeat. She felt a hollow sensation as if she had been weeping for a long time. 'Well...' she began. And then, suddenly, out of nowhere, an idea struck her. It was so alarming, so believable, that she sat up and stared at Sir Kenneth, almost shocked. And for a moment she thought that he, too, had been struck by the same understanding.

He was frowning at her. 'Mrs Frazier-Coombes...?'

'Do you think,' she said cautiously, hardly daring to say it; 'do you think it could be possible that Claudia...?'

'Possible? What?'

'I was just wondering... Do you think that Claudia might have already been pregnant when you and she...?'

Their eyes locked. He said, 'What are you suggesting?'

She hesitated. 'She was very manipulative, I think. Wasn't she?' He nodded once. 'I suddenly wondered if—if that evening with you—was a kind of insurance policy.'

'Why would she?'

'I don't know. But it seems to fit with her personality. I could be quite wrong. But it seems an unlikely thing for her to do—to have that brief relationship with you. And then give me your name. Doesn't it?' She hesitated again. 'Do you think it was her idea? Did she—well, take the lead?'

He was thinking, head bent, regarding the polished surface of the desk. She wondered if she had gone too far. But when he looked up at her, his eyes showing his distaste of the whole business, she saw that they were both thinking along the same lines.

'You could be right,' he said quietly. 'It hadn't occurred to me. But as I recall it,' his mouth pulled in with a kind of disgust as memories returned, 'she stayed late that evening, a thing she seldom did. And—good God!' He rubbed his hand across his mouth as if trying to remove a physical recollection. 'I think you may be right. Because it was all rather pointless. Rather—demeaning, actually.'

They sat in silence, linked by thoughts new to them. She felt for the first time that, given a different situation, they could even have been friends. She stood, knowing that an end had been reached—or a beginning. 'Thank you for seeing me. I'm sorry to have taken up so much of your time.'

He was standing behind the desk, and now he came round it to face her. 'Mrs Frazier-Coombes...'

She saw that he was having difficulty speaking, and she put out a hand in farewell. 'It's all right,' she said with a tremulous smile.

'Look! Look—I just want you to know—nothing personal, you understand. I simply...'

'It's all right,' she repeated.

'No, look!' He seemed exasperated. 'Oh, do sit down! We can't leave it there. Sit down—please!'

Wondering, she did so. He moved around the room, distractedly. 'This test,' he said quickly, turning to regard her with that direct, authoritarian gaze that had subdued many a great symphony orchestra, 'it's easy, straight-forward? Confidential?'

She hardly dared say it: 'Yes'.

'No one need know?'

'That's right. There's a sort of kit. You can do it here, at home.'

'And it will prove...?'

'So they say.'

He picked up a pen again and twisted it in his fingers, then replaced it carefully. 'Ring me this afternoon. I'll be here until four o'clock. Ring me just before that. I'll have your answer for you. But it will be final. Do you understand? Once I've made up my mind I won't change it. All right?'

Andrea nodded. Her voice had left her. She took a deep breath and whispered, 'Thank you'.

13

She rang Gerard. He was quietly pleased, she sensed. 'I'll ring Sir Kenneth later this afternoon, as he asks. Can we meet somewhere after that?'

'Of course.' He suggested a restaurant overlooking the river. 'Seven-thirty? OK?'

She agreed. 'Don't expect too much, Gerard. He was heavy going. But something happened. I'll tell you when I see you. Maybe he'll say no, and he says he won't change his mind, whatever the decision. But I feel more hopeful. I can see his problem. He's afraid of any publicity, and he made good points about it. But he has to see our point of view, too. After all, if Claudia had wanted to, she could have made a right royal stink about it. Having met her, I'm surprised she didn't. Especially since she had two babies to rear. Even then, that wouldn't have been cheap.'

As she rang off she thought of Cathy, and dialled her number.

'So what's new?' Cathy said cheerfully. Andrea gave a small, subdued laugh. 'Oh, it's like that. Won't he play ball?'

'I'm not sure. It started badly, but he's told me to ring him this afternoon and he'll give me his decision. It actually ended better than it started.'

'Well, that's hopeful. What's he afraid of?'

'Publicity. And he's right. I promised absolute secrecy, but he pointed out that once I had told my children and they had told theirs and so on, there was no way that secrecy could possibly be guaranteed. If it wasn't for that I think he might have said yes.'

'Yes, that's a tough one.'

With nothing to do until she rang Sir Kenneth, Andrea was at a loose end. She sat for a while, letting thoughts race through her head: Will he take the test? What will it show? Do I even want him to be my father? At that she had to suppress a giggle. The idea of that stiff, almost unbending personality being even distantly related was really ridiculous. She wouldn't want him in her life, in the lives of her children. So why was it necessary to find out?

If the answer were to be yes, if the test gave proof of his affair with Claudia, she would be stuck with it for ever. Wouldn't it be better to let the whole thing go, to come to terms with the mist that had always hidden her origins? She tried to imagine a scenario: *May I introduce my father, Sir Kenneth Frazier-Greenwood? Yes, we only recently met. He and my mother had a sordid little affair many years ago, nine months before I was born.* She smiled briefly. But it wasn't funny. It was painful. And for a moment she felt quite sorry for the man she had interviewed in the grand room, a man who had everything good money could buy, but had never had children.

But I have, she whispered to herself. I have two dear children. So why don't I leave him alone?

By three-thirty she had come to a decision. If he said no to the test, that would be it. She couldn't fight any more. She had found Claudia, discovered the unsuspected Gerard, knew something about the dim past. It would have to do. She would go back home, keep in touch with Gerard, perhaps invite him over east for a holiday and to meet the children and her parents. And she would work out a new dimension in her life, one that accepted that not everything could be known.

At three-fifty she picked up the phone. Sir Kenneth answered it with suspicious promptitude; he must be as anxious as she!

'Sir Kenneth,' she began, but he interrupted.

'I have decided,' he said, soundly faintly flustered. 'I will take the test. I find...' he hesitated for a moment, 'I find that I also need to know. Kindly ring me again tomorrow morning and we will arrange matters further.'

There was almost no time to say anything. Andrea managed a stammered 'Thank you. Thank you so much...' before his phone was replaced and she was listening to silence. For a moment she held the receiver in a shaking hand. Then she put it down very carefully, sat down and stared into space. He had said 'yes'. The realisation brought tears to her eyes. Then, trying not to sniffle, she lifted the phone and rang Gerard.

'He said yes,' she reported simply. 'Gerard, he said yes!'

Andrea organised the DNA swabs for all three of them. It was over with such speed and total lack of drama that she felt a sense of anti-climax once everything had been done. And, once it was completed, she felt as if she had crossed a bridge and, looking back, had seen it explode behind her and fall in wreckage into the river.

Gerard had waited in a small ante-room as she accepted the swab with a sudden sensation of excitement. She wondered at the fact that such a small action could carry the possibility of such large results. While she waited for Gerard to go through the same routine, she stared ahead of her at a poster on the wall, seeing nothing. There was a slight feeling of revulsion that this had been necessary; that Claudia, who even *in extremis* could surely have said something, anything, to clear up the mystery, had played her final trick with such aplomb. *My mother,* she told herself. 'Mother' had always seemed to her such a warm, loving word, indicative of nurture and all the good things of childhood. She would have to revise her thinking. There was plenty of evidence in this harsh world that not all mothers came up to her standard.

Gerard came out of the room and nodded at her, moving his jaw as if he still felt the swab inside. 'Not too difficult,' he said. But she knew that for him it had been invasive, something he would have been happy to do without.

'Thank you,' she said obscurely, and he glanced down at her as she got to her feet.

'My pleasure.'

'But it wasn't, was it?'

'It had to be done. I hope it will prove what you—what we want it to prove.'

'Which is?'

'Ah,' he said, softly, on a long note. 'What indeed?'

They drank coffee at a beach café.

'I think,' Andrea said slowly, 'I think I'll go home for a while.'

He looked at her sharply. 'Will you? Why?'

'To make sure I still have a home.' She smiled at him. 'See my parents, the kids.' It would be good, a break she badly needed after so much emotional stress. 'What about you?'

'I have things to do,' he said vaguely.

Unexpectedly, she found that she really wanted to know more about this man whose life had so suddenly and unavoidably impinged on hers. Though she acknowledged to herself that the impinging had mainly been on her side. 'What things?'

'I have a consultancy. I've been neglecting it.'

'What do people consult you about?'

'Money.' He was silent; then shrugged. 'You're entitled to know...'

'I'm not entitled—if you don't want to tell me.'

He pushed his cup away and stared at it for a moment. 'I've lived a solitary life,' he said finally. 'It's the way I am. Or the way I've been.' He frowned as if the words he needed were elusive. 'Good parents, no worry there. But reticent people, not given to—to...'

'To babbling everything out like I do!' She grinned at him. 'Could we *possibly* be twins, do you suppose? With so many differences.'

He didn't smile. He was still staring at his cup, searching. 'I have to say,' he began, hesitating over every word, 'I have to say that—that—well, I do enjoy your babbling, as you call it.' He looked up at last. 'Meeting you, whatever the outcome, has been something so—so unexpected, so extraordinary, that...'

Andrea put out her hand a touched his. 'Me too. Whatever—it's been really good to find you.' Then she sat still, taken aback by a thought she had not thoroughly explored in all its dimensions. 'If we are brother and sister, then for the rest of our lives we have "family"!' She bit her lip, feeling quite emotional. 'That's something to treasure, isn't it?'

He nodded briefly. 'And if we're not?' He looked her straight in the eye. 'If we're not, then what are we? Not family. So what?'

'Good friends? After all, we went through the same traumas as babies. That's special.' Then she shook her head quickly. 'But we are—I really believe we are. Twins! It'll just take a bit of getting used to.'

They sat in the airport lounge, silent amid the bustle of other people's departures. Andrea's mind seemed to her to be a muddle of conflicting thoughts. By coming early she had hoped to be able to say goodbye to Gerard without the rush to find the right place, the correct door to leave by. She wanted time to say whatever might need to be said—though she would have been hard put to decide what that might be. She would be coming back in a couple of weeks. So what needed to be said by either of them?

Gerard was quite a restful man, in a way. It was possible to sit with him silently and not feel that one should be talking to fill the gaps. Unless he was bored? She stole a glance at him. Perhaps he was! She knew there were things he wanted to get on with in this life of his that she had barely managed to enter.

If so, he was a master of tact. At no time had he given her any reason to think along those lines. He had gone out of his way to be courteous and helpful—no fuss over the DNA test that he had really not wanted to undergo.

As if he read her mind, Gerard glanced up and caught her eye. He gave his diffident grin that made him look like a shy schoolboy. 'Hate airports,' he said unexpectedly. Hate was not a word she would have associated with him. Too powerful. 'Like limbo, whatever that is.'

She smiled. 'Artificial. It's so difficult to make sensible conversation with someone who won't be there in a few minutes.' She hesitated. 'You go, if you want. I'll be OK.'

He shook his head. 'I'll see you off.' He glanced around him. 'So many people in one place for a split second of time—they'll never all be together in the same place again. Makes you think! In twenty-four hours from now some will be in the UK, some in Bali, some in the US...'

'Yes...' She leaned back, stretching the tension out of her body. 'How about...?'

'Just what I was going to say.' He stood up. 'Tea or coffee?'

She laughed. 'Psychic! *Must* be twins. I'm surprised we aren't wearing identical dresses.'

Gerard grinned. 'So you want coffee?'

'Thanks.'

She watched him as he ambled slowly towards the counter and joined a queue. She felt a real familiarity with the lanky figure that always looked as if another five minutes would have helped him to dress tidily. The auburn-brown hair, thick at the sides, was wearing thin on top, she noticed, and she felt a pang of affection for him, knowing that he could have no good idea of what he actually looked like from behind, the broad shoulders, languid walk, old shoes well-worn and no doubt well-loved, and the thin patch gleaming faintly through the reddish thatch.

And as she watched him, as he moved slowly up the queue with his hand in his pocket already searching out the right coins, Andrea felt an entirely new sensation running through her. For a moment she wondered what it was, this sudden *frisson* that made everything seem brighter, more colourful. She was aware of the beating of her heart. Her cheeks felt hot. Appalled, she felt sensations she had not felt since Joseph had been so remorselessly taken from her. Gerard had awakened in her...*not desire,* she begged. *Not that!* Not when they had just come to terms with their twin relationship; not when they were about to discover...

Through a haze of panic she saw him returning to the table with two cups and a plate of biscuits. *I'll have to go,* she was telling herself. *I can't sit here and pretend...'*

Gerard sat down and pushed the plate towards her. 'They'll feed you on the plane. Still...'

Andrea put out a trembling hand and pulled it back again. It would never do to let him see her confusion. He looked across at her. 'You all right?'

She nodded. 'Pre-flight nerves,' she said through lips that felt like rubber.

'I didn't know you suffered from them.'

'I don't usually.'

He was silent for a moment. 'I'll miss you,' he said suddenly. 'Take care, won't you?' It was impossible to look at him. She nodded again.

Into a silence that felt quite unlike the serenity of just a few minutes ago, she said, 'I'll ring you when I'm coming back.'

'Do that.' He lifted his cup and drank. *Thank God! It's only me. He's not feeling this—this...oh help, I'm blushing!* 'I haven't got your home number, have I?'

'What?' She took a deep breath and pulled herself together. A few days away from him should do the trick. Once she was home... 'Sorry! What did you say?'

'Your home phone number.' He was regarding her curiously, not quite smiling. 'The sooner you get on that plane the better.'

'Why?' She wondered if he had guessed what was really ailing her. But he took out his diary and opened it at a page, pen poised ready.

'It's better once you get going. Nerves! Much worse thinking about something than doing it. Number?'

She told him, the figures coming automatically to her lips.

14

Andrea found the visit to home ground difficult to analyse. Perhaps she had put too much expectation on it; once it was over and she was in the plane flying back to Perth, she had an unexpected sense of relief—until she recalled her unwelcome sensations as Gerard was buying coffee.

Lucy was warmly cheerful. No problem there. Harry, very busy in the garden, was happy to have her home, helping him, toting the wheelbarrow to the compost heap or pruning the plumbago. But not really talking. Perhaps he didn't know what to ask.

Daniel was home for a couple of days between holidaying at a famed surf spot with a friend and going on a vacation 'dig' with schoolmates and a science teacher. He was glad to see her, and made all the right noises, but her news did not exactly rivet him.

Bethany was more outgoing. She wanted to know about Claudia, warts and all, about DNA testing; and about Gerard—or Uncle Gerard, as she insisted on calling him with a wicked twinkle in the eye.

'Is he really nice? Good-looking? Do you get on with him? Is he coming here?' And finally, when Andrea had done her best to answer truthfully without giving anything away: 'It must be really weird, I mean *weird*, to meet a grown-up man who is your brother. I mean—*weird!*'

'He may not be,' said Andrea defensively.

'Woo-hoo! That's even weirder! Not knowing!'

'Bethany! For heaven's sake!'

Bethany curled herself into the corner of the couch. 'Aren't you excited?'

Andrea laughed her frustration away, ending with a long sigh. 'Too much has happened to be excited about it.'

'You might as well enjoy it, Mum. I bet it doesn't often happen.' And she disappeared into a magazine—where presumably the stories had better endings.

'*Subject closed,*' Andrea thought, not altogether sorry.

Lucy took her out for lunch. 'So that we can talk without being interrupted.'

So Andrea gave her a run-down on her activities since she had arrived in Perth.

'I wasn't really disappointed in Claudia. I think I'd prepared myself for whatever the worst might be. But I was—well, a bit annoyed that she was so reticent. Time was so short for her that I felt she might have made the effort. It was like pulling teeth—you know? And always that feeling that she was enjoying being so unhelpful.'

'But you've managed well enough without her help.'

'Yes—I suppose so. I couldn't have done it without Cathy.'

They talked about Cathy for a while, but Lucy could sense a change in her daughter: she seemed as if something had occupied a corner of her mind, so that she was never quite concentrated on the subject under discussion.

'So tell me about Gerard,' she said at last, and immediately felt she had found the source. Andrea fiddled with her knife and fork, regarding the remains of her pasta with more intensity than it warranted.

'Gerard? Well, he's a very pleasant person. Quiet.'

'What does he look like? Anything like you and Claudia?'

'No. He's tall, his hair is dark, a bit auburn, he was married but his wife died before they could have a family, he's not as keen as I am to find out about Claudia and all that stuff...'

'Why?'

Andrea looked up and saw from the expression on her mother's face that she had caught a glimmer of the truth. 'He was reasonably happy with the way things were—that's what he says.' She put the cutlery down and leaned back. 'He'll make a nice brother.'

'And will that suit you?' Lucy regarded her curiously.

'It'll have to, won't it?' She pulled a face. 'Yes, Mum, all right—you can see through me, but keep it to yourself. I spent the first weeks hoping he'd turn out to be my twin, and once I was pretty sure he was I suddenly knew I'd rather he wasn't!' She smiled a little grimly. 'At the airport. On my way here. Quite suddenly I felt, well, I felt differently about him. The first time since Joseph. So when I go back...'

'And what about him?'

'I don't think he realised. I hope not. And I certainly don't think he feels the same way.' She managed a real smile. 'You would have been intrigued by Sir Kenneth, Mum. That really was lions' den stuff.'

Lucy took the hint and they indulged themselves with a small mutual chuckle at the great man's dilemma.

'If he is, of course,' she said obscurely, 'then he's got away with it nicely up to now. But if not—well, I'm being a bit unfair. Because he couldn't really want that kind of publicity in his position.'

'And if he is your father?'

'I've no idea. It just doesn't seem likely, in spite of the evidence. Anyway, we shall know soon enough.'

Gerard was waiting for her at the airport. It was a typically lovely spring day, warm with a light breeze, and baby clouds floating on a blue sky. It was good to be back, and she was thankful that, after the initial tremor at meeting him, they fell back into their easy relationship.

They had agreed to call for the DNA results when she returned, and once they had the all-important papers in their hands they sat for a moment in silence without reading them. Then Gerard drove them up to King's Park and they found a bench. Below them the river sparkled, and between the water and the steep slope at the edge of the park ran the serpentine lines of cars on the freeway. She could hear the steady engine hum, like a distant bee-hive.

'Well,' Gerard said, 'who's going to open it?'

Andrea hesitated. 'You do it.' She was all at once intensely nervous.

He opened the envelope in his usual unhurried way, withdrew the papers and unfolded them. Andrea leaned over his arm to see. And what she saw silenced her.

'So now we know,' Gerard said, handing it to her.

It was quite clear. Sir Kenneth Frazier-Greenwood was not the father of Andrea Frazier-Coombes and Gerard Scobell. But neither were Gerard and Andrea related. Andrea was the daughter of Claudia Shepherd and, presumably, her husband Ben. But where did Gerard fit in? For he was certainly the other baby who had been taken into care. If he was not Claudia's child...

'So who am I?' he said, confused.

And Andrea could only say, 'I don't know.' If there was a wicked throb of pleasure that he was indeed not her brother, it was tempered by her own confusion. Who in fact was he?

Andrea sent a card to Sir Kenneth. Inside she simply wrote: 'Thank you!' She received no reply, which didn't surprise her.

For a couple of days she didn't see Gerard. She was quite pleased; there was too much going on in their minds for meeting him to be easy. Then he rang her, and she knew that something had to be done—done or said, she wasn't sure which. She went over the whole thing again and again; read the copied papers, listened once more to the dying Claudia's words: '...the other one?' If he wasn't Claudia's child, then what?

They met in the park; it seemed the one place where they felt comfortable. There was a slight chill in the air, a late spring whiff of southern waters ice, and she put on a warm jacket. Gerard was waiting for her at 'their' bench, and it was quite difficult to meet his eyes because of the confusion she saw there. After they sat down they were silent for several moments.

'So...where are we now?' he said at last. And she shook her head.

'I don't know. I've been puzzling over it, but it doesn't seem to make sense.'

'We're not related, it seems.'

'No.' She glanced at him quickly. 'Do you mind?'

'Do you?'

'No.' They fell silent again. She had no idea what he was thinking.

'Dead end, I imagine,' he said finally. She nodded. 'I can't see where else we can go. Even if we wanted to.'

At that she looked at him, but his face was turned away from her. 'You don't want to, do you?'

He drew in a long, slow breath. 'I won't say I wouldn't have liked to know what it was all about. It's a lot of loose ends that are probably going to be very annoying. But I'm no detective—I wouldn't know where to start.'

'But if...?'

'If there was something, anything, that would solve the problem, then—maybe.' He shrugged. 'It was always your thing, not mine.'

She felt some reproach in his words, and was momentarily annoyed. Looking back on the journey they had made to get to where they were, she had quite a sense of achievement. But she agreed: if they didn't clear up this final mystery it would bug them for ever. *Keep digging*, she told herself. *Don't give up now!*

'One thing occurs to me,' she said, trying not to sound as if she were meaning to appease him. 'I was going through the newspaper reports this morning and I wondered if this woman, Carding her name was, is still around. She was involved with the babies.' *With us!* 'I wonder if we could find her.'

'Probably dead,' he said, and she detected a hopeful note in his voice.

'But perhaps not. We might look in the phone book.'

'She may have gone anywhere by now, even if she's alive. Interstate. Overseas. It'd probably be a waste of time.'

'It would take a few minutes to look for the name. I'll do it when I get back to Cathy's.' She felt a sudden surge of energy.

Gerard stood. 'I'll get some takeaway coffee.' He walked with that lazy movement across the grass, and she watched him go. She sensed a warm affection in her that was less troubling than the sensations she had had at the airport. Perhaps it would be all right. Perhaps she would get over him. She smiled to herself and wondered why she had never expected to feel desire after Joseph. It was like being a teenager again.

As they drank they were silent. Then he said, 'Right! We'll see if we can find this woman. What did you say her name was?'

'Carding. Bella Carding.'

He nodded slowly. 'And if we don't?'

'At some point we would have to give up, I suppose.'

'But you hope not?'

'Yes—I think so.'

'You know about yourself, Andrea. Why does it matter about me?'

This stopped her short. 'I—I'm not sure. Unfinished business, perhaps. It puzzles me why you were there at all. Why your birth was registered by Claudia. Surely that wouldn't even have been legal, would it? For myself, I need to know. For you—well, if you say stop, then I'll stop. Or I might go on and find out and not tell you.' She looked at him quickly, half smiling. But he kept on staring out at the view to the far hills.

Then he crushed his paper cup; he walked over to a bin and threw it in. When he came back he stood before her and looked down at her. 'If you found out,' he said with a whimsical smile, 'you'd never be able to keep it to yourself!' He sat down beside her. 'OK, Sherlock! Let's do it!'

She nodded, not speaking. Once more she was in a state of confusion. There was something about him that made her heart beat a little faster. She might as well make up her mind to that, no matter how it ended.

'So...!' Gerard had the phone book in his hand, riffling through the pages. 'Carding! He ran his finger down a page. 'Carding—Carding...there's not many, thank goodness. Two B Cardings. What now? Ring them?'

'Why not?' But it wouldn't be that easy, would it? 'Perhaps she's married, changed her name.'

He grinned quickly. 'Not getting cold feet?'

'No.' But suddenly she wanted to pull back, to think a bit longer, not to open a door to more memories that might be hurtful—to herself, to Gerard. To B. Carding, if she still existed. She had not really thought that part of it through. What would the woman's reaction be if they did find her? And yet, she chided herself, they had come this far, she had forced the pace, now was not the time to withdraw.

Gerard was regarding her thoughtfully. She could almost see the same questions, the same decisions, mirrored in his eyes. He took a deep breath and let it out slowly. 'Today, tomorrow or whenever,' he said at last. 'If we're going to do it then perhaps we shouldn't leave it too long. Not after your experience with Claudia.'

'Ring, then.' She watched him go to the phone and dial the first number. She listened to the brief exchange that meant that Bella Carding was not to be found at first search.

'A man,' Gerard said. 'No Bella. Never heard of her.' He turned to look at Andrea. 'Second shot?'

She nodded. What did she really hope to get out of it, if Bella Carding were to answer? More information? Confirmation—of what? Her palms were suddenly damp and she rubbed them against her skirt. This had been such a roller-coaster, so many hopes and expectations, and at the end of it all she wondered if it really mattered.

But Gerard was talking, nodding as he listened. Andrea's heart did a sudden thump. He was talking to Bella Carding, a woman she had almost thought of as a figment of her own imagination. The same Bella Carding whose grainy newspaper photograph, taken more than four decades ago, had become a part of their quest.

'Yes,' he was saying. 'We wondered if we might come to see you.' A pause. She was obviously asking why. 'My—my friend has recently discovered that she is the daughter of Claudia Shepherd. Your name appears in the newspaper reports of the—the tragedy. She would like to meet you.' Another pause. 'No, I'm sure she won't.' He was persuasive. Andrea watched him as his expression reflected sympathy, firm purpose, a warm smile as he said goodbye. He *was* a nice man!

'Well, Miss Bella Carding will meet us. It was a near thing. She isn't keen. She hoped you weren't going to bring "those nasty newspapermen" with you.'

'What does she sound like?'

He pondered. 'Very spinsterish. Whatever that means. Nervous voice. Not a penetrating personality.'

'Funny,' Andrea said, suddenly struck by a bizarre idea. 'If she'd had her way she would probably have brought us up.'

'That's a thought.' He laughed wryly. 'It's daunting to think how haphazard life really is. Imagine—we might have spent our whole lives together.'

'And never known we were not brother and sister.' Andrea's laugh was hollow. The knowledge she had always had of being secure, of being loved by the only people who *should* love her, because it was her right as their child: this knowledge trembled within her like the intimation of an earthquake to come, a tremor that might destroy what was precious to her, instead of, as she had intended, consolidating her life by filling in the last small jigsaw puzzle pieces. 'So—when do we see her?'

'She said I could ring her again tomorrow morning to fix a time in the afternoon.' He regarded her, frowning a little. 'Has it upset you? You look a bit down.'

Andrea looked away. 'Just a bit. I was wondering—what will she be able to tell us that we don't know?'

'The one thing we need to know, perhaps. Where do I come into it? You know, for good or ill, what your background is. But what about mine? It never mattered before. But I think it does now.'

'Yes, of course.' Andrea suddenly relaxed. That was it. The murky background of her own beginnings was one thing. But Gerard's own personal mystery was still a matter for a spot of detection. Sir Kenneth was out of the equation; Claudia and Ben were both dead. Bella Carding was their last hope. 'What was it all about, Gerard? *Why* were our births registered together? It's so—so...'

'Confusing is a good word. Claudia was a very mysterious creature, obviously. I'm sorry I didn't meet her. It would have been productive to have got a bit more out of her.'

'I doubt if you would have.' She recalled that thin, paper-white face with the flash of malice that was the only expression allowed to escape. 'I do wonder what my turning up like that really meant to her.' She visualised again the torn photo. 'I mean, was she *really* that tough? Or was it a protective shield for someone who knew she was dying and hadn't the energy for emotion?' She stared out of the window, seeing nothing, her mind's eye on her doomed mother. 'Sir Ken didn't like her. He said so. I really can't imagine her as someone who had a one-night stand with her boss. Do you think she was trying to snare him, perhaps get him to marry her? Or was it what I said to him—that she was already pregnant, and he was her insurance policy?'

'We shall never know. The pictures show her as a bit cold, not what you'd call attractive.'

'But she'd been arrested for murder. It would make a difference. And that's something else I hadn't thought of—was she afraid? Defiant? Did she think she was justified in killing him—*him*, my father. If he was! Oh!' she exploded. 'It's all so unbelievable. Let's hope Miss Carding is more down-to-earth.'

She was waiting for them. They saw her dimly through net curtains, and by the time they reached the front door it had opened and Bella was standing there, a Christian before the lions, a heretic facing the Inquisition.

Andrea smiled reassuringly and held out both hands. 'Hullo, Bella. Thank you for letting us come.' Bella put out cautious fingers to be shaken, taking them back quickly when Gerard enclosed them in his own large hand. She held the door for them and they moved ahead of her into the front room, where she made a vague gesture indicating that they should sit down, but herself stood by the door as if she felt that escape might be necessary.

Inevitably there was an embarrassed gap to be overcome. Andrea glanced at Gerard, but he was clearly waiting for her to take the first leap.

'We've been so much hoping,' Andrea began, 'that you will tell us what you know.'

'It's been very difficult,' Bella said. 'I didn't sleep. I just didn't know what to do.' She closed the door slowly. 'But then I thought, yes, you were right. Claudia told you about—about...' she nodded towards Gerard, as if even speaking his name would be too personal. 'So if she told you that I suppose she wouldn't mind you knowing the rest. Claudia,' she said surprisingly, 'could be very devious.'

She sat down slowly, carefully, facing them. They waited.

Bella let out a long sigh. 'Oh, dear...'

'It said in the papers,' Andrea started, trying to help, 'that you said *you* could have looked after the two children—after us, that is—when Claudia was convicted.'

'Oh yes, yes.'

'Had you had much to do with us—before?'

'Yes.' Bella slowly lifted her gaze to Andrea's face, and there was such a wealth of feeling in those tormented eyes that Andrea was silenced. 'Yes. I looked after you from the time you were born. Claudia worked, you see. I didn't. So I—I moved in with her and Mr Shepherd—Ben—and I looked after you when Claudia wasn't there. I'm afraid,' she said primly, 'that Claudia was not a *natural* mother.'

'But you were.'

'Well, I suppose I was a bit better at it. I cared more.' She smoothed her skirt over her knees, folding and unfolding a pleat. 'Yes—I cared more.'

'She must have been glad to have you there. What about Ben?' *My father,* Andrea was thinking. *How weird!* 'Was he a good father?'

'Well, he wasn't a *bad* father. Men weren't expected to do much with babies in those days. He was quite kind.'

'Was he a nice man?' Andrea suddenly needed to know. 'Would I have liked him, do you think?'

Bella looked up at her again, and regarded her for a long moment. 'I don't think you'd have had much in common. He was quite an ordinary sort of person. I could never see why Claudia married him.'

'Were they happy?'

'Not happy. Not when I knew them. More—resigned to each other, I think.' She stared past Andrea, remembering. 'They didn't have rows that I know of, not till that last one. But I think that was because Ben knew it was a waste of time arguing with Claudia. No one argued with her. She made up her mind and that was it. That's probably why she and I got on well. I didn't have a mind to make up.' It was said without feeling. Andrea felt a pang of pity.

'Did you know,' she said carefully, 'that Gerard was not Claudia's child?'

The long silence that lay between them was a barrier to shared knowledge. Gerard shifted in his chair, his eyes on the slight figure opposite.

'Yes.' Bella closed her eyes. 'I knew.'

They waited once more, the air seemingly vibrating with a mingling of expectation and—was it dread? Andrea glanced at Gerard, and she knew him well enough now to sense a building tension in him. His gaze was fixed on Bella, whose thin cheeks now bore two spots of colour.

'You'll have to forgive me,' Bella said slowly, taking a handkerchief from her sleeve and twisting it in her hands.. 'I've never told anyone anything about this. I don't know where to start.' She put the hankie to her mouth.

'When did you get to know Claudia?' Andrea prompted.

'When she went to work for Sir Kenneth. She wanted someone to do her ironing.'

'So you knew her for quite a while?'

'Yes. I looked up to her, you know. She was everything I wasn't. Really quite striking-looking. Always knew what she wanted. And got it. Used people whenever she needed something. Used me all the time.' Was there a flicker of a rueful smile? 'But I didn't mind. I needed to be used. Mostly she ignored Ben, as if he had no importance.'

'Did you live at home? You were still quite young.'

Interestingly, the barrier rose once again. Bella turned her face away slightly, the more relaxed mood dissipating into withdrawal. 'That's not important. I did—yes, I did. But it's not important.'

Which means it probably is, Andrea thought, sensing a darkness she had not been aware of.

'Was Claudia good to you?

'Yes, in her own way. You didn't have to expect loving-kindness. That wasn't in her. But if she could see something in it for her—I'm making her sound horrible.'

'No. You're painting a picture—a good picture. You're helping us to understand.'

Gerard was still silent. Andrea shot a quick look at him. She had a strong sense that he was hiding a disturbance within himself, that to speak would, at this moment, be impossible for him. She turned back to Bella.

'Tell us about the babies—about us!'

Bella took a deep breath. 'I think I'll make a cup of tea. Will that be all right? And then...' she stood up, fingers twisting together, 'I'll tell you.' She turned at the door. 'You're very patient.'

'I know it's very hard for you.' Andrea moved as if to get up. 'Can I help?'

Bella looked startled, the reaction of a parlourmaid to a visitor who has just stepped over the conventional line. *That's what she reminds me of,* Andrea realised. *The excellent servant who knows where the lines are drawn.* 'Oh, no! No, thank you. Everything's ready.' She escaped to the kitchen, and Andrea turned to Gerard.

'Are you all right?'

'Yes. Why?'

'I sensed you were feeling a bit...'

'It's odd, isn't it?' He stretched his arms, releasing tension. 'At this moment I don't know where I came from. In ten minutes it may all be laid out in front of me, and I don't have any idea what I'm likely to feel about it.'

'You'd rather stay in the dark?'

He met her eyes thoughtfully. 'Perhaps. But I have to do it. If not today, some other day when not knowing becomes a burden.' He shook his head, the decision made. 'No, whatever it is, let's let the light in.'

Bella's tea remained untouched. While Andrea and Gerard drank theirs and took biscuits because they were there, Bella stared ahead of her with a look of such drawn distress that Andrea's impulse was to put down cup and biscuit and run for it.

Into the silence she said, 'This is hurting you, isn't it?'

Bella turned quickly. 'It's painful, yes. But I can see it has to be done. The thing is,' she clasped her hands tightly, 'will this all come out? Does anyone else have to know?'

'No, no, of course not. Just Gerard and me. It's been so confusing for us. First thinking that Sir Kenneth might be—you know—and thinking we were twins, then finding out that he wasn't and we weren't—oh, it's been *so* confusing!' Andrea looked to Gerard for confirmation and he nodded.

'Whatever you can tell us,' he said with a sincerity that seemed to reassure their nervous hostess. 'Anything. It will help.'

'During the night,' Bella began, her voice not quite under control, 'when I couldn't sleep, I wrote a letter to you.' She raised her eyes briefly to Gerard. 'I'll tell you what I can now. Then, when you get home, you can read it. After that, if you still want to see me, you can come back.' To Andrea she said, 'You must think I'm a very silly person. I know I ought to come straight out and say it, but I can't. It's as if it's been like a growth inside me all these years, and now it won't come out.'

'I'm just sorry we've upset you...'

'I've always known that one day...' She stopped. 'I'll tell you what I can, and the rest is in the letter.' She sat up straight, like a child about to recite a poem. 'Claudia knew that my home situation was not a happy one, so she was quite pleased to have me at their place for most of the time. I think it was partly because she and Ben were not very well suited. Claudia liked to entertain—she met some interesting people and they came to the house. Ben preferred not to have visitors. He was a bit of a *loner*, I think they call it these days. My picture of him is always sitting by the fire with a book or newspaper in winter, or reading in the garden in summer. He didn't read anything special, no history or biographies or anything like that—Claudia taunted him with having no brain. She wasn't kind.'

She glanced at their cups. 'More tea?' They shook their heads.

'So—Claudia had a friend. They saw a lot of each other. A younger woman, a girl really. One day Claudia told her that she was—was pregnant, that Ben had got fed up with always being put down by her, and that he had...' Painfully she searched for the right words.

'They had made love?' Andrea suggested.

'Yes—though there wasn't much love involved,' Bella said with a sudden spurt of malice. 'Anyway, Claudia was furious. The house wasn't a comfortable place to be. Nobody speaking to anyone. They sent messages through me. I really thought I'd have to leave. But Claudia said I must stay. So I did.' She straightened her cup on the saucer. 'Then the friend told Claudia that—she—was pregnant. An unwanted pregnancy.' For a moment she was silent. 'They were both about three months on, and Claudia came up with a plan. She knew her friend couldn't tell her family. So they agreed that when the pregnancies began to show they would go off together, somewhere no one would think of looking for them, and have the babies, and that Claudia would register them as her own.'

She stopped, and Andrea stared at her. 'But how—I mean, there would be all kinds of difficulties. Doctors, nurses, other people.'

'You didn't know Claudia. She believed that she could do anything practical that other people could do. She got books, information. She said women often had to have children in odd situations.'

'But what if there were complications?'

'With Claudia in charge?' There was a healthy sprinkling of irony in her voice. 'She was confident. There was never any room for doubt with Claudia. So...' She shrugged slightly. 'Off she went with her friend, and they found a country cottage at the end of a track, so that people wouldn't always be passing, and she got in everything that would be needed, and they waited.'

Bella fell silent. After a moment she looked up at Andrea. 'The friend gave birth first, in that little cottage. And it all went according to Claudia's plan. And a couple of days later Claudia's baby was born. And they gave themselves a month or so to get over it, and then they went back home, back to Ben.'

Andrea leaned back in her chair, letting her breath go. Gerard cleared his throat. 'What had he been doing all that while?'

'Ben's programme never changed. Meals at fixed times, out to work, back from work, read his books—he didn't seem to need variety. He was rather a boring man.' She gave the ghost of a smile, as if, now the major part of her story was done, she could relax a bit. 'Claudia was right about that.'

'Who looked after him, him and the house? You?'

She shook her head. 'He was quite capable of that. I wouldn't have stayed with him. He wouldn't have wanted me to.'

'So the babies were registered as hers and Ben's?' Gerard queried. 'But I was the child of the—the friend? The illegitimate child.'

'I'm afraid so.'

'A child is a child,' Andrea said forcefully. 'A child can't be illegitimate.'

'They thought like that then.' Bella's cheeks were flushed.

'And was there no way the friend could keep her child?'

'No.' It was a whisper. 'There were good reasons.'

'OK,' said Gerard. 'So we know now that I'm illegitimate, the son of a very young woman, and was to have been brought up by Claudia as hers.' He frowned. 'You say she liked her pound of flesh. What was she going to get out of it?'

'Two things, probably. Complete control over her friend, who would never dare to stand up to her. And I think she enjoyed the idea that she had a secret that Ben could never share. She'd got away with something. She liked that.'

'So what went wrong?' Gerard asked bluntly.

'Ben got the idea that—that the boy wasn't his.'

'How?'

'He didn't look like any of them. Certainly not a twin, even a non-identical one. Different build, hair colour, everything.' She bit her lip. 'They had a terrible row. She taunted him, and for once he stood up to her. *"I'm not bringing up someone else's little—little bastard!"* he shouted.' She gulped at the word. ' *"Get him out of here!"* Well, Claudia refused. She admitted that he—that you,' she said, glancing at Gerard, 'were not hers, and then he made the logical jump, that it was the friend's child. They were angry—so angry. The children were crying. I took them out. We went to the park, and when we got back everything was quiet. I went into the sitting room and Claudia was there, staring into space. I asked if she was all right and she said yes, but Ben was dead. Just like that! I thought, heart attack, but she said no, he'd got what he deserved for being such a pathetic human being—that's what she said—and I'd better ring the police.' She shuddered. 'I went into the kitchen and he was lying on the floor, and there was blood...I wanted to be sick, but the babies needed their tea, and...'

'How truly awful for you,' Andrea whispered, deeply shocked. Hearing it from someone involved was very different from reading about it in old newspapers.

'It was awful.' For the first time Bella met Andrea's eyes without flinching. 'I think I knew, at that moment...' She stopped.

'Knew what?' Gerard asked.

'That the babies would be separated. That they would be taken away. That Claudia's *friend* would never see her son again. That's why I tried so hard to keep you both. But of course it was useless. There are ways of handling these things—official ways—and the ordinary person doesn't get a look in.'

'And that,' said Andrea as they walked across the road, 'is one of the saddest stories I've ever heard.

Gerard was deep in thought, and grunted. 'This *friend*,' he said. 'This friend who was apparently never heard of again...'

'Yes, I wonder if it would be possible to find her. Would you want to?'

'I wasn't quite thinking that.' He stood still for a moment. 'My thoughts are going in quite another direction.'

Andrea considered this. As they reached the car she turned to him, suddenly alarmed. 'Do you mean...?'

'Get in. We've got the letter. She said it would tie up any loose ends. Let's find out.'

They drove up to King's Park. The sun was catching windows across the river, flashing messages they could not read. Small power-boats dragged willing victims across the water on skis. A ferry made its slow way to the south shore. Perth's few skyscrapers stood defiantly, as if to say their city was as prosperous and thoroughly modern as any twice its size. Andrea thought she could live here, if the future were to present her with that choice. She leaned back, opened the car window, and waited to hear Bella's letter read.

15

*D*ear Mr Scobell, (formal to the last, Gerard observed), *By the time you read this I hope you will have heard enough from me to satisfy you about your own early background. It is 3 a.m. and recent events have taken sleep from me. I know that I will not be able to give you every detail of that sad time face to face. It is too harrowing for me. But you are entitled to know the truth.*

I was Claudia's 'friend'.

'Oh, my God!' Andrea whispered. 'Oh, Gerard!'

I came from a very unhappy home. My mother and father seemed to be locked into a hate-filled situation from which neither apparently wanted to escape. I was the only child, and the only other person in the household was my uncle, Mother's youngest brother. When I was small he took an interest in me. We went on the river together, played ball in the park. But when I began to grow up his interest changed. I was uncomfortable with him. When my parents were out in the evening—a common occurrence—he would make suggestions to me which I prefer not to write down. I'm sure you understand what I mean.

By the time I was fifteen he had made my life a misery, but I had maintained my self-respect. When I tried to tell my mother she said I was imagining things. I would not have dared to tell my father.

This was when I came to know Claudia. She was looking for help in the house, and I was so thankful to have somewhere to go. She knew there was something unacceptable in my life, though we never spelt it out.

Then I was sixteen, and my uncle was not about to take no for an answer. Night after night he came. I was helpless. Sometimes I felt like killing myself.

And so, in the end, as I had feared I became pregnant. The rest you know. Some women would think it right to hate the product of such

109

unnatural behaviour. I never did. When you were born, Gerard (if I may call you that), I thought I had never seen anything more beautiful or so good. I called you Gerard after someone I had read about in a book I have quite forgotten. I felt that, out of all the ugliness, at least some good had come.

If you wish to see me again, please ring me.

Yours very sincerely, Bella Carding.

Silence. Then, 'Oh, my *God*! Gerard, what shall we do? That poor, poor woman!'

Gerard was still looking down at the papers in his hand. 'What can we do? There's nothing. She's lived with that for forty-six years. Longer. How can we make it better?'

'How wonderfully kind of her at the end—"*out of all the ugliness*". What do you want to do, Gerard?'

'I have to think.' He folded the letter and put it in his pocket. 'Andrea, that's my mother. I'm floored!'

'But you suspected. You more or less said so.'

'I didn't believe what I suspected. Didn't want to. Still don't.'

She regarded the profile turned to her. The placid man was shaken and—was he angry? Or frightened? Even perhaps ashamed of the reasons for his existence? She looked around.

'We could get a cup of tea over there.'

'Tea won't do it.'

'What will?'

'Getting drunk, perhaps.'

'Do you?'

'No. But maybe it's time I did.'

Then he managed a faint grin. 'OK. I'm sorry for myself. And for her. I was lucky not to be reared by Claudia, I suppose. It makes me thankful for my own adoptive parents. But I just cannot imagine what my life would have been if *she* had brought me up. Do you see her as a mother?'

'She said she was more motherly than Claudia. I think you might have done quite well with Bella. If she could have kept you away from her family.'

'It's confusing.' He relaxed and leaned his head back, looking up into the branches of old trees. 'My great-uncle is also my father. Or was. Let's hope he's shuffled off! Let's hope they all have.'

'*I* need a cup of tea,' Andrea said firmly. 'Come if you wish.' She walked the hundred metres or so to the café, turning at the door to see if he was following. But he was still in the car.

'I'd like just a cup of tea,' she said to the hovering waiter.

'Yes, madam. Nothing to eat? A sandwich?'

'No, thank you. Except—yes, I'd like some cake.' That's what she needed now. Cake, rich, sweet, buttery, probably with cream. Comfort food. For somewhere near her heart there was a hollow sensation that was crying out to be comforted. When Gerard joined her a few minutes later, she was wading through a splendid confection that, whether it was physically or spiritually comforting, was certainly making her feel better.

'Have some,' she said through a mouthful of chocolate and cream. 'It's delicious.'

'So what now?' Gerard said as they drove back to Cathy's place.

'Come in and talk to Cathy.'

'What about?'

'She's wise. She's experienced. And she's discreet. She'll have met many worse scenarios than this.'

'Poor Bella!' Cathy exclaimed when they had finished telling her the story.

'I was rather thinking "poor me",' said Gerard, who was uncharacteristically grumpy. Cathy leaned forward and patted his hand, smiling. 'Poor you, too! Oh, these family relationships—they tear you apart.'

'I feel...' He was searching for something that would adequately express the tumult he was so unexpectedly experiencing. 'I feel as if I never want to see her again. But I suppose that would be churlish. And cowardly.'

'No curiosity to see how it pans out?' Andrea watched his face. This was a mood she had not met.

'Not at present.' He stood restlessly and moved to the window, looking out and seeing nothing. 'At present I would like to go back six months and start again.' He caught the look on Andrea's face. 'I'm sorry, Andrea. That's how I feel just now. I wasn't a radiantly happy man, perhaps, but I was reasonably content with my lot. Now,' he shrugged, 'I don't know what I feel. What am I supposed to feel? Am I supposed to hold out my arms and cry "Mummy!" and make up to her for forty-five years of misery?'

'Of course not,' Cathy said sensibly. 'You'll have to work through it in your own way. There's no reason why you should have to take it another inch further if you don't want to. No one can make you.'

'I think I'll go home,' he said suddenly, going towards the door. 'I'm rotten company.' He turned to Andrea. 'I'll ring you—OK?

Thanks for the advice, Cathy.' And he was gone. Andrea watched him as he went down the garden path, heard him open the car door, start the engine, drive off. She sighed.

'I didn't think he'd take it this way. He always seems so calm, so controlled.'

'It's as well to see all sides of a person before you get too far in to get out.'

Andrea managed a smile. 'You see through me. Am I that obvious?' Cathy smiled. 'But you're great with the advice, Cathy. Thanks.'

'Been there, done that,' Cathy said ruefully. 'Tomorrow?'

'I might go and see Bella. Even if he doesn't. I don't like to think of her sitting there, worrying about what he thinks of her. Such a mess, Cathy. Should I have left it alone, do you think? Not bothered to find Claudia, or Bella. Or even Gerard?'

'Once you found Claudia the course was set for you.'

When she rang him later to say she had decided to see Bella, he agreed to go with her. His emotions were perhaps better under control. But at the last moment he rang to say he wouldn't be able to. He made it sound as if an important engagement had just come up, and Andrea, though really not wanting to go on her own, accepted his absence and was about to put the receiver down when he suddenly said, 'I just can't face her!'

His voice, tight and strained, surprised her. 'Well...' she began.

'You can't expect me to,' he said, as if she had argued the point. 'None of this...' He trailed off.

'Of course not. But she may want to see you.'

'I very much doubt that. You saw how she was with me. Hardly even looked at me.'

Andrea sighed. 'Gerard—she was shocked. You know she was. It must have been a huge shock, seeing you..'

'Well, it was a pretty bloody shock to me, too.' He was sounding quite belligerent.

'I'll go on my own. You have to remember what she said in the letter. She wasn't at all bitter about you.'

'I should hope not! *I* didn't get myself into her mess. I'd have been quite happy never to have found out...'

'Yes. Well, perhaps it would have been better.' Andrea's voice was cool; she was determined not to apologise for the chaos she had brought into his life. 'But it's happened—for both of us—and we've got to make the best of it.'

'Why?'

'Why what?'

'Why have we got to make the best of it?'

For a moment she was stumped.

'Because it's there!' she said, half amused, half irritated. 'We can't pretend, can we? It's a fact. Whether you like it or not, she is your mother. Claudia was mine. We didn't make the mess—but perhaps we can try to help clean it up.'

There was silence at his end of the line. Andrea waited. At last he said, 'You may be right. But I can't see her today.'

'I'll tell her you're busy.'

'Yes—right! I'll—I'll ring you later.'

The click of his replaced receiver sounded very final. Andrea put the phone down slowly. At what point, she was wondering, having set the whole business in motion, could she have stopped it? Should she have foreseen that he would take this attitude? He had seemed so unmoved, so calm. But obviously not. Well, she would go and see Bella, and after all it might be better that way, two women chatting, uninhibited by the presence of a man.

'He wasn't a happy chap,' she told Cathy. 'But I'm blowed if I'm going to take the blame. He *could* have said no.'

'Curiosity. It leads us into all kinds of complications.'

'So I'm going on my own.' She sounded as if someone was trying to stop her, and Cathy laughed.

'Of course you are!'

'Are you laughing at me?'

'Perish the thought! Have another cup.'

Bella was even stiffer and more reserved than in their first meetings. She stood aside for Andrea to go into the sitting room, shutting the front door with a sharp, annoyed click. Andrea bit her lip. She mustn't get fanciful. This was a woman who no doubt thoroughly resented the disturbance that Andrea and Gerard had brought into the life she had somehow managed to control. She must remember that.

'Thank you for seeing me again.' Andrea tried not to sound placating.

'You're on your own,' said Bella sharply. 'Where's—he?'

'Gerard wasn't able to come this morning. Something came up.'

'What came up?' This was a different woman, someone not prepared to lie down under stress. Andrea sensed the pain, the suppressed anger that had probably always been there but never had the opportunity to break out. 'He didn't want to see me?'

'He—it's been a bit of a shock for him.'

Bella gave a short, harsh laugh. 'A bit of a shock! Of course he wouldn't want to see me again. What sort of mother...?'

'It's not like that. Please! He needs time. But he is coming to see you, very soon. He—said,' she prevaricated, trying to soothe.

'He shouldn't.' Bella sighed suddenly and sat down. 'We should just...'

Andrea waited before saying, 'Should just—what?'

'Put it all behind us. Pretend it never happened. Any of it.'

'Could you?'

For the first time Bella looked directly into Andrea's eyes. 'No, I couldn't. What has happened—what happened all those years ago—the whole terrible mess...' She shook her head slowly. 'Of course I couldn't pretend it never happened. No one could.' She clasped her hands together. 'But I could let it go...for his sake.' There was pleading in the voice. 'None of it was his fault. There's no reason why he should have to suffer for it.'

Andrea was moved. She put out a hand and touched Bella's arm gently. Bella's reaction, hardly concealed, was again to withdraw, physically and emotionally. The eyes dropped, the arm shifted, the atmosphere, which had been growing minimally warmer, suddenly grew cool again. *She can't stand being touched,* Andrea thought. *Touching has always been a threat for her.*

'Do you have anyone, family, friends perhaps, you can talk to, Bella?'

Bella's harsh, grating laugh was answer enough. 'No!'

'No friends?'

'I keep myself to myself. I've never wanted to be close to people.' She turned her gaze briefly on Andrea. 'People have never been any help to me.'

'Not even Claudia?'

'Claudia did nothing for anyone unless she could see some value in it for her.'

Silence hung between them like a blanket. Andrea wondered how soon she could get up and leave. 'Gerard and I...' she began.

'Gerard and you,' Bella said, biting the words, 'are only interested in what affects you. Otherwise you would never have...'

'Oh, no!' Andrea protested. 'You make it sound...'

'So did you think coming to see me would give me a warm glow? Did you? Did you imagine me running towards my—my son and throwing my arms around him? Did you think it would be all hugs and kisses? Did you?' Anger was rising in her, anger that had never had a chance to become absorbed, that had lain silent like a lake of magma. *And now,* Andrea told herself, *now the volcano is ready to erupt. And I don't know what to do about it.*

'Oh, Bella,' she said, shaking her head helplessly. 'You're right. We shouldn't have tried to find you.' She picked up her handbag and shifted in her chair, ready to leave. Yet she knew it would be the wrong move. What would be the right one? How could she comfort this icy woman, reassure her that good could come out of what had always been a tragedy, prove to her that having a son could be, should be a pleasure, even at this late stage. *Gerard should have been here! He should have let her know that—that...That what? That he would care for her in her old age? Be a good son to make up for the lost years? Take her to concerts and barbecues and introduce her to his friends as 'my mother'? Get real, Andrea! It's not going to happen.* 'What can I do, Bella?'

Bella regarded her without speaking for a long moment. 'I was over it, you see,' she said finally, her voice dead. 'I'd come to terms with it, all of it, many years ago. I knew I never wanted another close friendship. My family were all dead. I could manage—somehow—by keeping myself to myself. I have little hobbies. I listen to the radio, sometimes watch the TV. I go shopping. Once a week I take myself out to lunch. Always at the same place. I don't want new experiences. I just want to run my life the way I always have since—since Claudia went. It may seem very stupid to someone else, but it suits me.' She stirred, glancing at her watch. 'I'll make a cup of tea, shall I?'

Andrea, unable to speak, nodded. While Bella was in the kitchen she stood and went to the window. The small garden was meticulously neat and tidy. The flowers stood up as if they knew what was expected of them. There was nothing there that would surprise. She suspected that flies, beetles, slaters, slugs, snail, caterpillars—all the denizens of the normal garden—would receive short shrift. At first glance the square of grass, the short stretch of crazy paving, the bird bath, all combined to make a pretty picture of what a garden should be. But there was a soullessness about it, a perfection that allowed nature no hand in the planning. She thought of Joseph's garden, its riot of colour, its constant need for pruning and weeding, and sighed.

Bella returned with a tray and put it down on the small table. 'Milk? Sugar?' She poured in silence; Andrea watched her with compassion.

Once they were settled again into what should have been a relaxed and companionable situation, but wasn't, Andrea said, 'Bella!' Those tormented eyes met hers warily, but she refused to be put off by the rejection she saw there. 'You're right. We came to see you for our own needs. Perhaps we shouldn't have done so. But when we rang you, that first time, you could have said you didn't want anything to do with us...'

'And you would have accepted that?' Bella's lips twitched as if she might be going to smile. 'You have a lot of your mother in you, Andrea.' It was the first time she had used her name, and Andrea was startled. 'Nothing would stop Claudia when she got her teeth into things. You inherited more than you knew.'

'Oh dear!' Andrea smiled briefly. 'Was there something about her that I would want to inherit, I wonder?'

'She was a hard worker. And honest, I think. Honest to herself. Knew what she wanted and went after it. And sometimes that meant that you got run over if you were standing in the way. But I think she was an honest person.'

'But not about the babies?'

Bella shot a quick glance at her. 'No. Not about them.'

'Did she know who—who was Gerard's father?'

Bella looked down at the floor. For a moment Andrea thought she had finally stepped over the line, that she had offended too deeply. But she was wrong.

'I think she guessed, but I never told her. She said one day, "Who's the boyfriend?" and I just shrugged. She never asked again.'

There was really nothing more to say. Bella would never descend to the level of a cosy chat. Andrea stood and gathered her bag and scarf. 'Will you be all right?'

'I should think so. I've managed on my own all my life.' There was a spark of sarcasm, which Andrea found encouraging.

'Can I come again?'

'Do you want to?' She sounded as if it would hardly be likely.

'Yes. And I want to bring Gerard. He needs to come to terms, too.'

Bella was silent for a moment. 'Ring me first. I don't like surprises.'

'Of course.'

Neither of them could find the words to bring an uncomfortable silence to an end. Andrea held out her hand and Bella let it touch hers before leading the way to the front door. As the door shut behind her Andrea let out a long breath of relief and frustration. On the other side of the door, Bella was doing the same.

Once she was alone, Bella moved slowly across the sitting room to the spotless, dustless mirror above the empty fireplace. In it she could see her face, controlled, expressionless, the neat collar of her blouse, pearl buttons on the pale mauve cardigan she had taken a full month to create, for it must be perfect. No 'purl' where there should be 'knit'; no left-handed cable in a row of right-handed cables. If it were not perfect she knew she would never wear it.

She could see part of the room, too. Everything in its place, everything as neat and controlled as she needed it to be—except for the cushion Andrea had been leaning on. Bella picked it up and plumped it, putting it carefully where it had always been—who else ever sat in these carefully placed chairs? She looked around her. Only the tea-try spoilt the museum-like precision.

She sat herself down, slowly, and stared into a torment of confusion. Perhaps she could arrange never to see Andrea again? She surely had the right to refuse entry. But that meant...

Gerard's face swam through the swirling mists. That meant never seeing *him* again. She thought about that. After all, for more than forty years she had managed without him, had actually managed to forget him—almost. Now, as if she had been hit by a tsunami, she was floundering, gasping for breath, looking for the piece of flotsam that she could hang on to, that would make sense of all this turmoil.

'Gerard!' she whispered. 'Gerard—my son!' Then aloud, passionately, so that her voice rang across the room (for who would hear her?), '*Gerard—my son!*'

And then she wept.

16

Gerard rang. Andrea, not sure whether to be pleased or annoyed with him, was less than effusive. After a few moments he said, 'OK, I was wrong. I should have come with you. I funked it. Sorry! Does that make you feel better?'

'Should I?' She gave a half laugh. 'It's your problem, not mine.'

He was silent. Then, 'OK, what happened?'

'I think she was sorry you weren't there. But it meant we could talk a bit more freely. She started to say we should put it behind us...'

'And?'

'I said, would she be able to? And she said no, she didn't think so. There's a lot of bitterness there. A lot of old anger. She asked if we thought it would be all hugs and kisses. I said no. Then she said she had been over it for years. Just wanted to keep herself to herself. Doesn't want people—they've never been any use to her.' Andrea paused. 'I wish there *was* something we could do for her. But the damage is too deep set. It's been there too long. We might be making it worse.' She remembered something Bella had said, and smiled. 'She told me I had a lot of my mother in me! Not the most flattering thing she could have said, really.'

'Are you going to see her again?'

'I think so. Yes, of course I am. I can't leave it there, can I?'

Gerard hesitated. 'Tomorrow? Shall I come?'

She was surprised. 'Are you sure?'

'If it's convenient. Would she see us?'

'I think she would like to see you, deep down. Do you want me to ring her?'

'I have to do it, don't I?' he said, clearly unwilling. 'There's no way I can act as if I'm her son, that she's my mother. It would be ludicrous to play-act. But I think I should see her again, perhaps just once. Try to end it all gracefully. What do you think?' He sounded nervous.

'I think you're right. I'll ask if we can come, and let her know that if she doesn't want to see us again we'll leave it there.'

'Yes. Yes, OK. Look, Andrea—I'm really sorry...'

'For goodness sake!' she said with more asperity than she intended. 'It's been a weird time for both of us. Let it go, Gerard! I'll ring her, we'll go and see her again if she'll let us, and then— then we'll decide what has to be done.' She sighed. 'I should never have...'

He interrupted her swiftly. 'Don't blame yourself. You had every right...'

'Yes, I suppose so. We couldn't have imagined the way it would go.'

'And...and I'm glad you did, really. We would never have met...'

'No, that's true.'

'And I'm really pleased...' He stopped, as if he felt he had said too much. *He sounds like a boy with his first girl-friend,* she thought, tempted to giggle.

'Me too. I'll ring you later.' She put the phone down and stood for a moment, her hand resting on it. Then she went into the kitchen, Cathy's kitchen that now felt like home, and put the kettle on.

'Do one for me!' Cathy called from her room. 'How was he?'

Andrea moved slowly until she could see across the narrow hallway. 'He's glad we met,' she said, keeping her voice flat.

Cathy glanced up from her work, raising her eyebrows comically. 'Oh-ho!' she said meaningfully.

'Oh-ho to you!' Andrea grinned suddenly. 'He was very apologetic. We're going to try Bella again tomorrow.' The grin disappeared. 'I'm worried about her, Cathy. So much baggage from the past. And I don't think there's anything we can do about it.'

'You mustn't try. If anyone can help her it won't be you or Gerard. You're too close to it.'

'What, then? Psychologist?'

'Some kind of counselling. Someone who can see the problems from the outside.' She regarded Andrea thoughtfully. 'Sometimes there are things we can do nothing about, Andrea. The wise thing is to recognise the fact.'

'But if we hadn't—if I hadn't...'

'If life was always different from what we want! If you and Gerard had never been born, if Claudia had been a nicer person, if she hadn't killed her husband, if, if, if! We're not God, my dear. We can't see into the future.'

Andrea leaned against the doorpost. 'And for so many of us who are adopted,' she said quietly, 'we can't see into the past, either.'

'Well, you can now,' said Cathy crisply. 'Are you pleased or sorry?'

Andrea pondered, her eyes on Cathy's face. 'On balance, pleased. As long as we haven't damaged her too much.'

'And Gerard?'

'Ah, yes. He's different. But I think—I think in the long run he'll be pleased.'

Cathy gave a wicked smile. 'I'm darned sure he will!'

The kettle whistled. 'What *do* you mean by that?' Andrea detached herself from the doorpost, suddenly feeling much better. 'Tea or coffee?'

She saw the car draw up, but Gerard didn't get out. She could see him, his eyes turned down as if he was deep in thought, or perhaps nervous of meeting her again. When she opened the passenger door and bent to look in he turned and regarded her with a whimsical expression.

'I don't know whether I'm mad or what. Should we be going? You saw her...'

'Good morning, Gerard,' she said pointedly. He gave the sudden grin that she found appealing, that she could imagine him using as a small boy to get out of small boy crises.

'Hi! Sorry.' He switched on the ignition. 'Come on, then. Let's get it over.'

With the car in motion, turning into the main street, she leaned back and regarded him. 'I don't think that's the right attitude.'

'Probably not. I don't know what the right attitude is. "Hello, Mummy!" Or, "Good morning, Miss Carding". What do you reckon?' She saw him glance at her swiftly.

'Feel her pain.'

'Ah, yes. But, you see, I can't. I can only feel my own confusion. I don't like the thought of how I was conceived. I find it very—well, if I'm honest, I find it disgusting. If we are the genetic offspring of those who created us, then what am I? The product of an evil man and a young, frightened girl. At least your Claudia was a strong-minded, sane woman.'

'Strong-minded, yes. I'm not sure about sane.' She turned towards him. 'Gerard—we're both the products of unfortunate situation. But we are ourselves. We can be what we want to be. We may bear the genetic traces of our parents, but we are unique. Aren't we? Gerard and Andrea, unique! Whatever was bequeathed to us, we are free to make whatever we want of it. Don't you think so? Don't you?'

He didn't answer, and she wondered if he was annoyed. Then he said, his voice slightly gruff, 'You're quite a remarkable woman, you know. You see things clearly.'

She was surprised. 'Well...thank you, Gerard. That's very flattering.'

'I don't flatter. It's what I think. I feel as if I'm wandering in fog. You seem to have come to terms.'

'Because there doesn't seem to be any alternative.'

'That's what I mean. I can see so many alternatives that I'm giddy.'

They fell silent for a long moment. 'Just now,' Andrea began, 'the immediate problem is what we're going to say to Bella. I was very worried about her yesterday. I've never met anyone with such a depth of despair in her soul.'

'I've never considered,' Gerard said, seemingly struggling with the concept, 'the state of anyone's soul. Not even mine.'

'Then it's high time you started,' she said quickly, not wanting at this particular time to get involved in spiritual matters. 'You'd better let me speak to her first. She may be getting used to me.'

The road leading to Bella's was unusually congested. They pulled into the first empty parking space they saw and stood for a moment as one does when there is a problem to be faced. Gerard regarded Andrea across the top of the car. He raised his eyebrows, silently asking if she was ready for whatever might be the outcome. She nodded, then put a hand to her mouth. 'I was supposed to ring her. I promised!'

Gerard shrugged. 'We're here now. I could get her on my mobile. What's the number?'

Andrea felt in her handbag for her notebook, in which she had collected all the small details of this strange quest. She gave him the number and watched his face as he called it, not expecting the sudden change of expression.

'Yes,' he was saying. 'I want to speak to Miss Carding. No, we're friends...'We're just at the end of the road. She was expecting us to call...'

'What?' Andrea asked.

'I don't know. It was a man. He says she's not available.'

'A man? How odd! Has something happened?'

'We'd better go and see. He wasn't going to say anything on the phone, obviously.'

The reason for the congestion became clear as they rounded the bend, and without thinking they broke into a run. There was a police car, and an ambulance, and the usual knot of neighbours looking for excitement. Andrea pushed through them and was brought to a halt by a policeman.

'No, we're not family.' She was careful not to meet Gerard's eye. 'We've recently met her, and she was expecting to see us this morning. I saw her yesterday.'

'Sorry.' The officer was polite but firm. 'No one can see Miss Carding.' He turned away.

'Is she...?' Andrea began cautiously, just as two ambulance men emerged from the front door with a trolley—on it a small figure lying still and very pale. 'Oh, no!' Andrea whispered, taking Gerard's arm.

'She's alive,' he said. 'They've got her on oxygen.'

'Thank God! Can't we find out what happened? Someone would tell us, surely.'

But they would have to go to the hospital. No one at the scene was prepared to talk, and they watched as the ambulance pulled out and moved off into the traffic and the neighbours dispersed, chatting among themselves. Andrea caught the sleeve of an elderly woman.

'We're friends of Miss Carding. Do you know what's happened?'

The woman regarded her without interest. 'Didn't know she had any friends. Stuck up old woman, she was. Never spoke to anyone.'

'But what happened?'

She shrugged. 'Dunno! Heart attack? Or suicide, maybe.' The thought seemed to cheer her slightly.

'Who told the police?'

'She was lying on the front doorstep. That's what I was told. The postie saw her.' She walked away. 'People should be neighbourly, that's what I say. Then this kind of thing wouldn't happen.' Andrea let her go. She turned to Gerard, who was standing next to the policeman.

'Where are they taking her?'

'St Jude's. Come on. Perhaps they'll tell us.'

The woman at the reception desk was as careful with information as such people always are. This is a consolation, Andrea was thinking, when it's your own information they are withholding, but really annoying when you want to get hold of someone else's.

'No,' she said again. 'We're friends. But I think you will find that Miss Carding has no family—and she was expecting to see us this morning.'

'I'm sorry. When she is conscious we will ask Miss Carding if she wants to see you. Until then...' the woman shrugged with a kind smile. 'And I have no idea when that will be,' she said, forestalling Andrea's next question. 'Perhaps if you were to ring this evening...?'

They walked slowly down the hospital steps. Neither spoke until they were in the car. 'I feel guilty,' Andrea said at last. 'Do you think I should?'

'No!' Gerard was quite vehement. 'We haven't done anything wrong. We may have been misguided—and perhaps it would have a good thing if none of this...'

'Oh, I know.' She sounded weary. 'Don't say it again. If I could go back to the beginning...'

'What would you do?' he said curiously, looking at her.

She thought for a moment. 'The same, I think. Because I really did want to find out where I came from. And once I'd started the ball rolling, I suppose it would have been just the same—finding Claudia, knowing what she said, everything!' She glanced at him. 'And finding you.'

He didn't reply at once. 'Would it have mattered,' he said at last in a subdued voice, 'if you hadn't found me?'

It's so difficult to break through the conventions. Why can't I just say yes?

'It would have mattered,' she said quietly, avoiding his eye. 'I enjoy being with you. We get on well.'

'Too well to be siblings.' There was a suspicion of laughter in his voice. She smiled quickly.

'Yes! Just as well, I think. Though you would have been a rather nice brother.'

He touched her hand briefly, then started the car. 'Well, we'll try again this evening. Let's hope she's conscious by then. Come on—King's Park. It's all been a bit of a shock. We need a stimulant.'

'We're both a bit worried, Mum. I'm just hoping it wasn't a suicide attempt.'

'Oh, that would be dreadful, dear.'

'She was very strange when I saw her yesterday. I should have thought—I should have expected...'

'Why should you, Andrea? It's not something you would think of.'

'But perhaps I should have.'

'Andrea—your father has suggested that we should come over...just for a few days.'

'Oh, Mum!'

'But I'm not sure...'

'Please, Mum—no! Not just yet. It would be...'

'That's what I told him. We'd just be in the way.'

'I don't want to hurt your feelings...'

'You're not, I told him it wasn't a good idea. Look, I have to go now. Ring me when you know about Miss Carding. See you, darling.'

'So now I *do* feel guilty,' Andrea said to Cathy. 'I should have said yes, come as soon as you like. But I didn't. I just hope I haven't hurt them. She said not, but...'

'Stop carrying the problems of the world, Andrea. Your parents understand. And even if they didn't, you have things to do that you can't just let go of now. Right?'

But she felt restless, crushed under the load of other people's woes. 'What if Bella...?'

Cathy gave her a little push. 'Go and put that kettle on! Enough what-ifs for one day. Where's Gerard? Is *he* carrying the world on his shoulders?'

Andrea managed a grin. 'Poor Gerard! He's still shaken up over the manner of his conception.' She wandered into the kitchen. 'More tea?'

'Poor thing indeed! Yes—bickies in the green tin. I'll have two.'

Andrea put her head around the door, regarding this new friend with affection. 'I honestly don't know what I'd have done without you, Cathy. I'd have been lost at sea.'

'My pleasure, chook! I'm hanging in for the happy ending.'

'As one does! I'll see what I can do about it.'

In the kitchen she suddenly felt like crying. *So many unhappy things for so many people—and I never knew until now.* She wondered what Gerard was doing. Moping? Having one drink too many to try to forget his ancestry? Visiting friends? It suddenly occurred to her that she knew nothing about him except what he had grudgingly revealed. What were his friends like? You could tell a lot about a man if you knew his friends. Did he have any? She smiled ruefully. What was it to do with her, anyway? When this—this *situation* was over and done with she could go back home, home to her real parents, to Bethany and Daniel, to playing in the orchestra, to going to the beach, to her favourite restaurant, to *her* friends. And probably, more than probably, she would say goodbye to Gerard and never see him again.

I'd send him a Christmas card, she thought facetiously. A birthday card for sure—because I shall never forget his birthday! And that will probably be for the best. She lifted the kettle. *And I don't want to say goodbye to him. I really don't want to!*

'Where's that cuppa?' Cathy called.

Andrea poured the tea. It would work itself out. It had to.

17

'M iss Carding has said she will see you,' the reception nurse said. 'But keep it short. She's very tired.'

'What happened?' Andrea asked.

'Doctor will see you if you want to ask. I can make an appointment for you...'

'Later,' Gerard said, taking Andrea's arm. 'Where is Miss Carding?'

They walked in silence down a long corridor. On the walls were prints of famous paintings. The carpet was inoffensive grey with a pale blue stripe. All was light and airy, and the rooms they passed were full of quiet, neatly bedded patients. *Every one of them a trauma*, Andrea was thinking, *Every room holding its own little drama.* She realised she was dreading seeing Bella.

It was Claudia all over again. A small body in a white bed, only her head and hands visible. Bella was staring up at the ceiling, absolutely still, only a slight twitching in her thin white fingers showing signs of life. Andrea stood for a moment, wishing to be anywhere but there. Then Bella, aware of movement, turned her head slowly and let her eyes rest briefly, first on Andrea and then, for a moment longer, seemed to be searching beyond her. Andrea went to the foot of the bed.

'Hullo, Bella.' The tired eyes slid away from Andrea's face and closed. 'We wanted to see you. To make sure you were all right.'

Bella opened her eyes again, and for a tiny moment there was a flicker of emotion in them, though whether it was amusement or annoyance would be hard to decide. 'I'm all right,' she said in a voice drained of strength and feeling. 'I'm all right—you don't have to worry about me.'

'But we are worried.' She pulled a chair forward and sat. 'What happened, Bella? Can you tell us?'

One hand moved briefly, dismissively. 'Not important.'

Gerard moved into the room. Like many men, he felt out of place in a hospital, and he wore a wary look. When Bella looked up and saw him, a faint flush coloured the pale cheeks. He nodded. 'Bella.'

'You shouldn't have come,' she said in that breathy voice. 'I'm all right.'

'What was it?' he asked. Andrea could sense the discomfort that made him sound brusque. But the tiny change of tempo, the abruptness of the question, seemed to bring Bella out of the dream world of her distress. She lifted her head a fraction so that she could see him better.

'Do you need to ask?' She was querulous, but there was greater strength in the reply. 'There are times, aren't there, when it's not worth going on.'

'Not a heart attack, then?'

She almost smiled. 'No, not a heart attack.'

He was staring down at her. 'What did you take?'

Bella regarded him as if seeing him for the first time and finding something about him interesting. 'Too many sleeping tablets,' she said at last. 'But not enough.'

'You were on the front doorstep,' Andrea said hesitantly.

'So they tell me. Perhaps I was regretting...it's the coward's way out, isn't it?'

'Sometimes it's very courageous,' Andrea hazarded. 'It depends on so much. Who, and why?' She turned towards Gerard without looking at him. 'Was it because we were coming to see you?'

'You needn't take this on you. I made the decision. My choice.'

Gerard was still staring down at her. 'Why?'

Bella's eye closed for a moment. Andrea put out a hand to Gerard. 'We shouldn't...'

But Gerard, his face stern, ignored her. 'Was it deliberate? Or just panic? Tell us.'

Bella looked at him with greater interest, tired eyes momentarily showing liveliness. 'Have you ever,' she asked in the voice of the very sick, 'come to the end of a road—and known there was nothing beyond?'

He shook his head. 'No.'

'You've been lucky, then. I came there last night...' The voice trailed off and her eyes closed once more. 'Very lucky...'

On an impulse Andrea said, 'But you've got us now.'

The pale lips twitched in the beginnings of a smile, but she was clearly losing strength. 'Have I? I wonder...'

A nurse appeared. Andrea said, 'Yes, we're going.' She put out a hand and touched Bella on the cheek. 'We'll be back.'

They sat at a table in the hospital café, the inevitable cups of coffee before them. Andrea felt the whole overwhelming business could probably be evaluated in the number of cups of tea and coffee they had drunk. She had been unable to face Gerard since they left the ward. Now she looked up at him.

'Weren't you a bit hard on her?'

He shrugged. 'Invalids can be tricky. Sometimes being direct is the best way.'

'Experience?'

'Yeah. My mother, a little before she died. Had me and Dad by the tail. Don't suppose she meant to, but being so sick...'

'What was it?'

'Cancer. In the bowel. Not recommended. She suffered.'

'Tell me about them—your parents. Do you realise I know almost nothing about you?'

She saw mild amusement in his face. 'That must be a great loss.' He put his cup down carefully. 'She died about ten years ago. Very nastily. She tried to be patient, but it got too much for her.'

'You said she had you and your father by the tail. How?'

'When you're lying in bed and everyone, including you, knows that it's a death sentence, I suppose you can go one of two ways. Your Claudia, tough and unbending, or my mother, complaining and keeping everyone on the run.'

Andrea pulled a face at 'your'. 'So both died of cancer. Not so much of a coincidence these days, I suppose. And how did your father cope?'

'He actually surprised me,' Gerard confessed. 'He was very gentle with her—and I have to say he hadn't always been. Nothing dreadful—just a bit impatient. He had the idea that women were inferior beings who needed to be organised and controlled.'

'What did your mother think about that?'

'Well—I think perhaps she didn't mind. She wasn't a very dynamic person really. A nice cuddly mum when I was little, but she never quite grew up with me. Do you know what I mean?' He glanced at her as if he felt he had said too much. But Andrea leaned forward.

'Did you love her—them?'

There was a long pause. 'As much as I was capable of,' he said at last. 'I think—I hope—that those last months were as good for her as we could make them.' He looked towards the counter. 'I'd like another cup. How about you?' Andrea nodded.

When he came back she said, 'So you learnt how to deal with a fractious invalid?'

'Yes. One day, when she had had everyone running about and feeling sorry for her I said that that was enough. And she looked up at me and I think she saw that I meant it. I wanted to say I was sorry, but I didn't. And for some reason she perked up quite a bit and started to take charge of herself again.' He shrugged again. 'I don't suppose it would always work. Just did that time.'

'It worked with Bella.' She watched him over her cup. 'What do you think we ought to do about her?'

He shook his head slowly. 'I've no idea. We've stirred up a wasps' nest, and now we've got to wait for the buzzing to stop.' He put his cup down carefully. 'We can't just disappear now, I suppose. That wouldn't be fair. So what's the next move?'

'I don't know. Wait and see how she gets on? They'll probably let her go home soon.'

'And then...?'

'No idea.' She grinned suddenly. 'Another fine mess I got us into!' Gerard looked puzzled. 'Laurel and Hardy. Joseph loved them.' The smile died. 'I haven't thought about him all day.'

'Is that good?'

'I suppose it's inevitable. Eventually. One can't mourn for ever.'

'Do you want to talk about him?'

'Not now. One day, perhaps, when all this is over.'

Cathy's attitude was that they had done everything that could be expected of them. Andrea disagreed with her, wondering as she did so why that was advice she felt she couldn't take. Gerard would probably have agreed without hesitation. Then she found herself wondering about that and decided to take the evening off and go to a concert. Cathy thought it was a good idea.

'Would you come with me?' Andrea said. 'Do you enjoy that kind of music?'

'I'd love to. I'm culturally starved at the moment.'

So they went, and without knowing what they were booking for they found themselves in the back half of the concert hall, waiting for—of course—Sir Kenneth himself to come on to the platform. 'I didn't realise...' Andrea whispered.

Cathy gave a small and wicked smile. 'Of course you didn't! Well, I've never seen him in action, so this will be part of my musical education. What's first?'

'Mozart—a symphony, I think.' (They had saved money by not buying a programme.) 'Then a violin concerto...'

She had hardly realised how much she had missed live music since she had begun her quest. The well-remembered sensations surrounded her, knowing what was happening in a work she knew well, and yet finding it renewed in someone else's hands. She watched the conductor, thankful that she need no longer wonder if they shared genes and a distant history. He was impressive on the podium, tall and elegant, strongly built but with a grace in his movements that brought out the lyrical best in the music and the players. Thankfully there was nothing about him that could cause her any kind of distress, however mild. He was a stranger, a man she had met in a bizarre situation, someone she could look up to for his musicianship and yet never need meet again. She settled back in her seat, prepared to enjoy the evening.

18

Bella, back in her own home, seemed somehow changed, stronger perhaps. Andrea, expecting to find a wilting violet, saw that something had been released in the normally withdrawn woman. She wondered why.

'You're feeling better?'

Bella raised her eyes briefly. 'I told you—you don't need to worry about me. I shall be all right.'

'We upset you,' Andrea said remorsefully. 'It would probably have been better if we hadn't been able to find you.'

'Perhaps. Perhaps not.' She hesitated. 'It has been a shock to meet—Gerard.' Still the difficulty in saying his name. 'But I'm getting used to it now.'

'He's a nice man.' She was curious to know how Bella felt about her son. But Bella didn't answer at once.

'He seems—very pleasant.'

'Does it feel as if he's yours?' Andrea asked daringly.

'I don't know how that should feel. Do you mean, do I love him? Because I'm not very good at love.'

'Oh, that's sad!' Andrea thought of Bethany and Daniel, of her parents—of Joseph. 'It's so necessary to love someone.'

'Is it?' Bella raised her eyebrows. 'I wouldn't know.'

'But surely...'

'I was brought up in a household full of anger and hate. My closest friend was Claudia—well, you've seen her. Love wasn't her strong point. I've lived on my own, keeping myself to myself for many, many years. I see few people. I know few people. I really don't want people.'

'And then Gerard and I blew in!' Andrea shook her head, but she smiled at Bella and was thankful to see the flicker of a smile in return. 'Would you let us make up for lost time? I know Gerard...'

'Don't answer for Gerard!' Bella said quite sharply. 'But—if you wish, I would be pleased to see you again. Gerard must make up his own mind. I won't be beholden to him.'

For a while they were silent and avoided eye contact. Then Bella said, almost shyly, 'I'm grateful to you for showing concern, you know. Just not good at— revealing myself. Out of practice.'

On an impulse, out of her mouth before she had fully thought it through, Andrea said, 'How would you like a couple of days holiday, Bella?'

The silence that this was received in almost made her laugh nervously. Bella sat as if turned to stone, her eyes fixed on some unseen distance where Andrea could not follow. 'Holiday?' she said, as if the word were from some obscure foreign language.

'It was just an idea.' Andrea was wondering what on earth had possessed her to make such a suggestion. 'Just a thought, Bella. I thought you might...'

Slowly, Bella turned her head and stared at Andrea. 'Why?'

'It might do you good. A few days away.'

'A holiday? Where?' The blank stare became a frown. 'Where would I go?'

Andrea took a deep breath. 'I thought we might go somewhere together. Not too far. Just—just wherever you like.'

'You are a very strange person,' Bella said at last. 'What is it you want with me?'

'Nothing,' Andrea said hastily. 'Really—nothing. I just wondered if it would be a good idea—you've had a bad time recently.' She stopped. Bella was regarding her with what almost seemed suspicion. 'I thought it might help...' She tailed off.

Bella's expression was unreadable. 'What on earth would I do on holiday?' She glanced around the room. 'Everything I need is here.'

'Only for a day or two.'

As if she were talking to herself, Bella said, 'I've never been on holiday.'

Andrea opened her mouth to speak, then closed it again. This was something beyond what she had expected. After a moment she said, 'You must have. At some time, Surely?'

Bella dabbed at her lips with her handkerchief. 'You know how old Gerard is. Well, that makes me well past sixty now. But young to have a son of his age. And you know why! Holidays weren't part of our lifestyle, I suppose you'd call it. Everyone was too busy hating everyone else. And when I got to know Claudia—well, holidays weren't on the agenda. Then she—went away. And I had to find a way to live without her, without my son, without anybody. And I did it! I found work, I supported myself. If I was lucky I had two cents left at the end of the week. You don't pay for holidays out of two cents.'

She clasped her hands together and stared at them, moving them backwards and forwards as if she wanted to get to know them. 'But I never wanted a holiday. I didn't want to get involved with people. It would have been no fun on my own. You don't miss what you never have.' She lifted her eyes slowly to Andrea's. 'I probably haven't been out of the city in twenty years. You can't understand that, can you? Everyone's on the move these days. You can't open a paper or a magazine without seeing advertisements for holidays. Spend, spend, spend!' She sighed, unclasping her hands.

'I didn't mean to upset you, Bella.'

'Oh, I don't think you've done that. I just don't understand what you're after.'

Andrea took a deep breath. She felt she was losing control of the situation. 'I'm not after anything. Believe me. It was just a suggestion. Think it over.' She stood up. 'I'll let you get used to the idea.' She gave a quick grin, which Bella did not return. 'I'll be in touch.'

Once outside the front door she let out a great sigh— frustration, annoyance with herself, everything! But at least Bella hadn't taken her up on the offer. She couldn't quite imagine going on holiday with that uptight, austere creature. For a moment she was no longer sorry for her. *She brings it on herself,* she muttered. *It really isn't my fault.* She closed the garden gate behind her with a sense of relief. At least she'd tried.

'You did what?' Cathy said when Andrea told her of the offer refused. 'You did *what?*' The look on her face was comical.

'It seemed right at the time.'

And, 'You did what?' said Gerard when she told him later that day. 'What on earth...?'

Andrea was cross with both of them. It seemed as if she was to blame for having Bella's interests at heart. 'I don't see why not. I still think it would be a good idea. But she said no. Very definitely, no!'

'Thank goodness for that.' Gerard started walking again. They were in their favourite spot, in the gardens of King's Park, where they could see the river now and then through a break in the foliage. It was a beautiful day, just the sort of day for a holiday.

'Why is it such a bad idea?' she demanded, hurrying to keep up.

He didn't answer at first. When she asked again, he said, 'Because, in spite of everything, she is not our problem.'

'Do you think we could sit down?' They were approaching a bench and she sank down gratefully.

Gerard remained standing, staring out to where a ferry was just visible crossing to the far side of the water. Andrea collected herself. When she felt more composed she said gently, 'Whose problem is she?'

He turned to face her. 'No—not mine, either. Sorry, Andrea—I'm not a hearts and flowers man. I don't know why all this has happened, but none of it is my fault.'

'Nobody says it is. Why does it have to be anyone's fault, anyway? It's just life. Odd things happen.'

'We don't have to accept them, surely?'

'Once something happens—it's happened,' she said obscurely. 'You can't change the facts.'

Andrea regretted the silent struggle now taking place between them; she didn't want to fall out with Gerard. Their meetings had grown to be a needed part of her life, of her daily activity. More than that she was not yet ready to admit. But a row, even a silent one, was not what she wanted.

Because she felt mildly hurt by the attitudes of these people she had grown to like so much, even Bella, her stubborn side emerged. *What on earth*, she said to herself, *is wrong with going on holiday, even with Bella? If I want to...I'll...'*

'What are you muttering about?' Gerard said. She looked up defiantly; he was smiling.

'Nothing,' she said with dignity, 'that you need worry about.'

He regarded her for a moment, then nodded slowly. 'So where are you thinking of taking her?'

First she was annoyed; then she saw the funny side and laughed. 'Have you taken up mind-reading in your spare time?'

They wandered together towards the end of the path and leaned on a stone wall to admire the view over the gleaming water. 'It's so beautiful,' she murmured. 'I think that's what I want for Bella—she's had such a rotten deal. I want her to see something beautiful, and know that it *is* beautiful. There's nothing wrong in that, is there?'

'No, there's nothing wrong with that, Andrea. It's a kind idea. Do you think it will work?'

She stared at the ferry as it made its slow way from shore to shore, leaving behind it a slowly disappearing wash. 'I have no idea. I just know that if I don't do it I shall always wonder.'

But Bella was withdrawn when Andrea saw her next. The subject of holidays hardly seemed appropriate when she was clearly not in the mood. They drank the inevitable cup of tea together, and then Andrea stood up to leave.

'I'm sorry!' Bella said suddenly. 'I'm a big disappointment to you. I've forgotten how to be grateful, even gracious, I think.'

'No, you've had too much on your plate.'

'You're being kind again.' Bella faced her. 'You offered me something I couldn't comprehend—friendship and thoughtfulness. I've been rejecting life for so long that I find it difficult—really difficult... Can you understand?'

Andrea held out her hands to her impulsively, and after a long moment Bella's hand crept out of hiding and she allowed Andrea to touch it. 'You see,' she whispered, 'I never touch anyone. I'd forgotten how to. Touching, for me, has been a threatening thing.'

'You'll get used to it,' Andrea said gently, 'if you let yourself.'

'And if I do, and then I'm let down again...what shall I do then?' She was looking, perhaps for the first time, straight into Andrea's eyes, and pleading and grief and wonder were all there in her expression. For a moment Andrea felt panic; how should she deal with this damaged soul?

'Bella—let's have that holiday. Just a couple of days away so that we can see things from a distance. It sometimes helps. It puts things into perspective.'

Bella removed her hand from Andrea's and turned away. 'I can see it might help. But the idea scares me. I wouldn't know how to...'

'You don't need to know. I'll arrange everything. I'll find suitable accommodation and let you know when I've fixed it.'

'You're very competent, aren't you? You know how to do things.'

'So?' said Andrea, smiling.

Bella sat down suddenly as if her legs had failed. There was a long silence, and Andrea let it go on without interruption. At last came a sigh, a long, fading breath that gave the answer without words. She nodded once, then looked searchingly at Andrea. 'If you're sure. If you really mean it. If you think I can...'

'You know,' Andrea said cheerfully, 'you've shown great courage all your life. You've withdrawn from people, but you've kept everything going.' She waved her hand around to indicate the house, the garden, Bella's whole way of living. 'You could have finished it all when you were young, or when you saw yourself getting older. You could have allowed yourself to lower your standards—and you haven't. The house is a credit to you.'

Bella stared around her, clearly surprised by this analysis of something she had known so long that she had barely regarded it—perhaps for years. 'Is that how it seems to you? How odd!' Bella murmured as if she hardly wanted to be heard. 'To me, everything seems...' She hesitated. 'Dead.' She finished flatly, unemotionally.

'It needs life,' Andrea said. 'People. Activity.'

This was met with a dry smile. 'I think it may have to wait.'

Good! Andrea said to herself. *She does have a sense of humour somewhere, unused. Now we have to get it out into the open.*

In the kitchen, Bella was no doubt struggling with these new concepts. The tea-cups rattled, and there was a sudden gush of water. She was washing up. Andrea moved cautiously into this room she had not been allowed to penetrate. 'Can I help?'

But they had not yet reached that level of mutual understanding. Bella turned, confused. 'No—no, I'll only be a minute.'

Andrea returned to the sitting room. *Don't hurry things,* she told herself. *We're getting somewhere.*

'So what happened?' Cathy asked, wiping her hands. Andrea put the tea towel away—thankfully, she was allowed into this kitchen.

'We're going away for a couple of days. She agreed, very cautiously. You'd have thought I was going to...'

Cathy looked at her, smiling. 'Going to—what?'

'Attack her with a chopper! The whole idea of a holiday seems to give her palpitations. I just hope nothing goes wrong. She'd never see me again. And by the way—this is where you come in.' Cathy's eyebrows went up. 'Where on earth am I going to take her? Do you know any cosy little B&B that wouldn't completely freak her out?'

Cathy laughed. 'As it happens, I do.'

19

'The sea!' Andrea exclaimed. She drew the car to a halt so that Bella could see the wide, rolling ocean, take in the sight of seagulls swooping and diving, comment perhaps on the waves crashing below them. Anything! They had driven from Perth in almost complete silence—except when Andrea felt it absolutely imperative that something should be said. But Bella sat as if turned to stone; the bush, the birds, the flowers by the wayside—nothing seemed to register with her. Andrea sighed and restarted the car, and they drove sedately down a winding driveway to a cottage surrounded by dunes covered in aromatic plants. It was one of the things that Andrea particularly loved: the dune country where the sandy hills crouched under this wide-spreading blanket of perfumed growth.

'It's mine,' Cathy had said. 'I go when I can. Just take a few bits of food with you. Everything else is there already.'

It was the right kind of day to arrive at the coast. The sky was blue, the birds were singing (or in the case of a few galahs and a seagull or two, screeching). It was a day for bees in blossom, for a picnic on the empty beach, for children to romp through the dunes and for parents to call out, 'Just watch out for snakes!'

It was a day for Bella to see what the world outside her neat home contained. But judging by the look on her face she was having real difficulty in coming to terms with the change in her environment. Andrea watched her for a moment, then opened the boot and started to remove the cases.

'Could you give me a hand?' Bella turned to stare at her. 'Just take your own bag.'

'Where are we?'

'We're a few miles south of Margaret River,' Andrea said patiently. She handed Bella's bag to her and began to walk up the short path that led to a timber cottage. 'Here we are!' Bella began to follow her, very slowly as if she were being pulled against her will. *How on earth*, Andrea was asking herself, *am I ever going to get her going?*

Inside, it was cool and comfortable. The two bedrooms were attractive, the bathroom clean and ready for use with soft towels. The central sitting room was colourful without being overwhelming; she sank down on to one of the chairs and looked around her. Bella was standing by the door, bag in hand, on her face the same blank stare that had been there since they left Perth. Andrea patted the chair beside her.

'Come and sit down. This looks nice, doesn't it?'

Slowly, so slowly, Bella moved forward and came to the chair. She sat on the edge as if she needed to be ready for flight. Andrea could think of nothing more to say. She had hoped that the move away from everything that Bella recognised would break the spell; that this silent, troubled woman would open up, begin to talk, perhaps even learn how to chat. Sadly, it looked as if the damage was too deep, too intense, to be healed in a magic moment. Perhaps never. Perhaps they would sit here for two days, silent, uncomfortable, achieving nothing. Perhaps everyone had been right, Cathy, Gerard, even her mother. She should have left well alone.

For a moment she thought she might ring Gerard and tell him that he had been right all along. But pride got in the way. How could she tell anyone that now, within minutes of arriving at this delightful place, she was ready to pick up the unopened bags and scurry home, beaten before she had started?

'I'm making a cup of tea,' she said, getting up and stretching. 'What about you, Bella?'

'I could do that.'

Andrea almost showed her surprise. 'Well...why not? Yes, you make the tea and I'll go and unpack my bag.'

They sat outside on a tiny veranda, drinking together. Bella was still silent, but there was a different quality about her muteness. She was thoughtful rather than dismissive, and Andrea was conscious of the change, and welcomed it. The sound of the sea, the gentle shirring as it drew back from the beach, the squawk of sea birds and a zephyr of a wind that blew the scent of dune plants towards them, all made for peace. Andrea stole a glance at her companion. Bella was gazing out towards the ocean, her hands lying still in her lap, her cup of tea momentarily ignored.

At last Andrea said, 'It's wonderful, isn't it?' For a moment there was no response; then Bella nodded, a brief movement of her head that meant more to Andrea than she could have expected.

'It's...very beautiful.' Her voice was low. 'Very beautiful...'

By bedtime, not much more had been achieved. But Andrea's spirits had risen; she believed now that there could be a breakthrough for this silently suffering woman. When Bella said, hesitantly, at about nine o'clock, 'I think I'll go to bed now,' she was thankful. The evening had been difficult, but there was always tomorrow, and she found herself looking forward to it.

Bright morning welcomed them. Bella, though avoiding direct eye contact, seemed slightly less withdrawn than usual; but it was still a minimal difference. Andrea opened the front door, and took a deep breath of sea-perfumed air. Behind her, she sensed, Bella was taking a more distant view, as if it was forbidden to her to outwardly enjoy something.

'Isn't it lovely?' Andrea said, as if she was talking to herself.

'Yes.' It was a breathy sound, but it was another step forward. Then Bella moved towards the open door. 'So long since I saw the sea.'

They stood together in silent admiration of the view before them. Neither of them wanted to break the moment with talk, and so they remained, closer, but still with that strange, invisible barrier between them.

At last Andrea gave a sigh of satisfaction and turned away. She put the kettle on and began to put out their breakfast. It interested her that for once Bella let her do it; *she* was still standing by the door, and when she finally moved away and faced Andrea there were the traces of tears on her face. Andrea pretended she hadn't seen them.

'Coffee?' she said cheerfully. 'And toast and marmalade? Or do you want something cooked?'

Bella shook her head. 'That will be ample.' Then she looked up at her companion. 'I want to thank you. You've been very patient with me, and I want you to know that I appreciate it.'

'My pleasure,' Andrea said.

But Bella shook her head. 'It hasn't always been a pleasure to you, Andrea. I'm well aware of that. And Gerard—well, I've been a real disappointment to him. I'm not sure what he...' She trailed off.

'Today,' Andrea said firmly, 'we can forget about Gerard. We are here to enjoy ourselves.' She poured coffee. 'What would you like to do today?'

The expression on Bella's face was almost comical. Andrea could imagine that, for someone whose days had been so orderly, this was an inconceivable decision to make.

'Well...'

'How about a drive along the coast?'

Bella nodded, clearly thankful to be relieved of the decision-making. 'That would be...' It seemed difficult for her to come to the end of a sentence.

'Then that's OK!' Andrea was determinedly cheerful. This day must work its miracle for Bella—she didn't want to have to admit defeat and let the past win the battle. There had to be an end to the situation for all of them, hopefully one that would satisfy, but in any case, there were lives to get on with, for her a family to get back to—and some kind of decision needed between herself and Gerard. Firmly, she pushed him into the back of her mind. *Bella first*, she told herself. *Gerard can wait!*

There was a point, about five kilometres along the coast, when Andrea was all at once aware that her companion had relaxed. It was a strange sensation, because there was nothing she could pin down; Bella was still sitting beside her, hands in her lap, saying nothing, not moving. Yet in some odd way the atmosphere in the car had changed.

They found a small café with a good sea view, and she stopped the car. 'Lunch here?'

Bella didn't speak. But she opened her door and picked up her handbag, standing outside the car and letting her eyes wander along the long coastline. Suddenly she turned to Andrea, looking at her across the top of the car.

'I've been a fool, haven't I?'

Andrea, caught unawares, shook her head. 'Of course not.'

'I've let life slide past me. And now I'm wondering why.'

'That's good. It's always good to take stock...'

'I was in a dream—no, a nightmare. I was in a nightmare that I couldn't wake up from.' She let her eyes roam across the wide ocean, the dunes, the whole landscape. 'And this was here all the time.' There were tears in her eyes. 'Thank you, Andrea...' Her voice broke. Andrea's eyes were no better.

'Come on. Let's get something into us. We both need it.'

Before long, it was becoming clear that Bella's change of heart was not a figment of Andrea's vivid imagination. There was a moment when the austere mouth slid cautiously into a smile—a very small one, but a distinct improvement on the tense, muscle-bound face she had brought with her to the ocean. Impulsively, Andrea let her hand fall gently on her companion's, expecting withdrawal; Bella let her own hand lie there unmoving, but with a subtle acceptance of the friendship being offered. For the first time in their precarious relationship, Andrea really could feel the stresses begin to lift.

Lunch was a quiet occasion. Afterwards they had found a place that overlooked a wide view of the ocean; out there were a few white sails, taking advantage of the light winds. They talked seldom, but now there seemed little need for it. Something had been resolved, and the rest would follow. Bella said suddenly, 'I was wondering—what it was like for you, losing your husband.'

Andrea was taken by surprise. For a moment she wasn't sure what her answer should be. But such a step forward from this woman who had been so damaged by her own experiences was something she must take seriously.

'Well—I was devastated. It was so sudden.' All at once she had a clear image of Joseph in her mind, his strength, his cheerfulness, the depth of their love. 'And I missed him—so much.' She felt tears come into her eyes and let them stand there, a visual demonstration for the woman who was watching her intently; watching and perhaps wondering how it could be that some women could be so deeply and lovingly involved with a man when her own experience had been so savagely different. Through tears, the sun's rays broke into prismatic fragments: *even in grief there can be beauty,* Andrea thought, then mopped her eyes and smiled. 'He was a good man, Bella. We all loved him.'

Bella sighed. 'I shouldn't ask. It's upset you.'

'No. I love talking about him. And I don't get much opportunity for doing that. People don't want to hear widows going on about their lost love.' She smiled quickly. 'They say you must put it behind you and get on with living. Well, I have done. But I would so much rather have done it with Joseph.'

'I don't think I've ever known a good man,' Bella said, staring down at her hands as they lay passively in her lap. 'Certainly not one I would have wanted to spend my life with.'

'That's sad. There are a lot of them about!'

'I did wonder...'

Andrea waited.

'I wondered about—about you and Gerard.'

For once, Andrea could think of nothing to say.

'Have I offended you?'

'No—no, of course not. Just—surprised me. You seemed to be so lost in your own problems...'

'I wasn't blind. It puzzled me. I don't see people much—you know that. And then you and Gerard...well, you seemed to enjoy each other's company in a way I had never seen before...there was friendship. But I think there was something deeper.'

Andrea's instinct was to say nothing, or to repudiate the suggestion. But Bella was now watching her with an intensity that was almost alarming. She really wanted to know.

'Nothing has been said,' she said slowly. 'It's early days, Bella. Gerard has his own life—and I blew into it and spoilt his placid existence.' She gave a small, embarrassed laugh. 'He wasn't pleased, I'm afraid. Thought I was obsessed. But once I had started, I had to go on. And so I burst into your life and his, too, and often I wondered if I had been very selfish and ought to get on the plane and go back to where I came from.' She looked up at Bella. 'You would have liked me to go, wouldn't you?'

'Once. Not now. Not now I know you.'

Andrea felt a rush of—could it be affection? Affection for this damaged woman who, until now, had been only a barrier to finding the truth? She held out her hand, and this time Bella took it; and she did not try to remove it.

'I have to learn about friendship,' she said slowly. 'I always felt it was a way for one to be in control, and the other to be controlled. That's how it was with Claudia.' Then she glanced at her companion. 'You and Gerard...it may be the right thing.'

So I have her blessing! Andrea was thinking later, as they made their evening meal together. But I mustn't let her influence me. This will still have to be Gerard's decision.

Outside, the sun was sliding slowly into the ocean. A light evening wind blew through the dunes; it was utterly peaceful out there, and inside the cottage there was peace as well—the peace that comes with acceptance. 'It was a good idea to come here,' she said, and Bella nodded.

'*Your* good idea.' The rigid expression was visibly softening; somewhere under that neat, controlled personality an old nature was being reborn. Andrea wondered what the young Bella might have been if life had treated her differently.

'What would you have liked to do with your life?' she asked impulsively. 'If all those things—those ugly things—had not happened, what would you have wanted to do, or be?'

Bella stared at her, plates in hand. At last, hesitantly, she said, 'I have never asked myself that. I have never thought there could have been anything else than what happened.' She set the plates down carefully. 'You pose some difficult questions, Andrea. I don't really know what I am, who I am. My life seemed to be preordained, I suppose.' She shook her head slightly, clearly puzzled. 'I shall have to think about that. What I would have wanted...No one ever asked me that before.'

'Would you have wanted to be married?' Andrea was cautious.

'I...I suppose so. Perhaps. My view of marriage was— unfortunate, you know. My parents, then Claudia. It didn't do much for the image.' She gazed out of the window to where the sun was about to disappear into its watery grave. 'There's a lot of beauty that I haven't noticed before, so perhaps there is a beauty in marriage, too.'

'With the right person.'

'That's the problem, isn't it?' There was a whimsical look on her face. 'And once you've made the choice, there's no way to avoid the pain if it goes wrong. I wonder—would I have been too particular? Too fussy?' She turned to Andrea. 'You and your husband—how did you decide that the risk was worth taking?'

'We were in love. It didn't feel like a risk. It felt like an adventure, an opportunity to make something good. I trusted him.'

'Ah, that's it, isn't it? I've never felt that sort of trust, not in a man or in a woman. Never. I've always been...'She hesitated. 'I've always felt people were out to hurt me.' Her voice shook. 'Until you came along, Andrea. I waited for you to hurt me, and you never did. You never did!'

Andrea said, 'I'm going to cry!' She held out her hands, and after the briefest pause Bella came towards her and they embraced, a momentary gesture, but such a step forward.

'No one should cry for me.' Bella stepped back. 'I made my own bed long ago, and you have pulled me off it and made me stand up.' She took her handkerchief from her cardigan pocket and touched her mouth with it.

The short silence between them was warm and friendly. Andrea took a deep breath. 'Let's eat! This is very hunger-making.' And for the first time they were able to laugh together. Bella's laughter was unpractised, but it was there. They sat at the table, in twilight as the sun finally disappeared, not needing to talk now, for it seemed that everything had been said that needed saying.

The morning was bright with sunlight, but there was a chilly wind blowing across the dunes. It looked as if there would be a change in the weather. Andrea put the kettle on and warmed her hands at the gas burner. She called to Bella: 'I hope you brought something warm to wear!'

Bella emerged from her bedroom. Andrea was wearing a housecoat: her shower could wait until the water had heated. But Bella was, as always, neat and tidy, not a hair out of place. The tea was good, and they toasted a couple of slices of bread. The atmosphere between them was more relaxed than it had ever been, and Andrea was thankful that the tensions of the previous days now seemed to have gone for good.

'Did you sleep well?'

Bella nodded. 'Yes, thank you. The bed is very comfortable.' She went to the window and looked at the dune grasses blowing in the wind. 'What a pity it's changed.'

'Just as well we're going home!'

'Yes.' Bella sounded less enthusiastic at the idea than she would have done a couple of days ago. Andrea went to stand beside her.

'You've enjoyed the break?'

Bella turned to look at her. 'Yes. I didn't think I would, you know. But it's been—very important, hasn't it? For us.'

'It has. I'm so glad.'

They sat down and ate breakfast. As Andrea was clearing the table afterwards (and she was intrigued that now Bella was letting her do these chores) her phone rang.

'Oh, Bethany, darling. How nice to hear from you!'

The voice at the other end of the line was tentative. 'Mum, there's something I have to tell you.'

An alarm bell rang in Andrea's head. 'What is it, Beth?'

'I wasn't going to tell you yet, but...'

'Tell me what? Bethany, what's happened?'

'I'm so sorry, Mum. So sorry.'

'Bethany! What is the matter?'

'It's—it's that—Mum, I'm pregnant!'

'You're *not!*'

'Yes—and I'm really sorry. But I need to see you, Mum.' She was crying. 'I didn't mean to—but now I really need you.'

Andrea sat down suddenly. This was so totally unexpected. Bethany had had boy-friends, but they were always good mates rather than partners; for a moment she couldn't think what to say.

'You there, Mum?' It was a timid voice. 'I'm really sorry.'

She wanted to say, '*Yes, well, it's a bit late now to be sorry, isn't it?*' But there was real distress in her daughter's voice. She needed to say the right thing, something that wouldn't alienate them at this crisis moment.

'I'll be home as soon as I can arrange it, Bethany. Don't do anything silly. I'll let you know when I've fixed a flight. And... darling...'

'Yes?' Bethany was sobbing now.

'We'll work something out. Where's Dan?'

'I don't know...'

Bella came out of her room and stood for a moment watching Andrea as she laid down the receiver. 'Is something wrong?'

Andrea was staring at the floor as if the answer might be there. She felt as if all the breath had been knocked out of her. Bethany! The lovely child, the lovely young woman, the person she trusted almost more than anyone she knew—how was she supposed to deal with this? There was someone there, standing behind her—but her mind was shaking, like her legs, and she sat suddenly. The person behind her said, 'Andrea...?'

'Yes...' She turned her head slightly, and of course it was Bella. Bella, with a look of deep concern on her face, one hand outstretched as if she wanted to touch Andrea's shoulder but didn't quite dare. 'Oh...Bella...'

'Something's happened.'

'Yes. Something's happened.' She heard feet moving away, and then returning, and there was a glass of water held in a shaky hand. She stared at it, wondering for moment what it was for. Then, as if she stood on a beach with a great wave coming towards her—and could do nothing to avoid it—she let out a cry of distress.

'Can I help?' Bella was saying. 'Would you like a cup of tea?'

Andrea nodded. The confusion had ebbed, like the ocean, and what she now felt was pain, an overwhelming sensation such as she had never felt before. Within the agony were the normal constraints that we learn as we grow: stiff upper lips and not giving way to grief, trying to keep the pain within her own orbit— surely this was not something she could or should share with Bella?

But when she sat, a cup of hot tea in her hands, and Bella's anxious face was fixed on hers with a look at once sympathetic and confused, she pulled herself together. She had to do something. There was no way she could say to Bella, 'No, nothing.

Everything's fine!' Not now her life had been turned around, her faith in her family shaken to its core.

'Sorry, Bella. Give me a moment...'

They sat together in a silence that, mysteriously, was restful; and, slowly, as Bella first sat quietly and then, equally quietly, finished clearing the table and straightening chairs and cushions, the simple chores that can be done without thought, Andrea's panic gently subsided until she found she could think again.

She began to apologise; but Bella shook her head. 'Tell me!'

'Bethany...' Andrea began, then swallowed down threatening tears; 'Bethany—is pregnant.'

'Ah...' Bella's quiet acceptance was like a balm. 'I thought maybe someone had died.'

Andrea regarded her for a moment. 'Rather the opposite,' she said, with a glimmer of her normal self. 'It means I need to go home.'

'Yes, I can see that.'

'I don't know how long for.'

'Of course.'

She stood and moved to the window. Everything outside looked just as usual; it was only in here, in her heart, that there was pain. Without turning round she said, 'I always thought Bethany was a really sensible girl. You see so many young people now who seem to have no ability to look forward, towards the consequence of their actions. But not Bethany. She was fun to be with, she seemed to have fun with her friends—but I never felt I needed to worry about her. Daniel is more likely to jump into something without weighing the pros and cons—but not Bethany. Or that's what I thought.'

She turned and looked at Bella. 'I really would have imagined... with my history behind us, and the knowledge of how complicated life can be when that kind of thing happens—but I just never thought...' She trailed to a halt. 'I should have been there with her. I should have known what was going on, instead of rushing about here looking for something that, ultimately, isn't important....'

'It's important to you.' Bella was sitting with her hands clasped on her lap. In some odd way she had become the strong one; Andrea all at once knew that she could trust her to keep calm, to show reason where she could see none, to offer the supportive hand to help her through. She saw this in a flash of time, and wondered at it. How long had she been worrying that, if she had to leave, Bella would go to pieces? She looked at her as she sat, prim as always; but now there was something new. She could go to Bethany, and Bella would survive.

'I *have* to go,' Andrea said, and Bella nodded. 'I'll ring Cathy and tell her.'

'Will you ring Gerard?' It was the first time Bella had managed to say his name without hesitation. Andrea nodded. She picked up her phone and pressed Cathy's number. They spoke for a few minutes, Cathy being her usual sympathetic but sensible person— and that was what was needed at this moment. Then she rang Gerard.

'So how's it going?' he said before she had time to speak. 'Have you survived the ordeal?'

Briefly, she was angry. Then she remembered that the last time he had seen her there was some doubt about the good sense of going away with Bella. 'We've had a good time,' she said. 'Better than either of us expected.'

He sounded as if he found it difficult to believe. 'No problems?'

'Yes...one.' She searched for the words. 'I have to fly home as soon as I can get a flight. Something has happened.'

From the tone of her voice he realised that this was a crisis. 'Tell me.'

She told him. It felt all wrong to be doing this on the phone, and he seemed to feel the same. 'I'll meet you when you get back here—both of you. How soon? And where?' She turned to Bella. 'Can he meet us at your place?' Bella nodded; she went into her bedroom and Andrea could hear her beginning to pack her clothes. She moved towards her own room, but stopped at Bella's door.

'All right?'

She nodded. It was very strange to feel that Bella was no longer in need of that carefulness that had cramped their style for both of them. 'I just wish,' Andrea said in a low voice, 'that Joseph was here.' Bella smiled gently and nodded. Andrea went on into her own room. Whatever happened next for her and Bethany, at least here she had been right to insist on this brief holiday.

The journey home seemed long and frustrating, especially when they began to run into heavier traffic as they drew nearer to the city. Neither of them spoke much, but it was a very different silence from the one on the outward journey. Andrea had never imagined, during that time of uncomfortable gaps in conversation and fragile moods, that she and Bella could ever be friends; but that was how it seemed now. There was something comforting in the proximity of the woman who had seemed damaged beyond repair.

'I'm glad we came,' Andrea said suddenly; Bella glanced at her quickly.

'Yes. Yes, it's been very good.'

They fell back into silence, but it didn't seem to matter. At last Bella said, hesitantly: 'I have so much to thank you for, Andrea. You must have thought I was a very unpleasant person...'

'Not unpleasant. Badly hurt.'

'I didn't know how to thank you. I couldn't understand how this man you brought into my life could actually be my son. I kept waiting for you to say there had been a mistake, that it was the wrong person. Even though I could see some faint family resemblance, I told myself it was imagination—that it was too astonishing to be true. I could see that Gerard didn't want to know me, but that didn't matter too much—he was a fact, he was my son...and that was so impossible to comprehend that I just put it all on one side and tried to forget it.'

'Why did you take the tablets?' Andrea said cautiously.

Bella sat for a while looking out at the passing scenery. At last she gave a sigh. 'Total confusion. I felt as if I had been taken up by a whirlwind, out of my nice, safe life that I had created so that I would never be hurt again, and dropped in a strange country. I saw you and Gerard, friendly towards each other in a way that I had never imagined between a man and a woman—no harshness, no anger, no ugliness—and I knew I would never have that happen to me. And suddenly it didn't seem worth going on in my sterile world. There was only one way out to avoid the pain.' She paused for a moment. 'And I couldn't even get that right!'

'And now?'

'It amazes me,' she said thoughtfully, 'that a couple of days away from home could make such a difference to me. That's why it's so difficult to say thank you adequately, Andrea. I realise that I was so close to living a—a *normal* life! But I suppose it's difficult to make the changes unless someone points out to you that you're on the wrong track.' She turned to look at her companion. 'I know Gerard didn't want you to do this. But I'm so glad you did. It can never be the same again, now.'

20

All the complicated emotions of the day brought Andrea to the edge of tears. She put out a hand and touched Bella's; and this time it was taken and held.

The next day was little more than a jumble of things to do and people to see, tickets to buy and clothes to pack. She rang Bethany and was relieved that there were no tears this time. But her daughter's manner was withdrawn, she was difficult to talk to—Cathy, of course, said that it was to be expected. The girl had a great deal of chaos to work through before her mother arrived home.

Gerard was helpful; he shopped for her, found a convenient flight and made sure, several times, that she had enough cash on her for the journey. After a while she surfaced, standing up from the bag she was packing, and glanced at him.

'Are you all right?'

'Me? Yes—of course. Why?'

'You're not worrying, are you?'

'Worrying?'

She felt, probably unfairly, a tremor of irritation running through her. 'Yes—worrying. Are you?'

He wasn't looking at her. 'Of course not.' He turned away. 'Just wondering. A bit.'

'Wondering? What about?'

He was finding it difficult to locate the right words. 'You are coming back, aren't you?'

'Oh!' Andrea bit her lip. 'Yes. Yes, of course.' She moved across the room towards him. 'But I don't quite know when, Gerard.' She put her hand on his arm. 'I have to see what the situation is before...'

'I can understand *that!*' He sounded quite sharp, quite flustered. 'But afterwards. When—well, when you've sorted everything out.'

'Gerard...'

He turned to her, and there was a look in his eyes that she had not seen before. Had he ever looked like that, and she simply hadn't seen it, his expression saying so much more than he had ever put into words?

'Because if you won't be—coming back, that is...you would tell me, wouldn't you?'

'Gerard...'

'Andrea,' he said urgently. 'Please—this is serious. I have to know! If you're not...'

'My dear...of course I would tell you. But at this moment there's nothing to tell. I have to put Bethany first. Somehow she and I have to work something out, something that will be best for the—the baby, and for Bethany and me as well. You understand, don't you?'

'I understand that. But I am—damn it, Andrea, I'm scared that you'll go back into your family life and I might never see you again.!' He took her hands in his and held them tightly. 'I don't know if it's the same for you, Andrea—but if you went...'

She let him draw her towards him until he was holding her hands against his chest. It would be easy now to let him put his arms around her, tell him that of course she would be back, or that he could come to Sydney once this mess was cleared up. *But what a time to choose*, the logical side of her brain was saying. *Now, when I really have to go...* 'I'll let you know as soon as I can. I promise. It may turn out to be easier than it looks from here.' *But there'll be such problems to solve. What's important now is that I mustn't lose Bethany...but I don't want to lose anything—or anybody!* She was looking up at him, searching his face. He was a dear! She was so fond of him. *But does that amount to—well, permanency? And is it more important not to lose him (if anyone has to be lost)?*

They had never stood this close together. She knew she must say something, something soothing that would make the parting easier. 'Gerard...'

'I didn't expect to feel like this, you know.' His voice was urgent, and he held her hands firmly in his. She could feel his heart under his shirt. 'I thought we'd sort out our puzzle and say it was nice to know you, and then part. Send cards at Christmas, perhaps. Andrea—I've never felt like this before. Never! Please...tell me you will be coming back.'

She was suddenly deeply moved; her voice would shake if she tried to speak. She nodded, her eyes still held by the confusion in his. He took a deep breath. 'Thank God!' And then, before she could stop him, he had her in his arms and she had a moment of surprise before he bent his head so that he could kiss her cheek and her ear and bury his face in her neck with a deep sigh.

After that, it seemed ridiculous to go on pretending that there wasn't something warm and wonderful happening between them, and she turned towards him and met his lips with her own sigh of thankfulness.

It felt weird on the plane. Wanting to think about Bethany, to try to work out a reasonable solution to an unwanted situation, her mind constantly slipped back to the moment, the unforgettable moment, between herself and Gerard. Somehow, with that one kiss, a whole heap of problems fell into place and became manageable.

Since Joseph had gone, too suddenly, there had been a strange combination of aches within her, sometimes hardly felt—but now, she acknowledged, always there. At times it was a longing to have her husband back, to know once again the closeness they had shared, the way they had not needed to spell things out because each knew how the other thought.

At times, she could now see more clearly, it was the basic need for a closer relationship—yes, she was very close to Cathy, enjoying their times together with an ease that both felt. But that friendship could never be totally fulfilling. And that one kiss had shown her why, so frankly, so openly, that she knew she and Gerard would never go back to the easy friendship they had been sharing. Having his arms around her, feeling his body so close to hers—all those things she had been missing without really comprehending or acknowledging it—was a closure to the comradeship they had had, pushed into it by external forces, kept going because of her own pressing need to find out the truth about her own beginnings, and then with an urgency to help Bella through *her* traumas. But with closure came the promise of something so much better.

Now, sitting in the plane, she had time to think; but she had meant to think about her daughter, prepare for their meeting at the airport, devise things to say if there were uncomfortable silences—all that. Instead of which she kept seeing Gerard's face after they had brought the long kiss to an end; Gerard at the airport, his expression torn between joy and concern for her predicament; Gerard trying so hard *not* to say what he clearly wanted to: ' *You will keep in touch, won't you?*' '*You are coming back, Andrea, aren't you?*' All the things that were flying through his head and leaving him both confused and amazed. As she left him to go into the departure area she turned once more to wave. He was standing, very still, but everything she needed to know was in his face.

'Oh, yes,' she whispered, feeling herself pulled in two directions, 'I'll be back, darling!'

The memory of that final moment stayed with her until, when she looked out of the window, she saw that they were flying over the Bight. She must pull herself together. Bethany needed more than a mother newly transformed so that she felt like a teenager again with her first love. And for a moment she resented the burden her beloved daughter was about to unload on her, the complications that she would have to try to unravel.

It occurred to her suddenly that she still had no idea who the young man was who had helped to bring this drama about. Who had Bethany been close to last time she had been home? She could think of no one special, at least special enough to have been close enough to her to... That line of thinking would get her nowhere. Anger or suspicion wouldn't help. This was a time for mature thought on both sides, for assisting these two young people *(who on earth could it have been?)* to plan for their future and the future of their child—*my grandchild!* she told herself all at once, seeing a macabre comedy in the fact that she, about to become a grandmother, was at the same time falling in love like any young girl.

At least this thought had blown her back on course, away from the temptation of wanting to think about Gerard. For the rest of the flight she managed—as the kilometres sped away beneath her—to concentrate on the challenges of the next few hours. By the time they bounced gently to earth in Sydney she was once again Bethany's mother, ready to solve her child's problems as she had always tried to do.

And where, she asked herself several times, *is Daniel?*

This was not a normal homecoming. The girl standing away from the crowd of people meeting relatives and friends, who would usually have run towards her mother and embraced her with glad cries and laughter, remained at a distance; and, just as

Andrea had seen on Gerard's face the feelings he could not hide, so Bethany's eyes revealed a confusion that was so unlike her that Andrea stood for a moment, unable to go to meet her. The gap between them seemed impossible to cross.

Then Andrea lifted a hand and waved; and Bethany, looking pale and anguished, gave a tiny movement of her hand that was presumably a wave. It was only a matter of a dozen steps for each of them, but neither knew what would happen when the divide had been crossed.

Andrea held out her arms and managed a smile. 'Hello, love!' Bethany, biting her lips, took a step, and then another; and like magnets they were drawn together, arms around each other, knowing somehow that this was not the end of their world. The sob that Bethany had been controlling came quite suddenly, and her mother held her back, away from her, to see the face, paler than was normal, and the eyes, in which emotions came too swiftly to analyse, but were somehow recognisable: the shame of the small child who has done something wrong; the defiance that comes after the shame; the fear that nothing will ever be the same again: all these were there in her daughter's eyes.

'Come on,' Andrea said firmly, not letting *her* emotions get in the way. 'I need a coffee.'

Bethany took her bags and they made their way to the Dome. 'I'll get it,' she said, subdued. 'The usual?' Andrea nodded.

What do you say at a time like this? Andrea sipped the coffee. 'Oh. I was ready for that!'

Bethany's eyes were down; but now she glanced up quickly, trying to measure her mother's mood. 'Why don't you say something, Mum?'

For a moment Andrea was stumped for an answer. Then: 'Because I don't know what to say.' She smiled at her daughter. 'Which will probably surprise you. I usually manage something, don't I?' She stared into the coffee cup. 'I don't think we *can* talk about this now, can we? Not until we are at home.' Then she asked, all at once, 'What about your grandparents? Do they know? Have you told them?'

Bethany shook her head. 'I've only told you.'

'Right, then. When we get home...' *What then? she thought. When we get home we have to face it. When we get home it won't be like any other homecoming. When we get home I have to start being wise and supportive, and Bethany is going to have to be sorry and scared, and...*

come on, Andrea! You're a mother—you can do it! She almost smiled, and Bethany said, 'What?'

'Have you finished your coffee? Let's get going, then.' She picked up her bags and stood, looking down at the girl she loved so dearly. 'Come on, darling. Let's get home.'

The house was clean and tidy. Andrea suspected there had been some energetic housework done once Bethany knew her mother was coming. There were flowers on the small table by the window, and the dining table had been set for two in readiness for the homecoming meal. What time was it? Andrea glanced at her watch: nearly six, thank goodness—she was hungry.

Bethany stood by the door, almost as if she was afraid to come right into the room. 'I've got something for tea. Fish, actually. Is that all right?'

'That will be lovely. Can I help?'

But Bethany was determined to show that she wasn't a complete disappointment; the fish, when they sat down together, was well cooked, and the vegetables were fresh, not frozen. There was ice cream and fruit for dessert, and Andrea was able to congratulate her on her efforts.

They moved into the lounge room; and suddenly there was the silence that had to be breached, the problem that had to be faced.

'Right!' Andrea said. 'Let's talk.'

She was two months into the pregnancy, Bethany said, keeping her eyes down. Andrea took a deep breath. 'And the father?' She watched the girl struggling with an answer, and the silence was unnerving. 'Do I know him?' Andrea asked at last, feeling her heart begin to bump in her chest.

Bethany pulled out a handkerchief and held it to her mouth. 'That's what's so awful,' she whispered.

'Tell me.' Andrea's voice was gentle.

And the tale came out. Not in a flood of emotion, but in short phrases full of anguish. 'I thought he loved me, Mum. Otherwise I wouldn't have...'

'Right...'

'We seemed to get on so well...'

'Go on, darling.'

'And it was only once...I didn't think anything could happen just like that, only once...'

So much for sex education! Andrea found herself thinking. 'Yes, Bethany, once is sometimes enough.'

'But you hear about people who—who try for years and years... don't you?'

'Yes. We're all different. Our bodies operate in different ways.' A thought struck her. 'Were you on the pill?'

'No!' Then the flood broke and Bethany began to sob. 'I didn't think we were going to...you see? He knew how I felt about—that. But I thought he loved me, and I loved him *so much*, and then it all went wrong...'

'Where is he now?'

'*I—don't—know!*' It emerged in a roar of pain. 'I told him as soon as I was sure about —it, and I thought he would be pleased. But he—he hit me, Mum! He hit me and called me a dirty name, and— and—I haven't seen him since...'

'Where does he live? Is he a local boy?'

'He's not exactly a boy, Mum.' Bethany was mopping her eyes furiously, as if any violence was better than nothing. 'He's—he's married, and he doesn't live here. He's from Brisbane—I think.'

'*Married*, Beth? Together or divorced or what?'

Bethany shook her head, almost unable to speak. Andrea stood slowly and wandered over to the window, her thoughts in chaos. Somehow she had imagined, as the other partner in this drama, a nice if misguided young man, one of Bethany's pals from her school days, the sort of boy she, Andrea, could deal with. In the back of her mind had been a scenario, a young couple who had jumped the gun, as so many did these days; it had been Bethany's distress on the phone that had alarmed her, perhaps more than the situation itself. She had in her more hopeful moments believed that a good talking to about adult responsibility, about the needs of the baby over the needs of the parents, about anything...she had seen the problems solved, even if there were to be rocky moments, and maybe even a happy marriage at the end of it, once the emotions had been reduced to a more normal state.

This was not the scenario she had conjured up.

She wanted to say: What were you thinking of, Bethany? You, who always seem so sensible, you, the one I could trust? How could you let yourself down like this?

As if she had heard, Bethany said in a choked voice, 'I know I've let you down, Mum. You trusted me to be able to cope on my own.' And then, torn from her almost against her will: '*You should have been here! It wouldn't have happened if you had been here!*'

Slowly, Andrea turned to look at her. It was so much what she had been thinking. 'Why? Why wouldn't it have happened...?'

'Because. Because I would have seen him through your eyes. I would have been warned by the look on your face. You would have known what he was like, and I would have known there was something wrong. I didn't understand...' She trailed off miserably.

Andrea sat down, her hands together tightly because they were shaking. 'I'm sorry. I just thought...'

'What?'

'I suppose—I thought you were old enough to be able to cope without me. I was so wrapped up in my own concerns...'

'I've spoilt that for you now, haven't I? I'm so sorry...'

Andrea managed a small, tight smile. 'Bethany, if we go on apologising to each other like this we shall get nowhere.' She took a deep breath. 'So—what are we going to do about it? What does your doctor say?'

'I—haven't seen a doctor.'

'Then I think that is one of the first things. How sure are you?'

'I did one of those tests. I'm sure.'

'Does anyone else know?'

'No.'

'No girl friends?' Bethany shook her head. 'Daniel?'

'Daniel's a boy!' She almost spat the words out. 'Why would I tell *him*?'

'Well—we must tell Grandma and Grandad. This has to be a family thing. It's not the end of the world, Beth, and we need to be sensible about it. What is important now is the baby.'

Bethany stared at her. 'But it's me...' she began to say; Andrea shook her head.

'If you are going to be a mother, Bethany, you have to start thinking like a mother. Whatever else, this is not the baby's fault.'

In a very small voice Bethany said, 'But I don't want it, Mum. *I don't want it!*'

Andrea regarded her. After a moment she said, 'It's too late for that, darling. There are choices and we shall have to work out what is best, for you, for the baby—perhaps even for me. But if you really are pregnant—you must remember that this is a child. Not a doll to put away because you don't want to play any more—and not just "a mistake". An error of judgement, perhaps, especially from what you have told me about the—the father. But you can't just rub it out as if it's a wrong word. Any choice you make is going to bring heartache with it. You need to face that *now*.'

They were silent. Outside, the evening was closing in. Andrea stood and pulled the curtains together. At last Bethany stirred.

'So what do you want me to do now, Mum? Do you want to tell Grandma, or shall I?'

'I think,' said Andrea slowly, 'that tomorrow we shall both go and tell them—together.'

21

Grandma glanced from her daughter to her granddaughter, and knew that she was facing a crisis of some sort. Andrea had let her know, the night before, that she was back home, and that there was something she needed to discuss. But it wasn't Andrea, was it? It was Bethany who couldn't quite meet her eyes; and in a moment of womanly intuition she felt she knew what was going to be said. She was glad that her husband was not there—just for this moment.

'So!' she said, smiling. 'Lovely to have you home again, Andrea.'

'It's good to be here.'

Lucy wanted to put off the moment, even though she knew it would come. If she was right in her guess, they would all need all the love and understanding she—and they—could muster.

It was unusual for the three of them to sit silently; but there was a barrier there, hanging in the air between them, and Lucy thought that maybe it would be up to her to cross it. She sat back and regarded her visitors.

'So,' she said quietly, 'what are we to discuss?'

Andrea looked at Bethany. 'Beth, darling...?'

Bethany closed her eyes. 'I'm—pregnant, Grandma.'

Lucy regarded her for a moment, then nodded slowly. 'I wondered...' She turned her head towards her daughter. 'Did you know?'

'Not until she rang me while I was down south, Mum.' She took a deep breath. 'Beth told me then. I think we need to plan for the future. Whatever that may be...'

'Then I need to know a bit more about it. Beth...?'

Bethany gave a sigh that was almost a sob. In a small voice she told her grandmother what Andrea already knew. 'I thought he'd be pleased. Then I found out—I found out that he's—he's married...and he was very angry and then he stormed out and I—I didn't know what to do. So I rang Mum...' Her voice faded, and she searched in a pocket for a handkerchief. 'I'm so sorry...I've been so *stupid*...it never dawned—I never thought for a moment...' and then the tears came, and the two older women sat and waited until the storm passed. It was not yet a time for comforting. There was too much to go through first.

'How far gone, Beth?' Lucy's voice was carefully controlled.

'Nearly two months.'

'Have you seen him since?' Bethany shook her head. 'So we can assume he's not going to support his child? Do you know who he is?' she asked Andrea.

'No.'

'How did you meet him, Bethany?'

'At a tennis party.'

'And how can we contact him?'

Bethany stared at her grandmother in horror. 'I don't know. But even if I did—I never want to see him again!'

'But this is his child. Perhaps he is entitled to know how his child develops.' Lucy poured herself more coffee, her face grim. 'We have to face things, Bethany. However awful they may seem.' She said, as Andrea had done: 'There are choices to be made.' She regarded the girl with compassion, but there was a hard edge to it that Bethany knew was going to demand proper thought, proper *adult* thought—and she feared she wasn't ready for that.

'What choices?'

Andrea began to speak, but Lucy put up her hand. 'There are ways to deal with this. Three main ones. Have the child, bring it up yourself as a single mother. Or have it adopted.' She glanced down at her hands that were lying in her lap, but the knuckles showed her stress. 'We know all about that in this family. It would mean never seeing your child again. Or...' she hesitated, 'abortion. Back to square one, sadder and wiser, free to live your life as you wish. But that means killing your child...'

'That's what Mum said.' Bethany was unable to meet their eyes.

'It's what has to be faced.' Lucy regarded her thoughtfully. 'Do you want to have your baby?'

The girl shook her head slowly. 'No, not really. It would be a horrible reminder...'

'Then what would you want to do about it?'

There was a long silence. Then Bethany said, 'I don't know. It's like a trap...'

'It's a trap you allowed to happen,' Lucy said.

Andrea, taking a deep breath, said, 'Mum, she has to have time...'

Lucy nodded slowly. 'I know. But the baby isn't going to wait long for her to decide.'

After a moment, Andrea said, 'What about Dad?'

'I'll tell him later.' She sighed then. 'I have to say that I am very much against abortion. My opinion, not necessarily anyone else's. It just seems to me to be a cop-out, something to make it seem as if nothing has happened.'

'Adoption worked well for us,' Andrea ventured. Lucy gave her a swift smile.

'Yes. But not so well for Gerard, from what you tell me. We were all terribly lucky. We got you, and, well, you got us!' She sighed again. 'It doesn't always work out.' She looked at Bethany, whose fingers were pulling at the handkerchief. 'What do you think, Bethany? Shall we have another adoption in the family? Shall we chance the baby's happiness?'

Bethany looked up, pale-faced and shaken. 'If I try to work it out, how long have I got?'

'For abortion, probably not very long. For the other two, a lifetime. Your child's lifetime.'

There was a long silence. Then Andrea stood. 'I think we need to go home, Bethany. You've had enough for now.'

She turned to her mother. 'Thanks, Mum. Come on, Beth.'

Lucy stood and held out her arms to her granddaughter, and Bethany, with another huge sob, went into a long, loving embrace. 'Think well, darling,' Lucy whispered, her own emotions now less controlled. 'We're with you—you know that.' She relaxed her hold and turned to Andrea. 'It won't be easy, my dear. But you are both sensible people. It will be all right. In the end, it will!'

In the car, Bethany said in a subdued voice, 'I've never seen Grandma like that. Really tough! She scared me.'

'I think she meant to. It's a scary situation. She knew we both had to understand what we're up against. But she's right, Beth—it *will* be all right in the end. We shall see to that.'

'What would Dad have said?' Bethany suddenly asked as she and Andrea finished their dinner. 'Would he have been *very* upset?' She met her mother's eyes cautiously. 'Do you mind me asking...?'

Andrea laid down her fork and stared across the room. 'I don't know,' she said at last. 'But he was a reasonable man. He wouldn't have exploded!' She smiled gently. 'He would have had something wise and kind to say, I think. But he would have been firm, he was always firm when it was something that mattered to him.'

They were both quiet with their own thoughts. Andrea realised she had hardly thought about Joseph since she had arrived home; Bethany was trying to remember the man whose strength and understanding had always been her calming base during the eruptions of her early teenage years. 'I can't quite remember what he looked like,' she said, feeling bereft. Her mother put a hand out and held hers across the table.

'I know.' At last she said, 'He would have been saddened. But he would have started planning. That was the way he worked.'

'I've saddened you,' Bethany said in a small voice. 'I can't keep saying I'm sorry. But I am.'

'I know.' With a sudden spurt of energy Andrea stood and moved towards the window. 'Enough for one day, Beth. Tomorrow we start planning. ' She turned to look at her daughter. 'And tomorrow you see the doctor.' She bent to kiss the girl. 'A baby is always a blessing,' she said, her voice not quite steady. 'And we will do the best we can for this one.'

Upstairs in her bedroom Andrea stared into the mirror. 'My grandchild,' she said, wonderingly. 'Oh, Joseph—you should be here!'

When Andrea got up the next morning she felt as if she hadn't slept at all. She caught a sight of herself in the mirror and pulled a face: hair standing up on end, eyes bleary, skin drawn—was this, she wondered with a wry smile, what happened when you suddenly became a grandma? She showered quickly, brushed her hair with brisk, harsh movements that expressed in silence the tensions she was feeling.

Making breakfast, she suddenly realised that all her thinking for several days had been centred on Bethany. What about Daniel? For instance, *where was he?* It was all at once a matter of concern to her. Why, she demanded of her damp but more acceptable mirror image, do we worry ourselves over our daughters and think our sons will be OK, whatever happens?

As if he had picked up her brainwaves, Daniel arrived in his usual burst of energy. The back door swung open and slammed shut; no doubting who had come in. '*Daniel!*' Andrea yelled. 'Where have you been?'

'Hello to you too, Mum!' he said putting his head around the dining room door. "I didn't know you were here.'

Andrea sat down, laughing. 'Both of us!' She relaxed. 'I came home a couple of days ago.' She put out a hand to him. 'Come in and tell me what you've been up to.'

'Didn't Beth tell you? There's been a science week from school. We've been digging holes in the ground. It's called archaeology. I told you, don't you remember?'

She shook her head slowly. 'I didn't know you were into archaeology. What brought this on?'

He sank into a chair. He was a bit grubby, untidy in clothes that clearly could do with washing, and he was tired, which he revealed with a huge yawn. 'Old Fletcher,' he said through the yawn. 'Science teacher. I've told you about him. He's a bit of a genius. Got us all enthusiastic about digging up dead things. It's fun, actually. We've been looking into an old burial ground up on the north coast. Not for bodies – for *artefacts*.' He brought out the word with a bit of style, proud of his extended knowledge. He yawned again. 'So what are you here for?'

Andrea felt the tensions return. 'I live here.' When he lifted an eyebrow at her she sighed. 'Daniel, have you talked to Bethany recently?' He shook his head. 'Well—I need you to be...' she stopped. What did she need from him? Sensitivity? Understanding? The kind of wisdom she would have had from Joseph? She shook her head mentally. *He's a teenage boy—don't ask too much from him.*

'Dan—we have a problem. I've come home because Bethany asked me to. She's very upset, so please be careful what you say...' It was so difficult to spell it out.

'So—what's going on?' He was so clearly longing to be able to go to sleep.

'Darling—Bethany's pregnant.'

His eyes shot open, and he stared at his mother. 'Crikey!' He sat himself up and rubbed his hand over his face. *Funny,* Andrea thought, *that's what his father used to do.* 'So, who's the dad?'

'She won't tell me. Do you know who she's been seeing?'

'No. There's been a couple of guys—but they weren't, like, serious, just an evening out sort of thing.'

An upstairs door opened and shut; Daniel glanced up. 'Would you rather I disappeared?'

'No. We have to face this. The thing is, Dan—whoever the man is has dumped her. She's been very upset.'

Bethany came into the room. It was clear at once that her mood had changed since the previous day's weeping. There was determination on her face, and her head was held high. 'Hi, Dan!' She went to Andrea and sat down next to her. 'I've been thinking, Mum. About what Grandma said. All of it!'

Andrea took her hand. 'And...?'

'I'm keeping the baby. It'll be hard, but that's what I'm going to do. And if *he...*' she stopped and gulped, 'if he wants to see—it— he'll have to think that one out. This is *my* baby!'

And all at once it no longer seemed quite so overwhelming. It was unlikely that the sun had suddenly become brighter, but that was how it felt.

Daniel was staring at his sister, almost open-mouthed. After a moment of surprised silence, Andrea leaned over and kissed her daughter.

Daniel said, 'Wow!' and then again, 'wo-ow!' For a moment Andrea thought he might say, *'wait till I tell the guys!'* but he didn't. He sat up in the chair he had been lounging in. 'Gosh, I'm going to be an uncle! Wow!' Bethany, her eyes wet, put her face in her hands and began to laugh.

'Yes,' Andrea told herself, and this time with greater certainty, *'it will be all right!'*

22

'I haven't asked you anything about Gerard,' Bethany said. They were preparing lunch together. Andrea looked up from the tomato she was slicing.

'He's fine. At least, he was when I left.'

Bethany was looking at her searchingly. 'Is he nice, Mum? I mean, nice to you.'

Andrea nodded. 'Yes, he's very nice. You'd like him, I think.'

'Is he coming here? I mean, sometime...'

'I expect so.'

'Did you hope—you know, before—that he *was* your brother?'

'I think so. It's difficult to remember now. We've moved on from that.'

'So—what's going to happen now? Are you going to...to...?'

Andrea was amused. 'Am I going to what?'

Bethany shrugged. 'Things don't stand still, do they? Are you just good friends, or...' She shrugged again. 'I just wondered...'

'You want a girl talk?' Andrea smiled at her. The tension had gone out of the house since the morning, and she was deeply thankful. Perhaps it was only fair to discuss her own affairs with this newly adult daughter. 'Well...'

'I don't want to be nosey. But we have been wondering.'

'We?'

'Well, Dan and I did talk a bit about it. You seemed to be staying over there rather a long time, and we—well, we just wondered.'

'We'll talk over lunch and I'll bring you up to date.'

They carried the trays into the room where the sun was pouring in through wide windows. Andrea sat in her favourite chair, staring out over the garden. What should she say about what had been happening, 'over there'? What in fact *had* happened? Now that she was at home again the events of the past weeks had, as things do, become facts that could be sorted before being relegated to memory. What if she decided not to go back to the west? Who over there would care? What would Bella do, what would Gerard do without her? Why *had* she stayed there so long? What did it all matter, anyway?

But—if she didn't go back, what would that mean for her, personally? Did she need Bella and Gerard? If she remained here (where, let's face it, it was where she was comfortable), what about Cathy? Did these people rely on her now for anything—did they ever, come to that? She hadn't really thought much about any of them since she had got off the plane: did that tell her anything?

Suppose she decided to stay here, in her own home: what was her own future? She was still a young woman. She might find herself alone for the rest of her life. Daniel would grow up and leave them, and she knew enough about him to accept that she would have to do the keeping in touch. Bethany—well, the complication of a baby made things hard to judge. That might tie her down to baby-sitting and 'being granny', available whenever Bethany wanted a respite—and what if Bethany were to have the child and then, in some dimly seen future, marry an obliging young man who didn't object to another man's child being foisted...? *Stop that!* she ordered herself. That's not helping.

'So, Mum...' Bethany's voice broke into her momentary turmoil. 'Bring me up to date.'

'I think we'd found out everything we needed to,' she said, a bit vaguely, wondering exactly what she wanted to say. 'About Gerard and me, anyway. It was Bella, really—she needed help. That's why I stayed on. Well, part of it.'

'And what about him?' Bethany said.

'Well—he's fine. He wasn't keen on my attempts to bring Bella out of her shadows.' She smiled. 'I just had this idea that if she and I went away together...'

'Why? She sounds really—well, weird.'

'She's not weird, Beth. She's been lonely, terribly lonely, and she wasn't coping.' She hesitated. 'She tried to kill herself. And I felt responsible. If I hadn't stirred up this hornet's nest...'

'But you had to, really. Didn't you?'

'I certainly *felt* I had to. But once you've found out everything you can, perhaps it's time to stop. I didn't. And maybe I pushed her over the edge. I don't know.' She shook her head. 'Gerard didn't think she was my responsibility.'

'But he went along with it, didn't he? He could have said OK, that's it, I'm off! Why didn't he?'

'I don't know.'

'Because he was afraid he wouldn't see you again?' Bethany raised her eyebrows, a clear question. 'Come on, Mum. What's the situation with you two?'

Andrea looked at her. She wasn't sure whether to be annoyed or amused. 'My business,' she said. 'I suppose you could say it's fluid—nothing's settled.'

Bethany curled herself up on the couch. She grinned; pleasant to find the tables turned. She was feeling so much better now her mother was there, opposite her, and particularly since she had come to what she felt was a mature decision about her own future. The agonies of the past few weeks seemed to have dissolved. She wanted this baby, much to her own surprise. She'd be a good mother. She'd take life a bit at a time, and not make hasty decisions. And her mother would be there to help. If she didn't go back to Perth again, of course. She wondered just what Gerard's feelings were.

'Does he fancy you?' she said, and Andrea turned on her with annoyance.

'I really don't like that word,' she said firmly. 'Fancying has nothing to do with mature people trying to come to terms with big decisions. We are fond of each other. But that's all...' She almost added 'at the moment', but felt that would only lead to more questions.

'Well—is he coming over here?' Bethany wasn't going to let it go.

'Perhaps. I don't know.'

'Will you ask him to?'

Andrea sighed, almost ready to laugh at her daughter's insistence. 'Does it matter to you?'

They regarded each other thoughtfully. Bethany frowned a little. 'Yes, I think it does. It's someone who is important to you, and I don't know him.'

Andrea almost said, *'you don't tell me everything, my girl!'* But she didn't. 'I'll ask him if he'd like to.'

'And Bella?' Bethany grinned.

Andrea stood up. 'That's enough,' she said firmly. 'The inquisition is over. I'll let you know when I've decided.'

'So how is she?' Lucy said when Andrea rang her.

'Seems much better. She's made up her mind to keep the baby...'

'*Has* she?' Lucy's voice rose in surprise.

'Yes. It seems to have calmed her. I'm going to take her to the doctor today and have her checked out.'

'Good idea.'

'Have you told Dad?'

Lucy gave a small, dry laugh. 'Yes, I told him! He sat and thought about it, then he said, "Ah well, life goes on!" And that was it. I imagine he'll say more when he's had time to think.'

'Maybe it's not the huge problem it felt like when I first heard from her. She's not the first, after all.'

'And she won't be the last.' Lucy was staring out through the window into her garden. *How odd*, she was thinking, *that Bethany could conceive, just like that, when we tried so hard with no result.*

'No. It's just such a pity that something that should be joyful brings with it such problems,' Andrea said.

'Well, if they won't wait...'

'I know. It's part of the modern thinking—I must have it *now*.'

'Well, I think it's very immature.' Lucy's voice was sharp. 'Even birds know to build the nest before you lay the eggs!'

Andrea burst out laughing. 'You're right, Mum. But I don't think I'll say that to Beth just yet!' Then she was quiet. 'But there will be problems. And we'll all feel better if we can face them with a smile.'

Daniel came home, muddy from what seemed to have been a successful 'dig'. He kept yawning.

'Did you get any sleep?' Andrea asked after the largest and noisiest yawn.

'Not a lot, Mum. We were in a long dorm, and some of them were playing cards to all hours...' He yawned again.

'Who's in charge? At night, that is.'

'We're supposed to be on our honour.' He grinned. 'In the end some of us laid down the law...'

'How?'

'We shoved their cards in the stove.' He rolled over on the couch. 'They weren't pleased...'

'I'm not surprised.' But he was asleep. Andrea threw a rug over him and left him to make up lost sleep time.

So it was back to normal, she was thinking. Panic over. Family relationships in place, no harm done. Well, perhaps not quite.

She still found it was difficult to come to terms with what had happened; and she was pretty sure that she had heard Bethany weeping softly in the small hours. But the immediate turmoil was over—for now.

Her conversation with Bethany the previous day came back to her. She asked herself now why she had managed to put all the happenings on the other side of the country on hold so successfully that she had hardly thought about any of it. And had hardly given any time at all to Gerard, to Bella and Cathy, or to the vague personalities who had come and gone as she had searched.

She sat down now with the inevitable cuppa and let her mind run back to the first sight of her birth mother. Now, so many weeks later, the memory was almost grotesque. Could that bitter, dying woman really have had anything to do with her? And why had she made such an effort to locate her birth father? At this distance it seemed uncharacteristic of her that she had pursued Sir Kenneth with such intensity. Would it have mattered—at all— if she had not seen him in his home, followed him through the embarrassment of DNA testing?

Then, more painfully, she took herself through the time when Bella had seen no hope in her own future. Surely she should have left the poor woman with the life she had devised for herself? What had got into her with this determination to make them all face up to something that, in the wider scheme of things, surely didn't matter? Supposing that attempted suicide had actually worked as Bella wished it to? *Then* how would she have felt? How lucky, she told herself firmly, that Bella didn't pull it off.

She felt herself becoming morbid. *But after all*, she was thinking, cheering up, *I took her on holiday—and it worked! Surely that was a good thing to come out of it?* The coffee was cold now, and she put it into the microwave to warm.

Bethany came down the stairs. She seemed subdued. Andrea turned and smiled at her. 'Ready to see the doc?' Bethany nodded slowly. It would be an ordeal; but she would go through with it. In this new altruistic mood she knew she could cope.

Only, from time to time, she wished she didn't need to.

They lunched together after the doctor's appointment was over. Neither felt much like eating, but it was a symbol of something, togetherness, perhaps. Bethany was relieved, slightly, that he had found her in good physical shape for pregnancy, and thankful that he hadn't asked her any of the embarrassing questions that she had anticipated. She was still determined not to tell anyone who the father was. Why she felt so, she didn't quite understand, except that somehow it seemed less shaming if he remained a pale shadow in her background, and nothing in her mother's.

While the doctor was examining her she had lain there, humiliated by the impersonal searchings and unemotional eyes of this elderly man she had known for many years. It would have been better, she told herself—too late— to have gone to a stranger. It brought back, in a thoroughly unpleasant manner, the other way in which her body had been 'used', by the man whose name she would not speak; she knew she had enjoyed it, in spite of knowing that she was letting herself down in her own eyes, but now she couldn't recall *why* it had seemed so pleasing.

Conversation had ceased, both women deep in their own thoughts. Andrea was wondering what the next step should be; it was too early to begin the planning for baby clothes and cots and things—that would come. She remembered suddenly that someone had told her once that 'in the old days' no plans were made until the baby could be felt moving. About four months, that was; and it was called 'the quickening'. How simple it all must have been in those days, she imagined, forgetting for a moment the childhood deaths and the mothers who didn't make it through the ordeal. '*Not to mention,*' she muttered to herself, '*the lack of anaesthetics when something did go wrong.*'

Bethany looked up from her plate. 'What?'

'Sorry! Just wandering in my mind.'

Bethany managed a small grin. 'Yeah—there's a lot of that about.'

Andrea gathered her belongings together with sudden energy. 'Come on! Let's go shopping.'

'What for?'

'For fun! Why not?'

'No—I meant what are we going to buy?'

'Well...' Andrea met her daughter's eye, and laughed softly. 'Not anything we need, anyway. Just let's go and do something to cheer ourselves up. Here!' She took two $50 notes from her purse. 'We'll have one of these each, and see what we can get.'

They took their trophies home. Andrea had a light-weight jacket, cream with an interesting squiggly pattern in brown. She put it on in front of her mirror. 'What do you reckon, Beth?'

'Cool!'

Bethany had done her shopping in secret, refusing to let her mother see what she had bought. Now she opened the bag and produced a vase, a cunning blend of modern and classic, its shape returning to earlier styles, its colour vibrantly new.

'Gosh!' Andrea was impressed. 'You have a good eye for colour. Where are you going to put it?'

Bethany shook her head. 'It's for you,' she said. 'It was your money anyway, and I've caused enough problems. I wanted you to have it...' She began to cry. 'Because I'm so sorry. Because I've ripped all our lives to pieces—but I didn't mean to, Mum!'

It was too much for Andrea, and they wept together, arms around each other. When they could both get their breath, she said, 'Babies *are* gifts, Beth, darling. They don't always happen when you want them to, but it's up to us to make it work. And this baby will bring blessings with it, just as you and Daniel did for us.'

'Really?' Bethany's eyes were red. 'Do you mean that?'

'Bethany, that is the last time we're going to cry about this. One day, perhaps, you'll tell me who the father is, but it's up to you. We're not going to think about this child as an intrusion into our lives. OK?'

That afternoon Andrea sat down and wrote a long letter to Gerard. All at once she felt as if she could cope with these very different emotions—Bethany at this end of the country, Gerard and Bella thousands of kilometres away on the far coast. It was suddenly necessary for her to know how things were. Was Bella coping? And then—was Gerard missing her, or was he relieved that he didn't have to have his life pulled apart in search of things that he really didn't want to know? She wondered what kind of letter he would write back to her. Polite, enquiring about Bethany's 'problem'? Detached, trying not to get sucked down again into her own search for truth—if that was what it had been? It came to her that she would feel quite upset if he only sounded friendly. But from what she knew of him, he was unlikely to allow his more private feelings to be displayed in a letter.

As she was addressing the envelope, she heard Bethany coming in from the garden.

'Letter for you!' she said, and dropped it on her mother's lap. 'From Gerard?'

'I don't know till I open it.' Andrea held it in her hand. 'I don't think I would recognise his writing.' But she knew. He had beaten her to it! Was that a good omen or not?

'So what does he say?'

'Beth!'

Bethany held up a hand and backed away. She was grinning. 'Just being a sticky beak.'

'If there's anything that affects *you*,' Andrea said, pretending to be austere, 'I shall tell you. Now, hop it!'

Bethany 'hopped it', shutting the door with intentional care. Andrea relaxed and smiled. Back to normal, and she was thankful.

23

'*My dear Andrea,*
    'I have been hoping to hear from you and wondering if everything is all right. I expect you have been busy in your usual way, clearing up other people's messes.'

She raised her eyebrows. He sounded almost peeved.

'But you do that so well that I'm sure order is being restored. I am assuming that you would like a report on things at this end of the world, and I hope you will be both pleased and surprised that Bella and I went out to lunch together yesterday.'

Andrea shook her head slowly, beyond surprise. She would not have expected it—and certainly not so soon after she had left them.

'I went to see her on Friday. Guilt, I think, on my part, because I had been determined not to get pulled into something I didn't want (this is a time for confession, as you can see—perhaps there will somehow be absolution at the end). But I was restless—I was missing you, of course, and all the challenges you throw at me!—and I found myself thinking about Bella and what she had been through when she was a girl, and I really did have a pang of guilt. So I went round to her place, and she was, as you can imagine, much taken aback by my sudden appearance. But she is of the old school where courtesy is concerned, and she invited me in and we had the (ever-ready) cup of tea. And we began to talk. Too much to write, Andrea, but when/if I ever see you again I will tell you. Will I? See you again, I mean? I know it's all the same country, just a bit larger than most, but you do seem a very long way away.'

Andrea put the letter down and sat, staring out of the window. It wasn't at all what she had expected. It was warmer, friendlier. It was—she reread a line or two: it was affectionate, and she felt a warmth spread through her. Somewhere, under all the stresses of her homecoming, her concern for Bethany, the turmoil that had been there, in the back of her mind, perhaps since she had first met her mother—somewhere there had been a small fear that Gerard would stop feeling about her the way she knew that she was feeling about him.

'Enough shocks for you for now. Please write to me—or even pick up the phone and ring me! I hope I did the right thing, seeing Bella. We were a little uncomfortable at first over the lunch, but when I came to think about it afterwards I thought we were probably as easy as most mothers and sons are who haven't really met for a long time! She had grilled fish and vegetables, very trad, and I had calamari, which was a bit chewy, but I found I didn't mind. I still can't quite believe it happened.

'Is it all right for me to say, "with love"? Well, I'll risk it!

'Looking forward so much to hearing from you, Andrea.

'With love, Gerard.'

Andrea was still sitting, letter in hand, when Bethany put her head around the door. 'Everything all right?'

Andrea smiled at her. 'Yes. I think everything is fine.' She folded the letter and put it in its envelope, 'He's well, and so is Bella.'

'And...?'

She placed the envelope carefully on the table, letting her hand rest on it for a brief moment. 'Everything's fine, Bethany. Really fine.' She relaxed.

Bethany regarded her with what used to be known as 'an old-fashioned look'. 'You can run, Mum, but you can't hide! In the end you *will* tell me what's going on. OK?'

'You have ways of making me talk?' Andrea laughed. 'When I know myself what's going on—then I will tell you.'

Bethany shrugged, amused. As her daughter closed the door Andrea picked up the envelope and dropped a quick kiss on it. *'Yes, with love is good, Gerard...'*

Lucy said, 'Bethany says you've heard from Gerard. How's everything over there?'

For a second Andrea felt annoyed. But of course, it was natural that Bethany should be intrigued by her mother's unusual behaviour. 'Yes, he's fine.' (Surely there must be another word instead of 'fine'. It seemed as if she had used that word to death).

Lucy picked up on the momentary reserve. She hesitated. 'Do you intend going back to WA?'

Andrea sank back in her chair. Decision time? She would have to come to it eventually; was she ready yet? 'I think so, Mum,' she said at last.

'After the baby?'

'Probably. I wouldn't leave her yet.'

'If you go, perhaps she and the baby could go with you?' She was very cautious.

Andrea pondered. 'That would leave Daniel on his own...'

'We would be here.'

'Yes.' She shrugged. 'I don't know. I really don't. Perhaps it would be a mistake to decide too soon. If Bethany has a good delivery and everything is good, then...' She shook her head. 'I can't make decisions yet.'

'What does Gerard think about all this?'

'Well...' She sighed. 'It's not really his problem, is it?'

'I don't know, Andrea. Is it? Is any of it?'

Neither spoke for a few moments. 'What you want to know,' Andrea said slowly, 'is do I have a future with Gerard?' Lucy nodded. 'Yesterday I would have said I really don't know. Today...' She thought of the letter, safely stowed in her handbag. 'Today, I think perhaps I do.'

'And is that good, my dear?' Lucy's eyes were full of the affection that had carried Andrea through so many teenage confusions.

'I—think it is, Mum.' She met those eyes and smiled. 'Yes, it's looking hopeful.'

In the early evening Andrea did at last pick up the phone, and rang Gerard's number. As she heard his voice, at first brusque until he knew who it was, then, all at once, warm, confused, perhaps even a little excited, it became very clear that the miles between counted for nothing. That night she went to bed without stress, for the first time in weeks. Everything would be fine—that dreaded, over-used word?—but how else could she express the relaxation, the contentment that she felt as sleep overcame her?

No dreams that night, but sensations of good things. '*Fine* things!' she whispered to herself. '*Very* fine!'

'So you'll be going back to WA?' Bethany asked. They were sitting on a bench overlooking the sea. Today it was calm, like blue silk, and it was as hard for Andrea to imagine it in stormy mood as it was to recall how she had felt before that phone call with Gerard.

'Probably.' She was still cautious.

Bethany watched her mother's face. She wanted a definite answer, but she was mature enough to know that she mustn't trample on risky ground. 'What about Dan?'

'Yes.' Andrea sighed. What about Dan? He had appeared again this morning, had a quick bath to remove the traces of the latest 'dig', scoffed a thick sandwich and a mug of tea, and left, waving vaguely as he shot through. 'I'm not even quite sure what he's supposed to be doing at the moment. When is this archaeology ending?'

'Dunno. But he seems to be enjoying it. Getting dirty suits him!'

They were silent again. Andrea was wondering if she had neglected him to a dangerous level. 'It's so hard to keep in touch with teenage boys,' she said. She glanced at Bethany. 'Has he got a girl friend? I ought to know, and I don't.'

'Not that I've heard of. It's probably difficult to fit it in as well as the digging.'

Silence. The euphoria she had felt had slipped away, and Daniel's problems had taken its place. She wondered if motherhood was always like this—one problem superseding another, over and over again. No doubt she would find out as time went on. 'We should do something together,' she said firmly. 'Like we used to.'

'When Dad was alive? Yes.'

Andrea paused. 'Yes,' she said at last. 'Like that.'

'Do you think about him much—Dad, I mean?'

'Do you?'

Bethany pondered. 'He's getting fainter,' she said at last. 'It's a pity.'

'We can't keep them with us for ever. Not like they were.'

'I suppose not. But do *you*? Think about Dad?'

'Yes. It's a good feeling. But I agree—it does get fainter. Now, I can think about only the good things, things that bring me happiness. Not the bit at the end.'

'And if you and Gerard...I'm not being nosey, Mum. It matters.'

The silence was longer this time. *What's the answer?* Andrea was thinking. 'If—*if* it comes to anything, well, permanent, then Dad will be a good memory—always. I loved him a lot, you know, Beth.

We were so well suited. It was a wonderful friendship as well as a marriage.'

'That's how it should be, I suppose.' Bethany was pensive. 'I thought it was just—exciting.'

'No one can be excited for a whole lifetime. I've always thought that marriage is like a cake, a really good cake, with good ingredients, the ones you choose for yourself. Fruit, maybe, or just a lovely sponge. If you mix it properly and cook it at the right temperature, you get a special cake.' She stopped. 'And then...sex is like the icing.'

'How do you mean?'

'You can have a cake without icing. But the icing enhances it in some way. The icing *is* the moments of excitement, the "good sex" that people always hope for. It helps when the cake needs a boost! Cake without icing is nice, but you can't have icing without cake. That's where people get it wrong—at least, that's how it seems to me. It's childish to think that you can eat the icing but not the cake.'

'I've never heard you say that before.'

'There never seemed any need to say it, darling.' She turned to look at her daughter. 'And you've already learnt that for yourself, haven't you?'

Slowly, Bethany nodded. 'If Gerard and you—would it be the same for you again?'

'That's what one has to find out. I'm very fond of him, but—well, time will tell.'

'And what about Bella?'

Andrea gave a small laugh. 'Bella will probably decide for herself what her future will be. She's come on nicely, I must say. A few weeks ago I would never have believed that she and Gerard would have a meal together.'

They sat companionably, without speaking. But the air was thick between them with questions and answers, with thoughts of life taking new patterns, new relationships and, no doubt, new problems to solve.

'Home!' Andrea said at last. 'I'm ready for a cuppa.' That, at least, was a real constant. Life without a cup of tea was not to be thought of.

Lucy dropped in later in the afternoon. She wanted an update on what was going on: Bethany, Andrea, Bella—and, of course, Gerard. Andrea almost wished she wouldn't ask; but she filled her in about Bella's lunch date, and Gerard's letter, and the phone call.

'It's still on, then?' Lucy said.

Andrea laughed. 'Of course it is. If you mean Gerard. It's just a question of —what *is* "on", at the moment. I'm not jumping into anything, Mum.'

'I'm glad to hear it. Your father was asking...'

'What did you tell him?'

'That you would tell us when the time came!'

They were laughing together when Bethany called from the top of the stairs. 'Could you come, Mum?'

'Just a minute, dear.'

'No, Mum—*now!*'

Andrea and Lucy looked at each other, and Andrea got to her feet. 'What now?' She ran up the stairs. Bethany was standing there, holding on to the handle of her bedroom door. 'I'm sorry, Mum—but there's blood!'

'Blood?'

'Mum, I'm scared...'

In the bathroom she held up her panties. 'Oh, God!' Andrea was saying, somewhere deep inside her. 'Not that!' There was indeed blood, and as she tried to decide what the next move should be, Bethany doubled up suddenly. 'What is it, Beth?'

Beth clutched at her abdomen. 'Pain. Cramps. I don't know...' She began to cry. 'What's happening?'

'I'll ring the doc. Come on, lie down on the bed. Here,' she took towels out of the linen cupboard, 'put these under you. I'm going to the phone.' As she ran out of the room she called down to Lucy. 'Can you come, please, Mum?' As they passed on the stairs she whispered, 'I think she may be losing it. She's in the bedroom...'

The doctor's receptionist was sorry, but the doctor was out on an emergency call. 'Ring for an ambulance,' she said. When it arrived, twenty minutes later, Bethany was pale with pain, her forehead sweaty, eyes panicking.

Andrea and Lucy sat in the waiting room at the hospital. Always waiting, Andrea was thinking. It was too reminiscent of the day when Joseph was taken from them. She dared not consider that she might lose Bethany too.

Lucy put a hand on hers. 'If she loses it,' she said, 'she'll be all right, you know. A miscarriage is not usually dangerous.'

'I know. I know, Mum. It happened to me, too. But it's all so ridiculous—she had come to terms with being a mother, and I think she was actually looking forward to it. And now this!'

'And were you looking forward to it, too?'

Andrea sat looking down at her hands, which she now had under control so that they had stopped twisting and turning. 'Actually, Mum—I think I was. Silly, isn't it?'

When the doctor came out to speak to them, his face was relaxed and cheerful. Andrea dared to feel hopeful. But he said, 'I'm sorry. Your daughter has lost her baby. But she's well, and she's asking to see you. Just for a few minutes. I want to get her properly looked at.' He put his hand on Andrea's shoulder. 'Don't worry. She's young and strong, and she'll get over this well.' He hesitated. 'Is there a father who may wish to see her?'

Andrea shook her head, and he nodded.

'Then we'll get her tidied up inside and you can see her this evening.'

Harry visited with his wife and Andrea. Bethany was staring at the wall opposite when they entered the room. She was pale, but when she saw them she smiled, and Andrea's heart leapt with relief. She had wondered if Harry's presence would inhibit his granddaughter.

He moved to the bed and looked down at the girl. 'All right now, dear?'

Bethany nodded. 'I'm sorry...' she began; but he stopped her.

'No need for apologies,' he said, quite firmly.

'*I* need to.' There was a new maturity in her voice. Whatever had happened, however much Bethany had felt abandoned, fearful, unsure of herself, that was now over. She had grown up. 'I messed things up for all of you—and I *am* sorry.' She gave a small, rueful smile. 'It won't happen again, I can promise.' She glanced at her mother. 'Lesson learnt, Mum. Cake before icing!'

When they left her to sleep they went down into the hospital café. Lucy and Andrea, as if they had timed it, each gave a huge sigh. Relief? '*Yes,*' Andrea was thinking. '*It is a relief.*' She smiled at Lucy, and knew that they had both been worried, deeply worried; now that it was all over...? All at once she wondered: back to Perth? Stay here and try to forget what happened over there? What was the next move? And why couldn't life just stop still for a few minutes so that she could catch her emotional breath?

As if she had read her daughter's mind, Lucy said, 'So, what now?'

Before Andrea could answer, Harry said, 'We're going out to dinner. We can all do with a break.' And they laughed and nodded.

It takes a man to cut through all the emotional hazards, Andrea told herself. A man like Gerard, perhaps?

'Now,' Harry said when they had ordered from a long menu, 'tell me about this guy Gerard.' He looked at Andrea over his glasses, a well-remembered gesture from early days. It meant *'and I want to know the truth'*. Andrea leaned back in her chair, relaxing.

'What do you want to know, Dad?'

'What sort of a man is he? I've been allowed to catch snatches of information from your mother...' (Lucy smiled and shrugged), 'and it's time I was put into the picture.'

Andrea returned his long look. 'Let's say,' she began, 'that I discovered I was thankful that he wasn't in fact my brother.'

Harry nodded slowly. 'Could have been a problem, I imagine.'

'He's nice. Tall, about your height, Dad, going a wee bit thin on top—unlike you...' Harry patted his own thick thatch self-consciously. 'Reserved, a bit defensive because he had to absorb a lot of information he didn't want.' She remembered the withdrawal in his face when he learnt about his mother. 'Not the sort of happy adoption I had. But not bad, just a bit uneasy. He said he was so different from his adoptive parents that it was always clear he wasn't their son. I never had that problem.'

'And what of the future? Do you have plans?'

She considered this. 'No-o. Not plans. Perhaps hopes.'

'Are you going back over there?'

'Yes. There's Bella, too. I owe it to her to see she's OK.'

Harry regarded her thoughtfully. At last he said, 'OK. You'll tell us when you've made a decision?'

'Of course.' She glanced at her parents, the stable element in her life. 'You'll know all about it.'

Lucy said, 'We'd love to meet Gerard and Bella. Would they come over here?'

Andrea grinned. 'They are fixed stars, I'm afraid. Glued to their own lives and places. But I can try!'

'Do that!' Harry said; and then the waiter arrived, and the evening turned back, briefly, to the problems of Bethany. The relief in Andrea's mind and body, now that the baby problem had in some mysterious way resolved itself, was prodigious. Suddenly she felt capable of achieving anything. Of managing the problems that still awaited her across the vast area that was Australia. Of coming to a real decision about Gerard.

24

Bethany was home, stretched out on the couch, being 'looked after', and enjoying the sensation. When her mother came in she turned her head. Andrea was carrying the cordless phone. 'You going to ring Gerard?'

'You must be psychic.' She sank down on the nearest chair. 'I've been wondering, Beth—will you come with me?'

'To Perth?'

'Of course. There's a lot of unfinished business there for me. And you are at present unemployed...'

'I've been thinking, too, Mum. I didn't know what I wanted to do—until now.'

'And...?'

'I thought I didn't want to go to uni—but I think I was wrong.'

Andrea sat back and regarded her daughter. Maturity seemed to be doing her a great favour. 'To study what?'

'English—something on the Arts side—I'm not sure yet. But I don't want to, well, waste any more time. I've wasted enough.'

'We'll go into it, Beth. Find out what's possible.' She hesitated. 'I would be very happy for you to do that. Very happy.'

Cautiously, Bethany said, 'All this—mess has actually turned out quite well, hasn't it?'

'That's life, darling. It always surprises. It's one of the amazing things—you never know what's around the next corner.'

'So—I'd like to come to Perth with you. Because I really want to meet these people, Cathy, Bella—Gerard. I really want to know that side of your life. Do you mind?'

Andrea shook her head, smiling. 'I want you to meet them, Beth.'

'Will *they* mind...if I'm with you?'

'Well, they'll have to get over it, won't they?'

Bethany grinned, resolutions made. 'You going to ring him, then?'

Andrea picked up the phone and dialled a number. 'I'm ringing Cathy to see if she has another bed available. You'll have to sleep somewhere...'

'She's coming to Perth with me,' Andrea was saying.

Lucy nodded. 'Good idea.'

'I'm glad you think so.' She searched her mother's eyes. 'You don't think it's a bad decision?'

'Well—even if I did, it's your decision, isn't it? She's your daughter. And she needs time to think.'

'Yes, she does. But she's been thinking...' She told Lucy about the wish to go to university. 'I'm really pleased.'

Lucy nodded again. 'What about Daniel?' she said cautiously.

'Yes—what about Dan?' Andrea hesitated. 'It's his last year at school. I don't want to shift him now.' She faced her mother. 'Could he stay with you—just to the end of the year?'

'And then?'

'Well, I don't know what I'll be doing by then, do I? If I decide to stay over there...' She laughed, shrugging. 'It's a fluid situation. If you would rather not...'

'I'll speak to your father.' Lucy's voice was firm. 'If *he* doesn't mind...'

'I love the way you two always talk things over! It's how Joseph and I...' Without warning, she found herself feeling tearful. 'Oh, dear!'

Lucy watched her for a moment, then turned away. For once she was unsure of what she should say. She stared through the window, seeing nothing. It always took her by surprise that she could feel such emotions over this grown-up child she loved so much. When, she asked herself, does one accept that one's child has become an adult—someone whose emotions one can dismiss? At last she said, 'You do what you need to do, my dear. Harry and I will support you.' She turned back, Andrea was wiping her eyes. 'We all miss him, you know. He was a special person. Tears are quite appropriate.'

Andrea managed a small laugh. 'What would he think? If he could see me like this?' She smiled then, remembering. 'He'd say "for goodness sake, Andrea! Life is for living! Get over it!" And he'd be right.'

'If Daniel stays with us,' Lucy remarked, 'he'll be subject to Harry's house rules. You'd better warn him!'

'The Inquisition all over again!'

'The Inquisition,' Lucy said, pretending grimness, 'will be a holiday!'

When Andrea broached the subject of his future lodgings, Daniel stared at her for a moment, then nodded. 'OK.'

'You'll have to behave yourself.'

'What makes you think I wouldn't?'

She shook her head. 'Just a warning, Dan.'

'You mean no loud music, home by ten, no parties, dress properly, and don't even think about alcohol and drugs?'

She raised her eyebrows. 'Exactly!'

'Not a prob! I'll be good.' He frowned at her. 'How long is this for?'

'Till you finish this year at school.'

'And then...?'

'By then,' she said, hoping she was right, 'I should have decided whether to stay over there or come back here.'

'It's this man, isn't it? Gerard.'

'That's part of it,' she admitted. 'But there's more to it than that.'

'You going to marry him?' His voice was sharp.

It was a moment for honesty. 'I simply don't know, Daniel. Perhaps. It depends on so much.'

'D'you love him?'

Andrea was silent. This was not a conversation she had prepared herself for. At last, 'I think so. But whether that is enough, or whether he feels the same about me...We need time. I hope to know by the end of the year.'

'Why then?'

'Well...perhaps I'm not prepared to let things go on for ever with no resolution to them. You will have finished school, Bethany is thinking of going to uni...'

'What? I thought she said she didn't want to.'

'She's changed her mind.'

A silence full of thoughts fell between them. After a few moments Daniel said, hesitating, 'This baby thing—it's made a difference, hasn't it?'

Surprised, Andrea nodded. 'To you?'

'I don't suppose anyone thought I was involved. But I was. One minute Beth was just my sister—then she was going to be a mother, and it seemed really weird, you know, like she was someone else. I couldn't talk to her or anything.' He looked at his mother and she saw a kind of pain in his eyes. 'Then, just as I was getting excited about being an uncle it was, like, all over. It was as if it never happened. Only it did.' He looked away. 'It made me think...'

'What?'

He gave it a moment's concentrated thought. 'Well, growing up isn't all fun, is it? You can't just bash your way through life and hope for the best. It's tricky sometimes.'

'You are so right,' she said, putting out her hand, which, to her surprise, he took. 'You'll be fine, Dan. There's so much of your father in you.'

He looked up at her, astonished.

'Is there? Am I like him? Really?'

She nodded, unable for a second to speak.

'Wow!' her son said, awe in his voice. '*Wow!*'

The moment of departure came, as it so often does, with smiles hiding tears. Lucy hugged Andrea, then Bethany, while Daniel stood back, not sure what his role might be. Harry, more emotionally disturbed than he had expected to be—for, after all, they were only going to the other side of the country; it wasn't for ever—waited until Bethany suddenly threw herself at him and held him tight.

'Thank you,' she whispered.

'For what?'

'For not nagging me and making me feel worse than I already did. I shall miss you—all of you.' She turned to Daniel. 'Hi, Dan!' He stared at her. 'Have a great time. Write to me sometimes.'

'Write?' He made it sound like an obscure tribal tradition. 'What about?'

'School. What you're doing. Anything...'

'You're only going to Perth!'

'So?' It was clearly one of those conversations that wasn't going anywhere. Bethany grinned and flung her arms around her brother. The expression on his face made Andrea laugh.

'Just behave yourself!'

He pulled away, not quite sure whether to be pleased or not. 'Everyone thinks I won't behave,' he complained. 'Grandpa is the only one who hasn't said it.' He looked at Harry, not quite meeting his eyes.

Harry put out a hand and patted him on the shoulder. 'It's us against them,' he said. 'Women always think they can't leave without proper warnings to us idiotic men. You'll get used to it.'

For a moment Daniel wasn't sure if it was a joke. Then his face cleared. 'Yeah—that's good!' Lucy smiled at her husband.

As departure time came close there was that strange silence between them that happens when conversation has run its course. Lucy took a deep breath. 'Well—time to let you go.' She turned to Andrea. 'Let us know, won't you?' and Andrea, knowing exactly what she meant, nodded.

Andrea dozed for much of the trip across the land mass that was Australia. Bethany, not sure whether to be excited or apprehensive, read magazines and watched the film flickering before her—one that she had already seen. She was so conscious that this was a different journey, one that might change her life, change the relationships she had known since birth. She glanced at her mother, and wondered. What was this man Gerard really like? How would getting to know him change things for all of them? And what would she, herself, do in this city she had never yet seen? Whom might *she* meet?

In the weeks she had spent in Sydney Andrea and Gerard had exchanged emails perhaps twice a week, once his letter had arrived. She had rung Cathy several times; and once she wrote to Bella, hoping that she was well, and letting her know she was not forgotten. It had been a deliberate ploy to isolate herself a little from the problems she had met in Perth, to give herself time to think, and to prepare herself for whatever her future might be.

Sometimes she longed to be over there, letting things just happen as they would; sometimes she wanted the whole series of episodes that had led to Gerard, to Cathy, to Bella, to disappear and allow her to continue as she had done since Joseph's death. There had been times when she had resented the impulse that had taken her there, made her go on until she came to some resolution. And from time to time she remembered Claudia, the birth mother she had had no emotional contact with, and who, by her determined opposition, had unwittingly spurred her daughter on to the place where she now found herself.

'I suppose I shall end up being grateful to her,' she thought as they raced towards their destination, and smiled as she woke up fully.

Gerard was not at the airport; she had asked him to meet them at Cathy's—lack of confidence? Fear of her own emotions?

She asked herself the questions as the taxi carried them through the city.

Bethany was leaning forward, looking at the buildings, the trees along the river, the houses, trying to imagine what they were coming to, where this future of hers was to be based. What she saw she liked; Perth was smaller, more compact, newer looking than Sydney; the great sweep of water in the centre of the city was impressive, and she watched a ferry make its slow way towards South Perth. All these things, she was telling herself, would become everyday surroundings to her once she had settled in—but now, when it was all new to her, she found it pleasing and even exciting.

When the taxi drew to a slow halt, there was the house where Cathy lived, there, indeed, was Cathy, standing at the door ready to welcome them.

'Wonderful to see you both!' she cried as they walked up the path. 'And this is your lovely Bethany.' She put out her arms, and gave the girl a hug, before turning to Andrea. 'And you—well, you're looking good, my dear. The break has helped you.'

Andrea's eyes went to the front door, hoping... Cathy laughed. 'He's there! Wouldn't come out until I'd spoken to you first. So tactful!' She whispered, 'Actually, he's making the tea.'

Andrea smiled. Tea with Cathy was so much a part of her Perth life. As they went inside, she turned to her friend. 'It's good of you to let Bethany come.'

'I wouldn't have missed the opportunity for anything. You know that!'

Gerard was standing by the kitchen door, wearing the guarded expression she knew so well by now. For a moment they stood silently, looking at each other. 'Hello, Gerard! How are you?'

He cleared his throat. 'Pretty good, thanks.' His eyes slid away from her to where Bethany was standing, regarding him with a cool gaze that hid her own confusion.

Andrea turned and brought her daughter forward. 'Gerard, I'd like you to meet Bethany.'

With an almost comic formality they shook hands. Bethany's cheeks were a little flushed. 'How do you do?'

Cathy broke the impending silence. 'Well, Gerard, is the tea ready?' She went into the kitchen, taking Bethany's hand and leading her away.

'So...how have you been—really?' Andrea went towards him and held out her hands, and he took them, drawing her closer until she was held against him.

'I've been OK. But you...?' He was searching her face. 'You've had a bad time, haven't you? Is she...(he balked at saying the name, nodding towards the kitchen) all right now?'

'Yes, she's good. It was difficult while it lasted, but I think it was the best outcome all round. Bethany is reconciled to it, and that's the main thing. She's in good health.'

'I found myself thinking—when I heard she had... had lost it—it would have been better if that had happened to us. Saved a lot of trouble for everyone.'

Andrea moved back from him, just far enough to be able to release her hands. 'And we wouldn't have met each other.'

'We wouldn't have known about it,' he said reasonably.

She looked at him, her head on one side. 'That would have been a great pity.' She said it deliberately, challenging him. 'I don't regret any of it. Do you—really?'

'If *you* don't...' He reached for her again, and this time he held her tight against him, her face buried in his jersey. 'I am so glad to see you, Andrea,' he murmured. 'I have been so sure that once you went home you wouldn't want to come back—I had to come to terms with that, never seeing you again.'

She lifted her face away from him so that she could see him. 'I'm here, Gerard. I need to be here...'

'Do you? Really?' When she nodded gently he bent and kissed her; and she felt the tension run out of him, his arm muscles relaxing; and he gave a long sigh that said more than anything else of the stresses he had created for himself, the control he had been under. 'I love you, Andrea.'

She was almost taken by surprise, not expecting his declaration so soon. But when she glanced up at him and saw the look in his eyes she gave a sigh that almost matched his own. 'I know, darling. I love you, too.'

She had expected to be confused, even embarrassed—even though she knew (or hoped) that they would come to some workable decision about...about what? Their 'relationship'— was that what it was, a relationship? But now, suddenly, only an hour off the plane, she felt wonderful. No confusion, no embarrassment. Just a good feeling that immediately took the place of all the hesitations, all the questions without answers. She looked up at him and laughed softly.

He was looking at her, a deep, amazed expression, as if he had found himself in a land of plenty following a long, hard drought. He put his hand against her face and bent to her again. She had wondered about this; would it be...she stopped herself. Comparing him with Joseph would get her nowhere. This was new life, she wanted to embrace it, hold it to her, experience it without hesitation or regrets for a past she would never want to forget. She lifted her face to him. How odd that a 'relationship' could change so easily, she was thinking. Not only friends, now. Lovers! It felt right.

Cathy came from the kitchen, talking rather noisily—and tactfully—carrying a tea tray. Behind her, Bethany was holding a plate of sandwiches. She was staring down at them as if there was something more interesting on the plate than slices of bread filled with egg. Andrea took it from her and gave her a quick hug. The room was full of an emotion she could not quite analyse, but her own heart was singing. She glanced at Gerard. He had moved to the window and was staring out as thoughtfully as her daughter had regarded the sandwiches. Andrea suppressed a desire to laugh. It would all fall into place.

25

Bethany couldn't meet her mother's eyes, and wouldn't look at Gerard. Whether this was shyness or rejection it was difficult to assess. Andrea ignored it. This was *her* moment, hers and Gerard's, even though he was as silent as Bethany. 'Sandwich?' she said, smiling, standing in front of him and holding out the plate.

He sat down rather suddenly and stared at the food as Bethany had done. '*Really,*' Andrea was thinking, '*we do seem to have created a bit of a shock wave!*' 'Sandwich?' she said again, and he took one and held it without taking it to his mouth. Cathy, deeply amused and as deeply touched by the small drama being acted out before her, handed him a cup of tea, which he held in the other hand seemingly unaware of what he was doing. 'Here,' Cathy said, moving a small table towards him, 'put them on there.'

'Thanks,' he managed.

'So—Bethany's been telling me how you have all been during these last few weeks.' She smiled at Andrea. 'She's looking very well.'

They took refuge in small talk, easy conversation. Cathy was used to people whose mixed up lives inhibited them from the delights of chatting, of getting to know other people; but she was determined that now, perils and traumas hopefully well behind them, these two people she cared about, and the daughter for whom she already felt affection, would sail together into their peaceful harbour. (*For goodness' sake,* she told herself, *don't get all sentimental. Peaceful harbour, indeed! Life doesn't work like that. I should know!*).

Gerard struggled to the surface eventually. He was finding it amazingly difficult to keep his eyes off Andrea, whose exuberance was extraordinary. He needed to get her on their own, to talk about this thing that had happened to them—to him—and try to make sense of it.

When he had arrived at Cathy's that afternoon he had not been sure of his future. Now, however incredible that might be, he seemed to have made the move that he had been so unsure of, the move towards Andrea that would change his life. That was where he had kept getting stuck: did he want to change his life so radically? Did he want to keep his daily regime, his protective armour of habit, unchanged for ever? He was nearing fifty—was that too old for what was happening to him, or perhaps even *young enough?*

And suddenly...all those hesitations, all those protections, had been stripped away from him. He seemed to have let them go without a struggle. What was next? He glanced at Andrea, who was sitting and talking to Cathy, looking totally happy in a way he had not seen her before, glancing at him sometimes with a smile in her eyes and on her lips.

He had to look away from the lips. Remembering the kisses that had blown everything that he thought sensible out of the window, he kept his eyes down on his plate and let the conversation swirl around him.

Across the room, Bethany was doing the same thing, not knowing what she should make of the emotions that were being stirred. After all, this was her mother! It was weird to see her own mother looking so happy simply because...She glanced quickly at Gerard. He looked quite ordinary, Quite nice, she supposed. Tall, a bit good-looking if you like older men—but what did her mother see in him that was worth changing all their lives for?

She tried again to remember her father. Had her parents been lovers, *real* lovers? Like she had felt with...she wouldn't even think of his name. Now she was trying to come to terms with the fact that *her mother* might be going to have the same joy of being close to a man, the same sensations when he touched her, when he kissed her, when he...but she couldn't go there. Not yet.

Cathy turned to her. 'How about we all go out for dinner, Bethany? Would you like that?'

She nodded. Anything would be better than this emotional wind-storm. Was anyone else feeling it, or was it only herself, enlightened by her own recent experiences? 'Yes,' she said in a small voice. 'Dinner would be great.'

'My shout!' Cathy stood, energised, ready for whatever would come next. 'How about you, Gerard?'

He looked up at her for a moment, then nodded. 'Thank you, Cathy—yes.' He turned towards Andrea. 'If Andrea isn't too tired.'

'Good idea, Cathy. Of course I'm not too tired.' She smiled at him. 'Never felt better!'

Dinner helped to calm everything down. They conversed; Andrea talked about her parents, about Sydney, about anything that would keep the conversational ball rolling. Cathy, a spark of mischief in her eyes, regarded this emotional journeying with more pleasure than she had expected to feel. Bethany managed to chat, just a little, with Cathy and her mother: she hadn't yet managed to speak to Gerard, and he was feeling the same reservations. Soon, he knew, he would have to break through the silence between them. He wondered whether Bethany was angry because he was there, whether this barrier between them would resolve itself or become a real problem for the future.

Cathy, sensing his difficulty, leaned over to him. 'Isn't Bethany like her mother, Gerard?'

'Yes—yes, I suppose she is.' He managed to look the girl in the face for a moment. 'Yes...'

Andrea raised her eyebrows, and turned to her daughter. 'Are you like me, Beth?' Bethany, confused by the turn in the conversation, blushed.

'Didn't think so,' she managed.

Andrea patted her hand. 'Poor you!' She laughed. 'Who is Daniel like?' Bethany shrugged.

'I'm looking forward to meeting him,' Cathy said. 'When do you expect him?'

'Not before the end of the year. He has to complete his schooling first. Exams and things.'

Gerard felt an unexpected pang of what he could only think must be jealousy. All at once he wanted this meal to be over, to go out into the evening, perhaps walk back to Cathy's with Andrea, the two of them alone, able to talk, to explore this new situation he was trying to come to terms with. It was one thing, he was telling himself, to fall in love with a woman; quite another to have to accept that she had prior commitments to her family. He wondered, his spirits sinking, if he could cope with that. He could hear them talking; but there was a cloud of doubt in his mind that would not evaporate. He looked across the table to Andrea, and caught her eye.

Cathy picked up the emotional mood. 'I'll go and pay. Then we can go back to my place. OK?' She pushed her chair back. 'OK. Gerard?' He nodded.

Outside the restaurant they fell, seemingly without thinking about it, into two groups: Cathy and Bethany ahead, Gerard and Andrea behind. She put her arm through his, and he glanced down, almost afraid of the emotions she could arouse in him.

'All right?' she murmured, and he hesitated for a moment. 'Do *you* want to go to Cathy's now?'

He shook his head. 'No. I want to be with you. Alone.'

She smiled at him. 'Me too. We have a lot to talk about.'

They walked together silently, letting Bethany and Cathy get ahead of them, and then branching off into a small park, where there was a bench under a tree. 'Won't they...?' he began, but Andrea shook her head.

'They know we need to talk.'

'Cathy, yes. But—your daughter?'

She turned to look at him, full in the face. 'Her name is Bethany, Gerard. Say it!'

'Bethany...'

'Well done!' He knew she was mocking him, but it had been really difficult to say that one word—that one lovely word, he was thinking: Bethany! Saying it seemed to make everything more personal, more intimate—perhaps, even, dangerous.

'I've lived alone,' he said, as if he was trying to explain. 'I'm sorry. I'm—I'm just confused. I didn't think...'

'Think what?'

He couldn't avoid her eyes. 'That it would happen so soon, or like this.'

'Not orderly enough?' She laughed gently. 'Life jumps out on us sometimes.' She leaned to him and kissed him on the cheek. 'But I'm glad it has, this time. We were wasting time, letting things slide.'

'I was. I don't think you...'

'I wasn't sure.'

'What has made you sure?' He turned towards her, taking her hands in his. '*Why* are you sure?'

She didn't answer at once, searching his face with eyes that seemed to measure, calculate, analyse him. She began to speak, but he lifted her hands to his lips and she stopped, her heart racing. 'Why, Andrea?'

'I wasn't sure how *you* felt, Gerard. I needed to know that you felt as I did. When I saw you today in Cathy's house I knew that whatever you felt I was ready for it. If you showed you didn't want me I would step back, clear things up here, go back to Sydney. I can have a life there with my parents and my children. But you *did* want me! I could feel it across the room. And when you kissed me I was sure.'

He put his arms around her and held her close. 'I'm sure,' he whispered, and the kiss was the one she had sometimes dreamed of, the one that set her blood on fire, that all at once made everything seem simple; the one that sealed their future.

Cathy and Bethany sat down together. 'They won't be back for a while,' Cathy said. 'Time for us to talk.'

'What about?' Bethany was at once suspicious.

'About your mum and Gerard.' Cathy smiled. 'It's going to happen, you know. They're in love.'

'It's odd, that's all.' Bethany felt a bit like crying. 'It's going to change everything. It was OK until she came over here.'

Cathy thought for a moment. 'It might have happened anyway, don't you think. Your mother is an attractive woman, she's still young enough, she's probably lonely in a way you haven't realised...'

'She's got us. And Grandma and Grandpa. And her work—if she comes home she can be in the orchestra, I expect, and do teaching—there's lots she could do.'

'And this is why you have to be very mature, very supportive. She has a long road ahead, and once you and Daniel have left home and may perhaps be living hundreds of miles away—once your grandparents become old and may need looking after—do you want her to do all this on her own, without a partner, without any support?'

'You're on your own,' Bethany said, daringly. '*You* manage.'

Cathy sat back, regarding the girl. 'Yes,' she said slowly. 'I'm on my own. My own fault. I did what you did—but I had my baby, and then had to have her adopted. It was fairly normal in those days.' A spasm of pain crossed her face as Bethany watched her. 'We are not created to be on our own. Being alone is all very well, but not as a permanent situation.'

'So why is it all right for you and not for Mum?'

'Because, like it or not, she has found someone she can live with and love and be companionable with. Someone she understands, because they have gone through a difficult time together.'

'Difficult?'

'The business with Bella, with all those complications—with Claudia,' she said carefully. 'Your grandmother.' She leaned towards Bethany, taking her hand. 'You are very important in this situation, my dear. If you show you have accepted Gerard, that you are happy for her, you will make it so much easier for them. Gerard is a nice man, a decent person. They can be happy together. Don't put stumbling blocks in their way.'

Silence between them. Then Bethany said in a small voice, 'I don't know what to say to him.'

Cathy smiled her encouragement. 'That's understandable. Just follow your instinct. If you are anything like your mother, that will work very well.'

Bethany stared down at the floor. Then she looked up. 'What happened your baby? Do you know where...?'

Cathy nodded. 'Yes. But I think she doesn't want to know me. She's a nice woman, I'm told. She's happy. I can't ask for more than that.'

'Do you think...?'

'That she will ever want to know me? No. But I can live with that. We all have to live with our mistakes, don't we?' She smiled at Bethany, and the pain in her eyes was clear to see.

'I'm sorry. It must have been awful for you. I suppose I was lucky really, that it all came to an end.'

'Still hurts, though, doesn't it?'

Bethany regarded Cathy solemnly. 'I can see why Mum likes being with you. You're very wise about things.'

26

They met the next day at a café by the river, Andrea feeling strangely breathless because this was the first 'date' since they had admitted their feelings, Gerard still wondering if he had been struck by something rather heavy. But it was all right. It felt right as they embraced, and then took their seats where they could see the water running slowly past.

Andrea put her hand out and Gerard took it; and then, as though the fog had lifted, he looked across the table and saw her, really saw her, sitting there, fresh in the morning sun, a tender smile on her face. He leaned across the tiny table and kissed her again, the tensions flowing out of him, leaving room for other, more pleasurable emotions.

She had a sudden ridiculous thought. 'Do you know,' she said, the smile beginning to turn to laughter, 'I have never, in all these months, seen where you live. Isn't that idiotic?'

'You want to?'

'Of course I do. It's where you have your life, isn't it? It's where you're yourself.'

'We can go there.'

'Now?'

'After we've had coffee!' He spoke to the hovering waiter. 'And then we'll go.'

'Didn't it ever strike you that I should see your home?'

'You never said.' They regarded each other with the open, intimate look that can only happen where there is love. 'I would have liked to see you there many times, but I funked it.'

'Why?'

'Because I knew that if I saw you in my house I would never get rid of the image of you there.'

She stared at him. 'Was I such a threat?'

'A threat?' He considered the word. 'More of a challenge. If you had gone away again I would have been left with an image that I would never be able to control.'

She flashed a smile at him. 'And you think I'll be easier to control now?' She slid her hand under his and it felt good. His hand was warm and strong and she wondered why it had taken so long to get to this point of intimacy.

'I hope I would never try,' he said quite simply.

Fifteen minutes in his car brought them to the northern part of the city, where the houses were comfortably set in gardens. 'It's an old one,' he had said, and she wondered what she would find. But she liked the look of it as they drew up in the driveway. Brick and tile, well kept, a wide porch that was almost a veranda; inside, when he opened the front door and stood back to let her enter, a short hallway leading into a large room with views into a garden with some fruit trees, and native plants in the borders.

'It's lovely, Gerard,' she said; and he shrugged, pleased. 'You weren't expecting me today, but it's so well looked after...'

'You thought it would be full of beer glasses and covered with dust!' When she turned to him, shaking her head and amused, he took her by the waist and held her in front of him where he could see her properly. 'Not all men are messy creatures who can't live without a good woman to keep them in line.' He kissed her. 'Probably that was half the trouble.' He slipped his arm around her. 'Come on—let's do the full tour.'

Three bedrooms, beds made up and ready for occupation. Bathroom and kitchen seemed recently painted, fresh and clean. Especially the kitchen. 'Have you redecorated?' she asked, looking at the equipment, the gleaming tiles, the slate floor.

'Last year. Before I got myself into this mess!' He was relaxing as she watched, the small grin turning to a smile, the tense face muscles letting his expression emerge, warm and loving. Andrea leaned against him and buried her face in his sweater.

'It's a lovely mess,' she murmured, her voice muffled. 'I'm loving it.'

Gerard held her, his face against her hair. 'I'm loving you...' He gave a sigh of thankfulness. ' Andrea...my darling...'

'We have to talk,' she said, detaching herself from him.

'What about?'

'Mainly, I think, my family.'

'Ah.'

He sat down in one easy chair while she sat in the other. 'This *mess*, as you call it, will change so many things. It's not just you and me getting together—it's how it will affect my children. So we really have to be sure that we know what we're doing.' His eyes were on her, and he nodded slightly. 'And it's a question of where are we going to live, and whether I'll be able to find work, and which of us will sell our own house, or...or what?' She stopped suddenly. It all sounded very difficult.

Gerard was silent for a moment. Then he said, 'One thing at a time, I think. If we try to solve every problem before it's even existed, we're going to be bogged down from the start.'

'That's why I don't want to run into it without thinking...'

'We won't do that. We're both sensible people, aren't we? We'll do what we can now, and then deal with things as they come up. First—what about Bethany?' He managed the word without difficulty this time. 'She's obviously not too happy about us. What's the answer to that?'

Andrea gave it thought. 'I think,' she said finally, 'that she is still pretty mixed up after the—the baby and losing it. You see, she had come to terms with the situation, and then, suddenly—no baby!' She looked up at him. 'It's just a matter of patience. And I think Cathy is doing what she can for us.' She smiled ruefully. 'Where would we be without Cathy?'

He shook his head. 'Not where we are, anyway.' He held his hand out and she took it. 'I should try talking to her—to Bethany, that is—and see if we can...'

'Would you?' She was eager, pressing his hand. 'Could you?'

'Yesterday, no. Today, yes!'

'What's the difference?'

'You. Me. Us!' He shrugged. 'I had no idea how it would change things.'

'How?' she said, wanting to hear him say it. His smile was something new to her. In all the months they had searched together for the truth, and so often found it distressing, he had so often been solemn, reserved, even inhibited; this new man, this new warmth and expression, gave her more pleasure than she could have imagined. 'How has it made a difference, Gerard?'

'Because now I know that it wasn't just me getting carried away. That you felt it too. I couldn't believe that for a long time. I could see no reason why you would want to be part of my not very interesting life, and I thought you would be disgusted by the background—all that with Bella—all that. So I kept myself under wraps, didn't want you to know any more about me, not how I am today, myself, without all that unpleasantness... Can you understand?' She nodded gently, her eyes on his. 'And when I thought that perhaps there was something, something *real* between us, I decided it was my imagination. I didn't want to be hurt any more than was necessary.'

'Did you resent me?' she asked in a small voice.

'No, never that. But I couldn't see anything good coming out of it. You are from the other side of a very large country. I have my business here—it's not world-shatteringly big, but it pays for the bread and butter. You have a family, I don't. I could only see the hazards—and now I can see the possibilities. That's it, really. A possible new life—for all of us. But I want it to start out without resentment from your children.' He stopped. 'What about Daniel?'

'I don't know.' Andrea was thoughtful. 'He's very much wrapped up in himself these days. Finishing his school time—exams coming up in a few months. Hopefully going to uni next year, or perhaps taking a year off—I don't know. He's not like Bethany. He doesn't show himself to people—you know what I mean? I think he would probably shrug and say "whatever!" That's all they seem to say these days.'

'When will you tell him?'

'When I've decided what to say!'

He regarded her seriously. 'Do it soon. His reaction matters. I have to know that he won't think I'm trying to replace his father.'

'Do you think he would?'

'I used to be a boy,' he said, lifting his eyebrows at her. 'I know a bit about them.'

'Tomorrow, then.' She leaned back in the chair. 'How nice if we could just take off and not have to explain ourselves.'

'An island in the sun with hot and cold running water and no one to bother us?' He actually laughed, and it was a good sound. 'We've gone beyond that, my love.'

'Say it again.'

'What? An islan...'

'No. My love!'

His eyes burned into her. 'My love,' he whispered. 'Oh, Andrea—my love!'

'I want to buy something for Cathy,' Andrea said on the way home.

'Good idea. I was thinking of flowers anyway.'

'Look, there's a florist in that row. Let's stop and get some there.'

She let him choose the flowers: lilies and carnations, pink against white. As they went back to the car she saw the shop next door, its windows tastefully arranged with china and glass. 'Look at that, Gerard! That in the middle. Isn't that exactly Cathy?'

It was a tea set, white with a pattern of green fernlike leaves. Delicate colouring, yet strong in its construction. Cathy wouldn't want something too dainty. 'I love it!' Andrea said. 'How much is it?'

They went in, and it was a strange sensation, buying something together. Andrea insisted on paying for it, and the woman behind the counter wrapped it for them carefully in two packages. As they went out into the street, Andrea stopped for a moment. 'That was a special moment,' she said softly. 'Doing something together.'

Gerard, carrying both parcels, looked down at her face and was caught again by the sensation of not quite being there. But the packages in his arms were heavy enough to convince him that this was reality—this was perhaps how it would be from now on. 'I can't kiss you here,' he murmured. 'There's a police car over there.'

'Do it!' she said, grinning. 'And to hell with the consequences.'

At Cathy's they left the car in the driveway and went to the front door, Gerard carrying the flowers. 'I'll come back for the parcels,' Andrea said.

'No. I'll do that.' Gerard led the way in and found Cathy in the kitchen. She was overwhelmed by the flowers, and insisted on kissing him warmly on the cheek. Slightly embarrassed, he took himself off into the lounge room.

'Had a good time?' Cathy was searching in a cupboard for a suitable container.

'Wonderful!'

'Seems like it!' She came across and put her arms around her friend, who was glowing from the inside in a totally new way. 'Have I told you how glad I am for you?'

'No—tell me again!' Andrea smiled, her eyes suddenly moist. 'None of this would have happened but for you. I am *so* grateful— what if I had come all this way and had to do everything on my own? I couldn't, that's the truth.'

'Glad to be of service.' Cathy laughed briefly, searching in her pocket for a handkerchief. 'Why do we always cry at the best moments?'

'Wait! I've got something for you...' Andrea went into the hallway—and stopped. She could hear voices, Gerard's and Bethany's. Gerard was saying, 'I've got some stuff in the car for Cathy. Do you think you could help me bring it in?' Andrea waited, holding her breath, to hear her daughter.

'OK,' Bethany said, surprise in her voice. 'If you want.' Andrea slipped back into the kitchen as the two went to the front door.

Bethany carried one parcel, Gerard the other. 'They're not really heavy,' she said, looking at him, and he nodded.

'But I don't want to drop them.'

She gave him a very measuring look. 'You just wanted to say something to me. Get me on your side.'

He stood still, regarding her with an expression she had not expected, a warm, friendly look that made her understand, all at once, exactly why her mother found him attractive.

'Neutral, anyway,' he said in good humour. 'My side if possible. Because your mother is on my side, and it would be nice if we could all...' He saw that she was not smiling. Perhaps this was going to be more demanding than he had hoped. He felt a little helpless—his experience with girls had been limited so far. He imagined that he was about to learn how tricky that could be.

Inside the house, Andrea was helping Cathy in the kitchen. Gerard wandered in, his face not revealing his frustration. Andrea came to him and put her arm through his.

'All a bit much?' she asked, smiling.

He smiled back. 'Nothing I can't handle.' He hesitated. 'Going to ring your mother?'

'Yes, I'm going to ring them this evening. In fact,' she glanced at her watch, 'I think I've left it a bit late. OK. Phone calls tomorrow.' She glanced mischievously at Gerard: 'Will you be here—to talk to my parents?' and was amused at his expression, compounded of love and a dawning alarm at what this new life portended.

'I expect I must,' he said, conceding.

'Of course you must,' Cathy said firmly. 'They'll love you.'

He cocked an eyebrow at her. 'Don't overdo it,' he said, and she was pleased to see he could let the protective armour down. He stood, pushing his chair back. 'Let's give Cathy her tea set.'

Cathy's eyes filled with tears when she saw her gift. 'I feel I ought to say "oh, you shouldn't have!" But honestly, Andrea—it wasn't necessary...'

'For us it was. We can't keep telling you how much you have helped us—but every time you use these you'll remember.'

'They're lovely,' Bethany said. 'Are you going to use them?'

'All the time!' Cathy was setting them out on the table. 'They won't be wasted in this house.' She hugged Andrea, then turned and hugged Gerard. 'I'll let you wash them up!'

They all laughed, tensions relieved. Gerard glanced at his watch.

'Time to go!' He held out his hand to Andrea. 'See me out?'

Bethany's eyes were still on the door after Gerard and her mother had left. Cathy said, not looking at the girl, 'You feel better about it?'

Bethany answered slowly. 'He seems nice. Mum seems happy.' She hesitated. 'I suppose I never looked at her as just being a woman—she was always "Mum", and really, Daniel and I...' She looked straight at Cathy. 'We probably never *really* thought how it was for her, losing Dad like that. Just one of the things that grown-ups have to cope with. And she did. She never complained. And when she started this—this hunt for her mother, it just seemed a weird sort of thing to do—but we were grown-up, too, we thought, and...' She bit her lip. 'And—I just wish...'

'That's over,' Cathy said. 'Put it behind you. Mothers expect to be hurt.'

'Do they?'

'If they're wise. So many things can happen in families.' She smiled. 'She's a great girl, your mum. And if she and Gerard really care for each other, that will be a bonus for all of you.'

'Yes...yes, I suppose so.' Bethany stared into space. 'She's still young, really, isn't she? Not fifty yet.'

Cathy nodded, smiling. 'Only the young think that fifty is old.'

'She and Gerard have a really weird history together, don't they?' She looked up at Cathy. 'How on earth did she find it all out?'

'Sheer determination, Bethany. Most people, finding Claudia and then Bella, would have turned away and gone home. Not your mum!'

'But I still wish,' Bethany burst out as she heard the front door shut and Andrea's steps approaching, 'that it hadn't happened!' Cathy stared at her in surprise.

Andrea came into the room. 'Run out of conversation?' She smiled.

'No—just pausing for breath.' Cathy stood, and went to the cupboard. 'So what's for supper tonight?' She brought out eggs and some ham and put them on the table. 'What do you fancy, Andrea?'

They discussed the meal. Bethany went into the other room and left them to it. Cathy, working her soothing skills overtime, kept the conversation going; and when they had eaten and cleared everything away she kept Andrea talking, while Bethany read magazines and turned on the TV in search of something to watch. By the end of the evening Cathy was out of ideas. She stood and hesitated for a moment, then moved to the door, her eyes on Andrea.

'Well, I'm for bed. All this excitement is too much for me!' She closed the door behind her.

'I think I'm ready for bed, too...' Andrea said.

After a moment Bethany muttered, in spite of herself, 'You're really happy, aren't you?'

She regarded her daughter with deep affection. 'Yes, darling, I'm happy.' Then, seeing the stubborn expression on the girl's face, she stopped. 'What is it, Beth?'

'I—I just don't...' she stopped, unable to shape her thoughts adequately.

'You don't what?'

'I don't want things to change! I don't want him for a sort of— of replacement father...I just don't! And I don't think Daniel will, either.' She turned her back and stood, stiff and angry in a way she couldn't herself comprehend. She knew she should be making things easier for her mother. She knew she was behaving like a silly child. But she couldn't get past the fact—the fact that was clear to her if no one else—that nothing would ever be the same again, for any of them.

They stood, the kitchen table between them, in a silence that hurt. Andrea, so recently warm with love, felt cold. Bethany was all at once afraid—of herself, of her mother's anger, of something so basic that she could not tell what it was.

'Oh, Bethany...' Andrea said at last in a voice that was no more than a whisper. 'I thought that everyone was happy now. Because I was.' She came to her child and put out a hand. 'Darling, Gerard doesn't want to be your father. *I* don't want that. But—' she hesitated. To confess her own need for companionship beyond what she could have with her children was dangerous ground at this moment. 'Beth, I'm not an old woman, you know. I may have forty or fifty years ahead of me. People live longer these days.' She took Bethany's cold hand in hers. 'You and Daniel will leave home and live your own lives. Grandma and Grandpa will eventually leave us, too, though I hope that won't be for many years yet. And I don't want to be on my own...'

Bethany refused to turn towards her. 'Couldn't you wait?' she said unreasonably. 'Until we go, Dan and I? Why must it be now, when we're a family, when we belong to each other? Why *now*?'

Andrea took a deep breath. She could feel the pain being replaced by anger, anger at this daughter she loved, and this was something she desperately didn't want.

'My dear, life sometimes takes us by surprise. You know that already. And I wasn't expecting to—to fall in love again, after your father. But he wouldn't want me to be alone...'

'How do you know that?'

'Because he was a sensible man, a loving man, and he would not want me to be forever mourning for him. He would want me to go on and live my life. If it had been me that died first, if I had known from some cloud up there in the sky that he was alone, I would have wanted him to find someone else. That's how it is, Beth. Like it or not, that's how it is.' She drew back, away from the girl. 'I think it would be a good idea if we went to bed now. I don't want to talk anymore.'

Silently, Bethany walked past her and took herself to her bedroom. Andrea, shaken, sank down on a stool and put her head in her hands. She had not expected that, and wondered now why. This put a different slant on everything; in no way was she prepared to break up her family, but it would be hard, very hard, to break it off with Gerard. At the idea she felt a pain in her heart, and buried her head in her arms on the table.

A few minutes later Cathy came quietly into the kitchen.

'Everything all right?'

Andrea sat up slowly. 'I thought it was, Cathy. Apparently I was wrong. Did you hear?'

'No. But I heard her in the bedroom. She's crying.'

Andrea sighed. 'I suppose I should go to her.'

'No.' Cathy was firm. 'She's a big girl now, Andrea. She has to fight through this herself. It's about Gerard, of course.'

Andrea nodded. 'I wasn't expecting it. I really thought tonight we were all happy with the way things were...' She stopped. 'I ought to go to her.'

Cathy sat down beside her. 'Give her time to think, my dear. You can't *make* her want it. She has to come to terms with it sensibly. She has to realise that you're not only her mother, you are a person with needs.'

'But I don't think she wants me to have needs like that!" Andrea gave a watery smile. 'She's only just realised the power of sex for herself. She doesn't want me to know about it too. Mothers are supposed to be immune!'

'Well, they're not! And she'll have to accept it somehow. Let it alone until the morning.'

Andrea stood slowly. She felt exhausted. 'Don't let Gerard know about this, Cathy. He'd do something silly like deciding that it was all over—and I couldn't bear that.'

'Not a word!' Cathy put her arms around her and kissed her cheek. 'You'll see! Everything will work out. This is so obviously right for you *and* for Gerard that it just has to happen.' She grinned cheerfully. 'I promise you!'

27

A t breakfast Cathy announced: 'Bethany and I are going to find a large department store in the city and do some girl things!'

Andrea glanced at the girl, who had hardly spoken since she had started eating. 'Sounds good,' she said quietly. 'When do you think you'll be back?'

'Goodness knows!' Cathy was unstoppably cheery, so Andrea smiled.

'Have a great day!' She opened her handbag and took out a couple of bank notes. 'Here, Bethany.' Deeply embarrassed, Bethany tried to refuse, but Andrea was adamant. 'Take it! You can't go shopping without money.'

Once they had left she took a deep breath and sat for a moment. She must ring Bella, if they were going to visit her. And then her parents and Daniel. What should she say? Last night it had seemed quite simple: '*Hi, Mum, I wanted to tell you that Gerard and I are engaged!*' Now, it seemed wrong, as if she might have to admit that...that what? That they couldn't be engaged because of Bethany's anger? She imagined Lucy saying, '*For goodness sake, Andrea —it's your life! Do what's right for you.*'

'And it is right,' Andrea murmured. 'I do have the right to control my own life.' As she argued with herself she heard Gerard's car draw up to the front of the house. When he gave a tentative knock at the front door, then entered and found her in the kitchen, she had quite lost that exuberance that had been so heady the night before. She was almost afraid to meet his eyes.

'What's wrong?' he said immediately. He stood inside the door and regarded her. 'Andrea...?' She stood and went to him, letting him fold his arms around her and kiss her cheek. 'Bethany?' he asked.

She drew her head back so that she could look him in the eyes. 'How did you know?'

'I half expected it.'

'Why?'

'Her attitude to me. A bit cool.'

Andrea laughed grimly, pulling away from him. 'I really thought...' She stopped, and Gerard patted her shoulder.

'You were happy. You weren't looking for negative vibes.' He held her with his gaze. 'You *were* happy, weren't you?'

'Oh, of course I was, Gerard. I still am. Just—what am I going to do about her?'

'She'll get over it, my love. She's a sensible girl...like her mother!' He touched her cheek. 'Come on, let's start the day again.' He sat at the kitchen table, pulling her down on his knee. 'Have you rung Bella?'

She shook her head.

'Your folks?'

'No.'

'Better do it, then.'

She managed to laugh; he hardly seemed the same man, who had had to be persuaded, cajoled, sometimes even convinced that everything was fine. Now, it seemed that nothing could persuade him that anything *could* go wrong. She relaxed in his arms.

'Go on—get the phone. Who first—Bella or your mother?'

She rang Bella. The well-remembered voice was unflurried, sounded almost pleased to hear from her. Yes, it would be very nice to see her...them...again. About eleven would be convenient. Andrea rang off. 'Eleven.'

While the phone rang again in Lucy's home, Andrea stood, eyes down, wondering exactly how she should put her news. Lucy sounded just as usual, warm and delighted to hear from her. 'How are you?' she asked, and then, 'And how is Gerard?'

Andrea took a deep breath and kept her eyes on him. 'I'm good, Mum. And so is he.' She hesitated. 'We just wanted to tell you that we're engaged.'

Lucy simply said, 'I'm so glad, darling! I hope you will be very, *very* happy together.' She paused for a moment. 'Is he there?'

'Yes!' She smiled at Gerard, who was looking slightly alarmed. 'Here—talk to your mother-in-law.'

He was warm, friendly, exactly how she wanted him to sound on this so-important phone call. Even though, when he handed the receiver back to her, he let out a mighty sigh of relief, she knew that Lucy would have been charmed. 'He sounds very nice,' her mother said. 'Andrea, dear, your father is out at the moment. Buying more tools or something. But I shall tell him the moment he comes in. Oh, Andrea, my dear—I am so pleased for you!'

'Right!' he said, duty done. 'Where are Cathy and Bethany?'

'Gone to do an all-girls thing at the shops. We are free to do as we like until Bella at eleven.'

'We'll start with this,' he said, holding her firmly and kissing her with enthusiasm. 'As a newly-engaged man I am entitled to decide our course of action.'

'Is that normal?' She smiled up at him.

'Not only normal—compulsory.' He pushed her away from him. 'So get yourself ready and we'll be on our way.'

'Where to?'

He held her gaze for a long moment. 'We have to buy a ring,' he said gently. 'It's part of the deal.'

She returned his gaze. 'I'd forgotten.' With her hands on his chest: 'Oh, Gerard, it's going to be all right. Isn't it?'

He shook his head. 'It's not *going to be*. It is! Completely all right.'

'Even if Bethany...'

'Whatever anyone does. This is something for us to decide, no one else. Believe me.'

As they drove into the city she stole a glance at him and was again astonished that love could make such a difference to anyone. She wondered yet again where the confidence had come from—or perhaps, she argued with herself, she should wonder where it had gone to... before? Where *had* this man been hiding himself? She leaned back in the car, her hand lying on his arm, and gave herself up to good thoughts.

Choosing the ring proved simple. They saw one immediately—a beautiful antique jewel, not the usual dazzling affair that newly-engaged couples like to show off, but a cluster of old-fashioned diamonds set around a ruby in a wide gold ring. It looked good; it felt good. She had removed her wedding ring that morning and was wearing it on her right hand; it had felt strange at first—but this ring, as Gerard slid it on to her finger, felt perfect.

'OK?' he said as she held it out to see the ruby glowing in a ray of sunlight; and she nodded, not quite sure of her voice.

The jeweller looked from one to the other and smiled. 'I hope you will be very happy,' he said formally. 'That is a very beautiful ring.'

Bella was ready, as always, with a kettle on the boil and the teacups set out. The brief warmth Andrea had felt in her during their holiday together had somewhat dimmed; and she greeted Gerard very sedately. But she seemed quietly satisfied when Andrea told her that they were now engaged, and showed her the ring.

'I hope you will be very happy,' she said, as conventional as the jeweller. She turned to Gerard, courage in both hands. 'Andrea is a very unusual woman. I owe her a great deal.'

He smiled at her—quite a different man from the one she had half feared for his silences, his desire not to be involved. 'I know. I'll look after her.'

She kept her eyes on him, almost puzzled. Then she drew herself away. For a few moments no one spoke. Then Andrea said, 'There are lots of things to sort out, of course, Bella. Where to live—you know. What am I going to do?'

'Do?' Bella said, unsure.

'I shall need to get a job. But where? And what?'

Gerard answered her, quite sharply. 'That will all work out. No need to worry about it now.' She looked at him, all at once wondering if this was another hurdle they had to surmount. Of course she would need to know what her future would be—even *where* it would be. But perhaps this was not the time nor the place. They kept to the kind of conversation that could raise no difficulties. 'So, Bella, how have you been since we last saw you?'

Bella seemed relieved.

As they were leaving Andrea said, 'I'd like you to come and meet my daughter Bethany. Can you come for tea one day? I can come and pick you up. I know Cathy would like to see you.'

Bella looked as if she had been asked to fly to the North Pole. 'Oh—I really don't know...well, perhaps another time, Andrea...'

Gerard, who had been silent for several minutes, said, 'Of course you'll come, Bella. You enjoyed our lunch together, didn't you? Well, then...' He kept his eyes on her, and after a confused moment she gave a small nod.

'Yes, of course...that would be very nice. Thank you...'

Once in the car, Andrea looked across at Gerard. 'Iron fist in velvet glove?'

He smiled. 'She needs pushing a bit. Who should do that but her loving son?'

'You're being a bit devious, aren't you? Loving? Really?'

He didn't answer straight off. 'While you were away,' he said at last, 'I thought fairly deeply about this total confusion you had caused me.' He threw a quick grin in her direction. 'Was I going to accept it or do whatever was necessary to get out of it? That's why I took her out to lunch. I had to see if there was anything there worth me making an effort for. And I could see that under all that hesitation and pain there might just be someone worth knowing better. OK,' he said, seeing Andrea about to speak, 'so I didn't follow it up. But I do think that she is owed a bit of pleasure in her life. And I doubt if she can go back completely to what she had before, which is a sterile existence. And no, I'm not a loving son. I don't feel anything for her as my mother. But I can see that life has been pretty mean to her, and perhaps I can make it up to her a bit.' He stopped and put his hand briefly on hers. 'And now that *this* has happened I feel as if I can do it.'

'I'm glad,' Andrea said quietly. 'I got to liking her while we were away. She has a family now, even if neither of you feels a strong link. In fact, I shall be her daughter-in-law, like it or not!'

'That's a daunting thought.' He drove into a restaurant forecourt and stopped the car. 'Ready for lunch?'

Later, they sat together on the bench they had used in the early days, when they were trying to plough a way through the confusions of DNA and obscure family links. Now, they sat hand in hand, close together, looking down over the sweep of water that filled the centre of the city. 'You didn't want me to talk about our future, did you?' Andrea watched his face.

'Not in front of Bella, no.' He hesitated. 'Of course there are things to be planned. But at the moment it's enough for me to know that it has happened, that I love you and you seem to love me...'

'Seem?'

'OK,' he smiled, 'you love me. For some reason which is beyond me just now. Let's not rush the future. It will happen.'

'You're probably right. I can't help it...'

'You're an organiser.' He was amused. 'You can't help planning things. All in good time.'

'You know,' she said lazily, 'I really don't know all that much about you. You know just about everything to do with me, but...' She looked at him with a thoughtful frown. 'I know you said you do something with finance—but I don't know exactly what.'

'It's not very exciting.'

'But it's part of you...'

He was silent for a moment. 'I help people who have financial problems. Not big businesses—ordinary people who get into strife over money and can't see a way out. People who come into money through bequests and don't know how to handle it. The best one was the family that won fifteen million dollars on Lotto. I helped them to invest wisely.'

'Did they offer you ten percent?'

'No.'

'I peeped into your office when I was in the house the other day,' she confessed. 'It was very neat and tidy.'

'It's a small thing, my job. I don't make a lot out of it, so I hope you weren't expecting to marry a rich man.'

She shook her head, smiling. 'That's one reason why I need to know what *I* shall be doing. I want to pay my way.' She paused. 'You've just bought me quite an expensive ring. You're not exactly short of it...'

'Shorter than I was before I bought it!' He grinned. 'No, I'm not a poor man either. But I've been used to supporting only myself. Two don't necessarily live as cheaply as one, not in the modern world.'

'You seem to be able to make your own times for things you want to do.'

He laughed then. 'You took up a lot of those times, Andrea, my love. I had to work half the night to catch up with things.'

She leaned against him. 'Oh, Gerard—what has happened to us?'

'Come to our senses, perhaps?'

'Mmm...' She felt contentment slide over her like a warm blanket. 'I expect I could find something musical to do...' She sat up suddenly. 'I suppose I shall have to decide what to do about my house!'

He pulled her back towards him. 'Andrea! Could you stop thinking? Just for a minute? It will all work out—I mean it.' She sank back against him, trying not to giggle, and they sat together in silence until he said, 'Time to go back?'

At Cathy's, Bethany and her hostess were in the latter's bedroom, the bed covered with packets and parcels and tissue paper. No need to ask if they had had a good day—the air was full of bubbling laughter.

'We had lunch at a funny little café,' Bethany said. 'It was Italian, and the man said we were both *bellissima*—is that right?'

'Your daughter knows how to spend.' Cathy picked up a tunic-style top, white and lime green, and held it against Bethany. 'What about that, Mum?'

'It's lovely, Bethany. What else?'

Gerard left them to it and went to the lounge room. He stared out of the window, seeing the traffic going by without noticing it. Somewhere along the line he seemed to have found a whole new aspect of himself, someone that he had never really known was there, lurking, waiting for the right moment to appear. Was this the result of his upbringing? His life with the people he called his parents? Why, since he was descended from the rigidly silent Bella and her unspeakable uncle—who was, quite horrifyingly, *his* great-uncle—had he discovered, or uncovered perhaps, this side of himself that he had not truly suspected was there; a side that wanted love, that could enjoy love, that was now ready to *give* love?

He needed a rest. All this emotional self-discovery was very tiring.

Bethany came into the room first. 'They're coming,' she said shyly; then, in a sudden burst of confidence: 'I was behaving very badly, Gerard. I'm sorry. Cathy's sorted me out.' She tried a small smile. 'So please forgive me. I won't do it again.'

He was moved. 'Bethany, my dear girl—it's been a momentous time for you. We're all allowed to make mistakes now and then.' He regarded her appreciatively. She was attractive, now she wasn't scowling at him; she was a bit like her mother, which was good; and he felt so relaxed in all these new relationships that he could only be thankful if she felt the same. 'The main thing is for your mother to be happy with the situation. She's a special person!'

'I know.' She sat down opposite him. 'Did you have a nice day?'

The tea-party next day with Bella had its own stresses. Unused as she was to social occasions, she sat upright in her chair and spoke only when spoken to. Andrea and Cathy kept the conversational ball rolling; Bethany sat on the far side of the room and stared at the visitor with mild astonishment, hoping that no one would expect *her* to join in.

Gerard put up with it for nearly half an hour before he moved into the attack.

'So, Bella, what's the next thing for you? Another holiday?'

She looked as if he had struck her. 'Oh...oh, no, I don't think so.' She smoothed her skirt over her knees. (*She always does that when she's upset*, Andrea was thinking. *Protective?*)

'We'll be sending out invitations once we know the date...' Andrea started. Bella stared, not understanding. 'When we have a date for the wedding.' Andrea glanced towards Gerard. Bella was doing the same.

'Here?' she asked in a small voice. 'Not in Sydney?'

'Probably here.' Andrea asked Gerard with a look. After a moment he nodded. 'So then we shall need some help with the arrangements...'

'Arrangements?' The voice wavered. 'What do you mean?' Bella's eyes went round the room, not resting on anyone. She looked almost scared. Andrea sighed. Obviously the wrong topic for *this* conversation.

"You'll have your invitation when the time comes.'

'Oh...yes...' The voice died away. Andrea picked up the hot water jug and went towards the kitchen.

She was standing by the window when Gerard came in. 'She's like you,' she said, not looking up. "Like you used to be, anyway.'

'How do you mean?'

'Isolated. Holds herself in. Can't blend.'

'Never had the chance to learn how to.' He put his arms around her. 'I wasn't really like that. It's self-protection, you know. Probably she doesn't want to be that way, any more than I did. But she has never found out how it works.' He kissed the top of her head. 'But I found you—or you found me!—and look at me now!' He turned her round. 'Any complaints to the management! Give her time—she won't be able to resist you, either.'

She closed her eyes and leaned against him. 'No complaints, that's for sure. Bethany seems to be struck dumb by her.' She laughed softly. 'Is this going to be a marriage or a self-help group?'

He turned her face up to him and looked down into her eyes. 'I love you, so I don't care what it is as long as you love me.' There was a hint of a question in his voice.

'I love you,' she whispered.

'When? When did you know?'

She smiled. 'When you went to buy coffee at the airport.'

He looked astonished. 'That far back? Good heavens! Why?'

'I suddenly knew that I didn't want you to be my brother.' That silenced him. 'What about you?' she said.

'When I saw you coming across the forecourt at that café, that very first time...' He stopped and grinned. 'I thought "here's trouble".'

'But...?'

'The second time I saw you I thought that maybe there was more to it than that.'

'And...?' She waited, smiling.

'When you started being so nice to an old woman who seemed to me cold and totally withdrawn, I thought—I thought that *this* woman could be something in my life that really mattered. And when you went back to Sydney I was lost. I couldn't believe that I could miss anyone like I missed you.' He bent his head to hers. 'OK?'

'*Very* OK, darling.' She frowned suddenly. 'You know...'

'What?'

'When you think of where we two came from—all the stresses, the dramas, your thing with Bella, mine with Claudia—murder and adoption and all the rest...isn't it amazing that we are so...?'

'Are what?'

'So...*normal!*' She stared up at him. 'When you imagine just what could have gone wrong...'

He put a finger over her mouth. 'We are us! And from today we don't need to think about all that. Not ever!' He kissed her lips. 'We put it right behind us—this is Day One of a new life. OK?'

She regarded him solemnly for a moment, then nodded. 'Absolutely!'

They stood together in a personal mist of satisfaction. In the hallway the phone suddenly rang, ripping through their daydream. Cathy answered it.

'For you, Andrea! Your dad.'

She moved away from him, her eyes on his. 'You'll talk to him?'

'Of course.'

'Hello, Dad!'

'Hello, my dear girl. Your mother has told me the glad news. I am very, very pleased to hear it.'

'Thank you, Dad. We're all feeling good about it.'

'Is Bethany there with you?'

'Yes.'

'And...is it OK there, too?' He was very cautious.

'Yes, she's coping with it very well.'

'Lucy felt there was a bit of a problem with her and...and Gerard. OK now?'

'Yes, Dad. All blown over.'

'That's good.' He sounded really pleased. 'You deserve the best, my darling. Be very happy!'

'Yes.' Her eyes were wet. 'Thank you, Dad. So much!' She turned to look at Gerard. 'Would you like to speak to Gerard? He's right here.'

She handed the phone over, and Gerard took a deep breath. 'How are you, sir?'

'The name's Harry, Gerard. And I'm very well, and very happy indeed to hear your good news.'

'Thank you...Harry. We're all feeling a bit surprised by the way things have turned out...'

'Make her happy, Gerard. That's all we ask you.'

'I intend to.' He caught Andrea's eye and smiled. 'It's not difficult. She's a buoyant person.'

'Buoyant! That's a good description of our Andrea. Look, Gerard, we hope to see you both quite soon...'

'Come over and see us here, Harry.'

'I think we will!' He sounded quite excited at the prospect. 'It's many years since we've seen Perth. Yes, that will be a very good thing to do.'

'I'll hand you back to Andrea...'

'He sounds like a nice man,' Harry said to her.

'Yes—he is.'

'I've got another nice young man here, wanting to speak to you.'

'Oh—Daniel! Yes, that's wonderful!' There was a silence for a moment, then a gruff late-teens voice came on. 'Hi, Mum!'

'Hello, Dan! How are you? Is everything OK?'

'Yeah, it's fine.' He hesitated. 'This engagement? You're going to marry him?'

'Yes.' She waited for his reply, hoping that this was not another little hiccup along their way.

'Right! So...like... where will it be? The wedding.'

'Probably here, fairly soon.'

'Am I coming?'

'Of course you are! We can't have it without you.'

'Why?'

'Because! It's a family thing.'

There was a short pause which neither of them tried to fill. Then: 'Mum, will I like him?'

'Yes, I think so, Dan.'

'Is he good at sports? Footy?'

She laughed. 'I don't know. I'll ask him later. Do you want to speak to him?' Daniel was vehement, and she laughed again. 'OK, love, another time.'

'Mum...'

'Yes.'

'We don't have to, like, *forget* Dad, do we?'

'Oh, Dan—of course not, my dear. He will always be there. Gerard knows that. Just as I hope Gerard will always be your friend.'

'OK then!'

'You're sure?'

'Yeah. Just wanted to say...*cool*! You and...and him. Really cool!'

'Thank you, darling. Thank you so much.'

She heard the phone click off. 'All well?' Gerard asked.

'Yes, everything's *wonderful*.'

They went back into the lounge room, hand in hand. All eyes turned to them. Bella, trying to find her way into what she had never known—a family—showed a flicker of interest; Cathy, stalwart friend without whom none of this would have happened, was almost licking her lips for news; Bethany, so much loved daughter, had her eyes on her mother's face, trying to see if the phone call had been successful. Andrea's heart warmed within her.

'So?' Cathy said. 'What did Daniel say?'

Andrea smiled at them, her eyes shining with the tears she did not need to shed, and then turned to Gerard. It *was* wonderful—wonderful to feel so safe, so wanted.

'He said it was...*really cool*.'

END

About The Author

BARBARA YATES ROTHWELL lived, married and brought up six children in Surrey, England, before emigrating to Western Australia in 1974 with her musician husband and their two youngest daughters. Her other children arrived in Australia in due course.

Also a musician and a trained singer, she was for 10 years in the 1980s a music reviewer for The West Australian newspaper. In the UK she had been Women's Page Editor for a large group of weekly papers.

After founding and running Yanchep Community School in Western Australia for 8 years, and having successfully written and sold short stories in several countries, Barbara decided it was time to break out into novel writing. Her teenage historical novel, THE BOY FROM THE HULKS, was published in 1994 by Longman Cheshire, and in 1998 her historical novel largely based on the Yanchep area, DUTCH POINT, was published privately in the UK.

Since then she has been publishing with Trafford in Canada/America, a Print on Demand company that gives her full control of her books. This has been a very satisfactory development. She has brought out 8 books (this is #9) with Trafford, and there are more in the pipeline.

Barbara has also written plays, of which two full-length and some one-act comedies have been performed by community theatres in Wanneroo, Perth and Coonabarabran, NSW, and one short play for a young cast in Bunbury, which won a commendation.

~~~

Some of her books can be found on her website: www.
barbarayatesrothwell.com and they are available from internet book
stores. She can be reached at the contact page.   Emails welcome!

Printed in the United States
By Bookmasters